GRIMALKINS DON'T PURR

BOOK 4 OF THE VALKYRIE BESTIARY SERIES

BY KIM MCDOUGALL

Grimalkins Don't Purr
© Kim McDougall 2021
All rights reserved.

Published by Wrongtree Press.
Cover and book design by Castelane.
Cover art by Sergey Velikoluzhskiy.
Editing by Elaine Jackson.

This is a work of fiction. Names, characters, places, and incidents either are the product of the author's imagination or are used fictitiously, and any resemblance to actual persons, living or dead, business establishments, events, or locales is entirely coincidental.

Hardcover ISBN: 978-1-990570-00-1
Paperback ISBN: 978-1-7776401-9-4
eBook ISBN: 978-1-7776401-8-7

Version 1

FICTION / Fantasy / Urban
FICTION / Fantasy / Paranormal

BOOKS BY KIM MCDOUGALL

The Hidden Coven Series:
Inborn Magic
Soothed by Magic
Trigger Magic
Bellwether Magic
Gone Magic

Valkyrie Bestiary Series:
Dragons Don't Eat Meat
Dervishes Don't Dance
Hell Hounds Don't Heel
Grimalkins Don't Purr
The Last Door to Underhill (Novella)
The Girl Who Cried Banshee (Novella)
Three Half Goats Gruff (Novelette)

Writing as Eliza Crowe

The Shifted Dreams Series:
Pick Your Monster
Lost Rogues

For Nosy, Dozy-piffle-puff-a-muff, Radar, Nefertiti, Rusty, Scooter, Puddin' Head, Brawny, Casey, Moe, Pasha, Griffin and Tobie the Terrible. Each of you left a golden vine around my heart.

From the Archives:

No Coco Crunches for Pookas!
April 20, 2079

It's easy to underestimate pookas. They're so stinking cute with their big eyes and twitching antenna ears. Don't be fooled. Critter wrangler rule number ten: cute kills just as much as ugly.

To be fair, under normal circumstances, the worst a pooka would do is steal your lunch. They are always hungry despite their whip-thin frames. And they never stop twitching, dancing, or tapping their toes. Watching a pooka stand still is like watching a hummingbird hover over a flower—they vibrate with potential energy. Potentially explosive energy. This state of constant agitation takes a lot of fuel. They spend about eight hours a day eating, and another eight scrounging for food.

The real trouble happens when a pooka gets hold of certain substances that react badly with its brain chemistry. Chocolate for one. Caffeine is another. These substances are carefully controlled anyway because of their rarity. But any reputable shop keeper or restauranteur knows not to sell them to a pooka. A diligent business owner will make sure that cocoa and coffee wastes are disposed of properly. Pookas like to dumpster dive, and that can lead to disaster. The east end fire of '76 comes to mind.

My pest control business was finally starting to take off that year. I'd won a couple of jobs through Hub, our local police force/militia/judiciary. I was earning myself a reputation as the person to call when you've got something wild and whacky on your hands. So when Hub found two pookas hopped up on Coco Crunches, they called me. By the time I made it across town to Jarry Street, the old flea market was in flames. Crazed pookas had gone on a rampage, turning over tables and garbage cans. It was cold, even for November. A vendor had been using a kerosene heater to keep warm. The pookas knocked it over, and well, it was a hot time in the old town that night. Twenty-four people died. The market was decimated and has never been rebuilt.

To this day, when I get a call about a pooka, I take it seriously.

I'd love to hear your experiences with pookas, especially if you have any tips or tricks for apprehending or neutralizing a strung-out pooka. Comment below.

COMMENTS (9)

We had pookas living in our barn for a season. They were nesting while the female gave birth. My mom used to give them sweet tea and biscuits. They were very polite. We had no problem with them and they moved on at the end of the spring. Of course, we haven't had chocolate here since...ever. Is it really as good as they say?
Homestead-mage499 (April 20, 2079)

> Ooh! I've never seen a baby pooka. Was it cute? And yes, chocolate is divine. I treated myself to a bite of milk chocolate for my last birthday.
> *Valkyrie367 (April 20, 2079)*

>> Soooo cute. There was a litter of three little fluff balls with ridonkulous ears.
>> *Homestead-mage499 (April 20, 2079)*

—•—

Vet here. I use a pheromone nebulizer for anxious kitties in the exam room. Maybe you could rig something like that to help with crazed pookas?
NorthShoreAnimalHospital (April 21, 2079)

> Hmmm. That's an interesting idea. I have some alchemist friends who might be able to help me with that.
> *Valkyrie367 (April 21, 2079)*

—•—

Your a waste of good air. Your blog should be flagged for stirrin up hate cause now everyone I know is going to want to go out huntin pookas. If someone gets shot in the crossfire, thats on you.

PercivalPapa (April 21, 2079)

> …"everyone I know is going to want to go out hunting pookas" ??? Maybe you're hanging around with the wrong crowd.
>
> *Valkyrie367 (April 21, 2079)*

How many pookas does it take to change a light bulb? None. They're too stupid to change lightbulbs. Better to roast them over a low fire. A little sweet chipotle sauce is tasty with pooka.

BigGameGuy (April 21, 2079)

Sigh. I'm shutting off comments.

Valkyrie367 (April 21, 2079)

Wheels spun on gravel as I bolted out of my parking lot. My truck's engine whined at the abuse, but I didn't let up on the accelerator. Debbie's frantic voice came through the tinny speaker of my widget.

"Kyra! He's gone crazy! I don't know what to do!"

A loud crash echoed through the speaker. Then silence.

"Debbie? Are you there?"

I held the widget to my ear. Errol watched me with wide eyes from the passenger seat. The three-inch bodach clung to the seat belt buckle as the truck swerved.

"Debbie?"

I heard muffled banging noises, then Debbie's whisper. "I can't get to the door. You've got to help me!"

"I'm coming." I put my foot on the floor. "Just stay on the line. I'll be there in ten minutes."

"I don't know if I can—" The connection dropped.

Crap.

I dumped the widget on the seat beside Errol.

"Mglfrbngt." His words were an unintelligible muddle, but his meaning popped into my head, loud and clear. *What is it?*

"Pooka. Hyped on chocolate."

Errol grumbled.

I skidded onto Morgan road. Debbie's convenience store was located near the overpass next to the high school and catered mostly to bored teens cutting class. But if a pooka snuck in and stole a couple of chocolate bars, it wouldn't be a safe place for kids right now.

I broke the speed limit on the old Highway 20 even though it was pitted with potholes. I had other places I needed to be today and wouldn't have taken this spur-of-the-moment job if Debbie wasn't the cousin of an old boyfriend. I couldn't turn down her panicked pleading. Hub would eventually show up, but pookas were low on their priority list.

Ahead, red tail lights blinked on as the traffic came to a halt.

Now what?

I slowed the truck. A long line of cars had pulled up at an intersection that didn't normally have a stop. Today, a web blocked the road. It spanned from a lamppost on one side to a grove of maples on the other. An unmarked van was parked beside it and two Hub militia in their black uniforms stood with blasters targeting the web. Incidents like these were the reason convenience store owners had to deal with pookas on their own.

More vans with flashing lights raced up the shoulder of the road. Behind us, cars were piling up. Some entitled alpha-hole leaned on his horn. As if that would make things better.

I peered out the side window for a better look. The web's black silk strings were as thick as twine. Magic vibrated through the strands like music in the seconds after a bow is lifted from a violin. And it stank—hot and sour—like someone had tried to cover up rotting meat with a lemon-scented oven cleaner.

"Damn." I slumped back in my seat.

"Bflg?" Errol asked.

"It looks like a Venus spider."

I picked him up and sat him on the dash. His worn boots, with a hole near one big toe, slipped on the vinyl. His feet and tiny walking stick got tangled in his long white beard and he fell over. My truck's radio flared to life and then crackled with static as Errol worked through his frustration. At least he didn't blow out all the electrical in the car. He was getting better at tempering his magic. When he finally settled, he studied the scene through the windshield.

"Fbltgnt." *Terra is pissed.*

I had to agree. In the past week, a giant nest had appeared overnight on the roof of the public library. It had a clutch of basketball-sized eggs in it, but no mother in sight. No one was brave enough to disturb the eggs. Hub had the nest under surveillance. In another part of town, a telephone wire broke and spontaneously turned into snakes. All the birds disappeared from the city overnight, and Denis Street was locked in a blizzard even though the rest of the ward was dealing with an early summer heat wave. Coincidences? Hardly.

And while the pundits in the senate debated the unusual magic spike, I sat in my truck, drumming my fingers on the steering wheel, stuck at the intersection of Morgan Road and old Highway 20.

"Ghtbtn." *She mourns the Queen.*

"Leighna?" My lip curled in an involuntary snarl as I said her name. Not because of any disdain for the dead queen. I'd admired Leighna Icewolf, late Queen of the fae. My disdain was for the way she died. The sight of Polina raising Leighna's fresh heart to the sky would haunt me for the rest of my days and nights.

"You think her death is the reason for all this?" I waved a hand at the colossal spider web. Hub was bringing out the flame throwers.

Errol chewed on the end of his mustache and nodded. He might have been right. Queen Leighna was a founding member of the Triumvirate that built Montreal Ward. Her magic was embedded in the shield that protected the town. She had always been the voice of reason among the bickering political factions. Now it was silenced.

Whatever the reason for this spontaneous manifestation of a spider web, I couldn't idle at a roadblock today.

I stepped from my truck and grabbed a soldier as he ran by.

"There's a stoned pooka tearing apart a store on Elm. I need an escort to get out of here before someone is killed."

The soldier was green, fresh from the academy. His mouth dropped open and worked at a response, while his eyes darted to his superior officers, who were already firing the web with their flamethrowers.

I shook him and pulled out my Hub ID. Working for the man had its perks sometimes.

"I need an escort, now!"

The soldier nodded. He didn't look old enough to drive, but he jumped into a van and blared the siren. I made a dicey three-point turn, nearly tipping my truck into a ditch and followed the kid along the shoulder.

Blaster fire erupted behind us. In the rear-view mirror, I saw the Venus spider had returned to her nest and wasn't pleased to find it a bonfire.

I skidded away as the officers let out another volley of flames. There was nothing I could do here, but maybe I could still help Debbie. If I wasn't already too late.

Five minutes later, I parked in the corner lot where Elm met Fairway Drive. My Hub escort left his lights flashing, but silenced the siren as I pulled up beside him. The strip mall housed a few stores, and about a dozen cars were scattered throughout the lot. A train rumbled by on the tracks running parallel to Elm Street, heading for the West Gate and the alchemist compound on Perrot Island.

I studied the facade of Deb's Convenience. The lighted sign above the door flickered. But that meant nothing. Most of the stores in this mall were rundown. The shoe repair next door had one boarded-up window.

Inside Deb's, the lights were on but nothing moved.

"What should I do?" asked the Hub officer.

"Just keep everyone away." I pointed to a few people now poking their heads out of other stores. Thankfully, it was too early in the day for much high-school traffic.

The window in front of Debbie's store exploded. I ducked behind my truck. Someone nearby shrieked. Peeking around the tire well, I spotted a can of beans rolling on the asphalt. More cans came hurtling out, breaking the second window. A high-pitched giggle followed them.

Errol rode on my shoulder, steadying himself with the hilt of my sword that stuck up from the harness on my back.

"Cfgltbd." *Let's do this.*

"Let's." I grabbed my homemade dart gun from the back of the truck and dithered for a minute over what size darts to use. The sedative in the darts was a ketamine base with a few herbs added to make it work faster and last longer. It was a Gita Special. My banshee roommate was a whiz with medicinal plants.

The pooka wouldn't be much bigger than a raccoon, but if he was high, he'd have abnormal strength and his metabolism would be all wonky. And like a raccoon, he'd have claws and teeth sharp enough to rip open a garbage can.

Another deranged laugh and barrage of foodstuffs told me I was out of time. I slid two darts into the chamber—enough sedative to down a horse.

Critter wrangler rule number nine: sometimes overkill is just enough kill.

Crouching, I crab-walked to the corner of the shoe repair. The owner stood behind his counter with a rifle pointed at the door and a determined expression on his face. I waved him down, knowing it would do little good. Since the Flood Wars, people had learned to protect their own.

I crept along the brick wall between stores and peered into Debbie's. The store was in shambles. Shelves of goods were toppled into the aisles. The fridges along the back wall were demolished, and the floor was covered in brown glass. The hoppy smell of beer filled the air.

I could hear Debbie's sloppy sobs, but I couldn't see her.

Good. Stay out of sight.

I craned my neck, looking for the pooka. He hung by his tail from the light fixture, swinging like a bored monkey in a zoo. About three feet from head to tail, he was covered in dark bronze fur that darkened to black on his legs and cat-like head. Stubby wings flapped behind him and bat-like ears swiveled constantly, hearing dangers from every shadow and corner. His eyes were the size of golf balls and veined in red. He was definitely strung out, ready to crash even.

No store owner in their right mind would sell a candy bar to a pooka. Debbie had been in the biz long enough to know better. The little bugger probably stole it. One bite would entice him to grab another. Two Caramel Fudge Nuggets would push gentle Dr. Jeckle into Mr. Hyde mode.

The pooka swung over a half-toppled shelf. His long fingers latched onto a box of matches. He lit one, dropping a handful of matchsticks into the mess below. The match burned down to his fingers. He yelped when it singed him and giggled when he dropped the still-lit match.

I glanced at the one intact display beside the front counter. It held an assortment of low grade fireworks for the upcoming Founders' Day that celebrated the creation of Montreal Ward. If the pooka got hold of those, he could do some real damage.

Even without the threat of a multi-hued explosion, I had no time for this. Mason expected me at his place in an hour. We were leaving with Nori to find a cure for Jacoby today. I needed a clean shot at the pooka and I needed it now. But hyped up on chocolate, he was now bouncing around the store.

"Can you get the lights?" I asked Errol. "Something spectacular to distract him."

"Hgtb." *Yes.*

"Okay. On my go."

I swung out, gun ready, and filled the space in front of the broken window. "Errol, now!"

I keened a magic surge from the bodach. The light fixture buzzed, flashed, sparked, and died. Fascinated by the light display, the pooka didn't see me coming.

I shot him in the ass.

He squawked. His mouth hung wide, his tail went slack, and he fell to the ground with a thud.

CHAPTER

2

Once I calmed down a hysterical Debbie, I packed up the pooka and drove to Hub Station to fill out the endless paperwork required for the catch and release of a class two fae.

"What am I supposed to do with that thing?" The dispatch officer jabbed a finger at the pooka sleeping in the cat carrier.

"Let him sleep it off, I guess. Not my problem anymore. I'm off the clock." Waving goodbye behind my back, I dashed out the door.

I coaxed my truck back to life, then glanced at my widget. I was already an hour late.

Errol was asleep on the seat beside me. His mustache swayed with each tiny snore.

Morgan road was clear of spider webs—thank the gods—and I sped past the Hub vans left cleaning up the mess. I'd wasted too much time with the pooka. Time was always my commodity to sell, but now it took on even more importance. Because my time was Jacoby's time. My dervish was slipping away like the last sands in an hourglass.

I shouldn't have even left the house this morning. I needed to get ready for our trip to Iona Park in the foothills of the Pocono Mountains where we'd find the Life Tree—my father's Life Tree. Nori insisted that I could use it as an anchor while my astral body searched for Jacoby in some place ominously called the Nether. And I hadn't even packed my bag yet.

I'd left all my other chores for Gita that morning. As I parked my truck in the cracked lot outside my apartment-office building, I hoped she'd been able to complete the critter feedings. Then I could throw clothes in a bag, grab Jacoby and my sword, and be at Mason's in under an hour.

Emil's car wasn't in the lot. He was probably out running errands. So far, he'd fit right into the void left by Gabe, my old assistant, even though I refused to believe Gabe was gone for good. After years of mediocre to disastrous assistants, Gabe had spoiled me for anyone else. He was organized, efficient and best of all, he didn't run away when things got bloody. Or furry. Or mucusy.

But Gabe needed time to sort out some family business. His father was the head of the Saivites, one of the largest godling clans in the city. And with the Triumvirate in disarray since Queen Leighna's death, the godlings were in the perfect place to finally garner support for the fourth political party they'd always wanted. At best, it would mean a bitter battle in the courts. At worst, their demands could plunge Montreal into its first civil war.

The fact that I was entangled in the events that led up to this destabilization didn't escape me. I relived those events every night in that uncomfortable space between wakefulness and sleep. I saw Leighna's last breath. I saw Jacoby exploding in a whirlwind of fire. I saw my blade slicing through Mason to get at the witch's heart.

I really had to stop cutting up my boyfriends. A girl could get a reputation.

I unlocked the office door and heard a crash.

That was never a good sign.

Gita's wail raised every hair on my body.

I rushed through the office and threw open the door to my apartment.

Cages lay open and trampled. My troll bats swooped and looped around the room. One plant stand lay on its side, pots cracked and spilling black soil across the parquet. The other stand had crashed through the sliding patio door. Chunks of glass littered the ground. Gita's shrine of pillows and fresh flowers for Jacoby had been toppled. The dervish lay like a corpse on the floor. Hunter, my pygmy kraken, sat on his chest, guarding him. A thumping sound came from above—Mr. Murray pounding for silence.

From his seat on my shoulder, Errol shook his walking twig at the chaos. His agitation caused the lights to flicker and the microwave to beep.

Something had blown through the apartment like a tornado, and one critter's conspicuous absence made it clear who was to blame.

I dumped Errol beside his bonsai, stormed through the ruined living room, shot a glance into my empty kitchen, and stomped into the bedroom where I found Willow, my gray cat, cornered by a fifty-kilo hell hound.

Willow yowled, hissed, and swiped a razor paw at Princess's nose. The hound bowed and wagged her tail.

I sighed. "Willow doesn't want to play. Leave her alone." At the sound of my voice, Princess bounded over and put two giant paws on my shoulders, knocking me back into the doorjamb.

The cat skittered around the corner and disappeared through the broken patio door.

Princess washed my face with her cow-sized tongue.

"Okay! Enough!" I pushed her off me and wiped my cheek on my sleeve. "Look at the mess you made!" The hound wriggled like I was praising her for bringing back a roadkill rat. I dragged her by the collar to the destroyed plant stands. "Look at it! You've ruined Gita's herb garden!"

From her closet, the banshee's cry rose in pitch.

Princess's tongue lolled from the corner of her mouth.

"It's a good thing you're so damn cute."

I ruffled the fur around her ears and ran a finger along the smooth bone plating that covered half her face. I couldn't stay mad at her. But I couldn't keep her either. This rampage wasn't the first time she'd caused a mess. It wasn't fair to keep such a beast locked up in my small apartment. I would have to find another home for her, some place she could run and use up her boundless energy.

The thought made my heart clench like someone squeezed it in a fist.

The Princess dilemma would have to keep until I sorted out the Jacoby dilemma. One critter rescue disaster at a time. But I couldn't leave for gods-only-knew-how-long and let Gita deal with the hound. Princess would have to come with us.

I cleaned up Jacoby's nest and settled him back on the cushions.

"Good job guarding him." I held out my fist and Hunter bumped it with one tentacle. I rewarded the kraken with some time outside in his new pond. When I returned, Errol had quit jacking the electricity and gone to nap inside his treehouse.

The troll bats settled upside down on the curtain rod above the ruined patio door. I swept broken glass and dirt into a pile and tried to save a few potted plants.

When Gita finally made an appearance, tears cut a path down her craggy cheeks.

"That beast is a demon." She pointed at Princess, who was now curled in one corner of the living room, chewing on a bone big enough to be a dinosaur. The hound raised one eye in a sorry-not-sorry gesture. Gita sucked in a breath, readying herself for another major wail.

"It's okay." I stopped her with one hand on her wrinkled, leathery forearm. "I'll take her with me. And as soon as I get back, I'll find her a new home. I promise."

Emil arrived with a canvas sack of groceries. He stood in the doorway, shaking his head.

"Looks like a portal to hell opened up in here," he said.

"I'll get it cleaned up before I go."

Emil would be staying in my apartment while I was gone to help with the critters. I didn't want to leave him with this mess. But I could feel time passing like a belt around my chest—a belt that was tightening with every second.

The curtain rod over the patio door fell with a clatter, and the bats exploded into the air. Princess jumped up from her snack and barked at this new fun game of catch-a-bat. Gita let out a sniffle-scream and ran to her closet, slamming the door behind her.

My throat closed. It was too much. All of it. My knees buckled, and I slid to the floor among the glass and dirt. My eyes felt hot and when I wiped them, my fingers came away wet.

"Let me have that." Emil crouched and took the dustpan from my hand. His handsome, boyish face wore an expression of deep concern. "Don't worry about any of this. I'll take care of it."

I sniffled. He took my hand and pulled me upright. "You go pack and get out of here. I'll clean up and board up the window. Easy as pie."

"Are you sure?" I hiccup-gulped and wiped my cheeks.

Emil grinned. "You smeared dirt across your face."

Of course I did.

"You sure you can handle this?" I repeated. "It's a lot."

"I'm sure. Gabe said he'd be on standby, if I need help. And who knows, maybe if I act like the damsel in distress, he'll coming galloping in on a white horse."

"Stranger things have happened."

Emil's feelings for Gabe were obvious to everyone except Gabe. Maybe the two of them did need to fight some battles together. It worked for me and Mason.

With that last thought, I went to pack my bag.

"Princess, let's go." The hound stretched and rose slowly. Sure, now that I was in a hurry, she was all docile and sleepy. I thumped Gita's closet door twice.

"We're leaving now." I got a blubbering response that might have been, "Have fun."

I'd been gone a lot lately. Guilt at leaving Gita again so soon weighed heavily on me.

Guilt seemed to be my default emotion these days.

I scooped up Jacoby and grabbed my sword from the umbrella stand as I ran out the door.

parked behind Mason's house, near the old barn. Princess didn't wait for me to open the door. Instead, she squirmed out the window from the back seat. Tad and Tums, the youngest of the goblin children, squealed with glee when she zoomed past the barn where they were stacking wood. They were well-mannered enough to ask permission from their older brother, Dekar, before chasing after the hell hound.

Dekar leaned on his axe, watching them disappear into the forest. He was young and his gray-brown skin hadn't taken on the weathered-wood texture that was common to adult goblins. And he would never be brawny, but his thin arms wielded the axe with skill.

Mason and I had met Dekar and his father, Arriz, camped on the road to Montreal over a week ago. They were refugees hoping to win coveted passes inside the ward. When we spied the pack of younglings hiding under a tarp in Arriz's wagon bed, Mason offered to find them work on his estate. I wasn't the only one who took in strays, it seemed. I was glad to see Mason had found jobs for them. The entire family looked half-starved and in need of a good rest. Maybe they'd stick around for the summer before moving on.

The twins took turns riding Princess like a pony. I didn't worry about the hound. With their stick legs and arms, the goblin kids couldn't weigh more that ten kilos each. Dekar watched his younger siblings with a frown.

"They'll be safe with Princess," I said. Not much would take on a hell hound, not even the creatures of Dorion Park.

"I'm not worried about the twins. I'm worried about what they'll do to your poor dog."

Princess dashed through the yard again with one twin riding her like a bronco and the other tumbling alongside.

"She's strong enough to hold a couple of kids. And she needs the exercise."

I turned back to the truck and my other passenger. Jacoby lay like a discarded rag in the front seat. Only my deep keening probe could sense any life in him. His ashen fur drooped instead of curling around his eyes—eyes that I hadn't seen open in over a month. Nori, our kitsune healer, had been dosing him with her own magic, just enough to keep him alive, but she couldn't sustain him forever.

We needed to bring Jacoby home now.

I cradled the dervish in my arms and hip-butted the door closed.

"Let me help you." Dekar put down the axe and reached for Jacoby. I jerked him away.

"I'm sorry," I said when I saw his look. People often mistrusted goblins. I didn't want him to think I shared that prejudice. "It's not you. I feel responsible for him. I guess I'm having a hard time letting anyone else care for him."

"I know what you need." He ducked into the barn and came back a few minutes later carrying a leather bag with straps. His sister, Suzt, followed him.

"Oh! Look at the poor dear thing!" She reached out. I hesitated only a moment. It would be a long journey to Pennsylvania if I didn't let anyone else carry him from time to time. Suzt took him from my arms and cooed. Dekar grinned.

"Suzt has a way with little ones."

It was a good thing too, since their mother had died some years ago in the Inbetween. Suzt and her brother had to be a blessing to their father in raising the little horde of goblins.

Dekar laid the leather pouch on the ground. Suzt tucked Jacoby inside it and then picked him up, contraption and all. It was a baby backpack. I tucked my arms through the straps. Jacoby nestled between my shoulder blades, leaving my hands free.

"You can wear it as a sling around your front too." Suzt adjusted the straps and nodded at her handiwork. "It was a lifesaver when the twins were babies."

"You sure you don't need it?" I asked. I'd been worried about trekking eight-hundred miles into the Inbetween lugging an unconscious dervish. This was the perfect solution.

She shook her head. "The twins are too big for it now."

Arriz stepped from the barn. It was hard to tell his age. Goblins had rough, weathered skin that made them all look old. Silver flecked his cast-iron black hair, but he was spry and sharp-eyed. He'd have to be to keep up with seven children. He wore a tool belt around his waist and carried a hammer in one hand.

"Da, is it okay if I give Kyra one of the baby slings?"

"Of course." Arriz's voice rumbled like a rockfall.

"Your gift will make the trip easier," I said, avoiding the pitfall of thanking a fae.

Suzt nodded, and the brother and sister returned to their chores.

"How are you settling in?" I asked.

Arriz pinched his lips as if holding back something nasty. "Bah! Fine enough. I suppose."

"What's wrong?"

He twisted the hammer in both hands, looking down.

"Arriz, tell me. Are you not getting along here?" Other than Mason, the Guardians often stayed at the manor. Maybe goblins and gargoyles didn't get along.

"No, it's not that. Everyone has been kind. Too kind."

"What do you mean?"

He shuffled the dirt with one toe, still not looking up. "I mean, Mr. Mason offered me a job, but this?" His arm swung toward the barn. "I fix up an old barn he doesn't even use. We pull weeds and dig gardens. Chop wood. For what? Mr. Mason is never here. He doesn't need us. This is charity, not a job."

I laid a hand on his arm. Like all fae, his heart didn't beat in a steady rhythm. Instead, it burbled like a meandering brook. I waited until he raised his face and met my gaze.

"That's not how Mason feels. We'll be leaving today. No telling how long we'll be gone. I'm sure he likes to know that you're taking care of things in his absence. Can I see what you've been working on?"

Arriz waved a hand inside the barn. I stepped through the big sliding door. It was a big old bank barn, built into the side of a hill. The only other door was closed and the light inside was too dim to make out the far wall.

But the place was spotless. Someone had cleaned out the two horse stalls. The floor was swept clean, cobwebs dusted away. And repairs had started on the stairs leading to the garage above.

A younger goblin came in carrying two-by-fours that he dumped beside a table-saw.

"Please excuse me," Arriz said. "I want to finish repairing the stairs this morning."

"Of course." I left him to his work, wondering if Mason really was creating a charity job to keep the goblins busy and fed, or if he had plans for the barn.

A MONTH AGO, Mason's old nemesis used Jacoby to split a bloodstone and bring back his lover, Polina. Jacoby shouldn't have been in that lab that night. I'd asked him to be there. And now—because of his loyalty to me—his spirit had been split from his body. According to Nori, he was lost in the Nether, a world between worlds.

And that was on me.

Nori was an amazing healer, but she had no bond with Jacoby, no way to find his lost soul.

But I could. The only stumbling block was that I was completely untrained in healing and without an anchor, I'd never find my way home.

Enter Timberfoot Greenleaf, dryad, fae hero and my absentee father.

When Timberfoot sacrificed himself to close the last door to Underhill, he transformed into a Life Tree, an oak of massive proportions with roots penetrating the veil between worlds. Because his roots clung to Underhill, someone with enough power could open the door to the fae home world again. I'd seen the results of that when Queen Leighna's younger brother tried his little coup last year.

But Underhill wasn't the only world out there. Dimensions, worlds, realms, whatever you wanted to call them, they bumped and rubbed against each other continually. And where they bumped, the veil was thin, making doorways between worlds more accessible.

For reasons I didn't fully understand, the Nether was a world with countless doors to other realms, like the airport hubs of the old days. Lost souls were inevitably drawn to it, willingly or not. The Nether was a kind of way station—part purgatory, part holy shrine. But it existed between time and space, and the only way to access it was by projecting my spirit. A dangerous business without an anchor to keep me safe.

Since the day Dad's little swimming seed had spawned me, he'd never given me another thing. I'd even changed my name. But he could be my anchor when I sent my spirit to find Jacoby. He could give me this.

Now, I just hoped that Mason had figured out the transportation. Timberfoot's tree was deep in the Inbetween, about a hundred and twenty kilometers west of Manhattan Ward. Making that trek on foot would take weeks.

Jacoby didn't have weeks.

I went inside to find Mason and Nori leaning over a map on the dining room table.

Mason lifted his gaze, and a tired smile softened his face.

"Did you find a route?" I asked.

"The railroad is our best option. And Oscar sealed the deal."

"How so?"

"I'll show you, but look at this first." He pointed to the map.

This map was new. It showed the rail line that Gerard Golovin had built in the last two years, linking Montreal with Manhattan. It was a brilliant feat of engineering, considering that the magic of the Inbetween caused flora to grow over anything man-made in a matter of weeks.

Golovin was a genius. Too bad he'd also been subjected to the madness of falling for Polina. She had a way of twisting a man's affection, hardening it like a spear tip tempered by flame. At her command, Golovin had blown up his own railroad—destroying the business he had been nurturing for years.

With his finger, Mason traced the rail line. It was a straight shot from Montreal to Manhattan.

"You're assuming the tracks are clear," I said. It had only been a few days since Gerard had blown up the ward protecting the rail line, but that was long enough for the Inbetween to claim back the cleared land.

"At least part of them are. Manhattan is intent on re-establishing the link with Montreal."

I didn't ask how he knew this. Mason had connections in Manhattan.

"So we drive it? Or are we taking horses?"

Nori wrinkled her nose. "No horses."

Her glossy black hair was pulled back in a ponytail, and the skin around her eyes looked over-stretched and brittle.

"No horses," Mason agreed. "Too slow. We'll be driving. That's Oscar's surprise."

He led me through the French doors leading to a large patio. Nori stayed behind to watch Jacoby.

"Is she all right?" I asked.

"She's agitated. She wanted to go to your place this morning to check on the dervish. I had to convince her twice that you'd be here any minute."

"I was late. I know. Pookas on chocolate."

Mason nodded, as if that made sense. We descended the stone stairs to the garden and headed around the house.

"And what about you?"

"What about me?"

Tough guy. It had only been a week since I'd impaled him on my sword. Without the gargoyle healing magic, he'd had to recover the old-fashioned way—with the power of a healer kitsune.

"You feeling up to this trip?" I asked, knowing he wouldn't tell me if he weren't.

"Of course I am. A little stiff getting out of bed this morning, but as a newly minted mortal, that's something I'll have to get used to." He grinned as if sore joints and his inevitable death were fun times.

We approached the garage above the barn, and I could hear the table-saw whining below as Arriz and his son worked on the stairs. In the garage, Oscar, the Guardians' lawyer who moonlighted as an alchemist, was tinkering with his latest invention.

"We're driving in that?" I pointed at the bizarre vehicle.

"Isn't she a beauty?" Oscar straightened from where he'd been inspecting a tire and pushed his thick glasses up the bridge of his nose. A streak of grease was smeared across his balding head, but a smile lit his round, gnomish face. "She'll do a hundred on a straightaway and mow down anything in her path. No worries about berserkers this time."

The vehicle looked like a black metal cargo crate on wheels, with no windows and only one hatch-like door.

"Um, Oscar? I don't mean to tell you your job, but how are we going to see?"

"Cameras, sort of." He scratched the fringe of hair at the back of his head. "More like photosensitive plates on all sides." He pointed to a strip of shinier black metal running along the top edge of the car. Then he cranked the door handle and it opened with a squeal of metal hinges.

Inside, screens lined one entire wall. A console table and two chairs were bolted to the floor in front of these. Benches ran along two of the interior walls. Oscar sat at the console and fiddled with the computer. Screens lit up, showing the dim interior of the garage. Out in the field, they would give a panoramic view of the landscape.

Oscar explained the controls to Mason and me. With the three of us inside, the car was already cramped. And we'd be adding Nori and Princess to the mix. It would be a fun ride.

"You still think the railroad is our fastest route?" I asked when he'd finished his tutorial. The wards protecting the tracks had been down for days. No telling what we'd find. The road could be overrun by venomous bison. Or the forest might have reclaimed the land already.

"Kester assures me that at least the southern half of the track is clear. They're working on getting the ward up and running too," Mason said.

Ah, yes. Kester Owens. The New Manhattan representative, my onetime captor, and Mason's buddy. He was also a demon, so I wasn't keen on trusting him.

"The rail tracks are the most efficient way to travel," Oscar said. "Watch this." He hit a button on the console. The car lurched upward, then slowly sank. I poked my head out the door. The fat rubber tires had recessed, allowing metal train wheels to fall into place.

"It will run quiet and fast, just like the train. Takes less fuel this way too." He hopped out to show us a storage trunk at the back of the car. "You've got two ley-line batteries and two extras. You'll have to charge them in Manhattan before you come home, but it should be enough to get you there."

I wasn't fond of should-be's, but I'd learned not to expect more when traveling the Inbetween.

"Good enough." Mason squeezed my arm. "You ready to go?"

I really wasn't. But delaying our departure wouldn't help Jacoby.

"Hold up!" Oscar stepped in front of Mason and crossed his arms over his chest, trying to look threatening. Since he was a full head shorter than me and looked like a grizzled old gnome, the effect was a bit diluted.

"Last time I lent you a vehicle, it came back looking like you'd driven it through a tornado. I expect this one to come home in better shape."

Now it was Mason's turn to cross his arms. He could pull off the threatening look. "You know I can't promise."

A sly grin twitched Oscar's mustache. "Of course not. That's why you're going to promise me something else. You'll put your name in for Alchemist Prime Minister when you return. Then I'll forgive any past and future damage to my inventions."

Mason's expression closed down. He didn't like to be pushed into anything.

Since Leighna's death, Montreal had become a rudderless ship. The queen's top advisor, Merrow Farsigh, took over for the fae, and though she was competent, she had none of Leighna's diplomatic grace. The human arm of the triumvirate wasn't faring much better. They had yet to choose a new leader since Minister Tremblay was injured in what people were already calling The Witch's Uprising. And Oscar filled in for Golovin after his death, but the Alchemist Party needed a strong leader. Mason had declined this role before because of his gargoyle affliction. He had no such excuse now.

"I promise I'll think about it," he said.

Oscar clapped him on the shoulder. "Deal!"

CHAPTER

4

n hour later, we were ready to roll out. Mason and I stood in the yard waiting for the goblin twins to herd Princess into the car. He tilted his face up to the summer sun. Seeing him in the sunlight was still a treat. His black hair shone with blue highlights, and he'd even taken on a tan. It suited him.

"How does that sun feel?" I asked.

"Like heaven." He took me in his arms. "The only thing better than the sun is holding you in the sun." His lips brushed mine. "And this time, you won't be going into any battles alone. In fact, I'm not letting you out of my sight."

"Um…yay?" I wasn't sure how I felt about this new hyper-attentive Mason. "You know I've been taking care of myself for a long time before I met you."

His response was to pull me tighter against him and give my butt a good squeeze.

Princess chose that moment to crash at our heels, knocking us both into the side of the car.

Nori arrived with her pack. It was twice the size of mine.

Mason quirked an eyebrow at her. "You brought your entire wardrobe?"

"I'm not going to Manhattan unprepared." Nori frowned. "And you guys might get away with a simple change of clothes, but every time I shift, I lose my pants."

It was a valid argument. As a kitsune, Nori could change into a red fox and back to human in an instant, but her clothes never made the journey.

"And besides, some of this stuff is for the ritual."

"Fine. We'll make room." Mason took her bag and rearranged things in the trunk to make it fit. He frowned. "There's something back here." Then he was pulling out a gangly arm, followed by a scrawny goblin. And another. Tums and Tad.

"Stowaways!" Mason said.

"We want to come!" Tums cried. His twin was right behind him, but Tad rarely spoke, letting Tums communicate for both of them.

Mason crouched to meet them at eye level.

"Not this time. You need to stay here and help your father with our special project. Remember?" He winked.

The boys looked at me and grinned. "Special project!" They dashed off.

"What's that about?" I asked.

Mason looked smug. "Nothing for you to worry about."

We all piled into the car. Nori chose the bench on the long wall, and I laid Jacoby beside her. Mason and I took the two seats in front of the control console. Princess filled the rest of the small hold.

"Lie down," I commanded. The hound cocked her head. "And what's that smell? Oh, gods. Did you roll in something dead again?"

"Wonderful." Nori wrinkled her nose and tucked her feet away from the beast. Princess sprawled on the floor and waggled her feet in the air. I shut the hatch and it sealed with an ominous clang. The small car suddenly felt even smaller.

It was going to be a long journey.

On the dozen console screens, we watched Oscar and the goblins wave us off. Mason put the car on auto-drive. It easily navigated the road from Dorion Park.

The twins had done their job by wearing out Princess, and the slight hum of the car's engine lulled her to sleep. Nori also closed her eyes and either slept or meditated.

We passed the wrought-iron gates of Mason's estate. The car jolted as if something hit us. A scratching, grating sound came from the roof.

"What was that?" I asked.

Mason scrolled through the cameras. A red and yellow bird popped up on the main screen.

Clarence perched on the roof and gripped the forward rail in his talons.

He flexed his wings, settling in for the ride. Sitting, the roc was three-feet tall, covered in red and yellow feathers, with a whip-like tail. His beak curved to a wicked point, sharp enough to tear flesh from a carcass, and the fists made by his toes wrapping around the rail showed off the power of his talons.

"How does he always know where to find you?" Mason asked.

"No idea."

Since his transformation, Clarence had an uncanny ability to locate me wherever I was. But his appearance ramped up my nervous-o-meter. Anything could happen to us in the Inbetween. I was already putting Nori, Princess, and Mason in danger. And now Clarence.

"There's no point in telling him to go home," I said. "He wouldn't listen any more than you would if I asked you to stay home."

"That's one of the things I love about you." He leaned in and kissed my neck. "You know when to pick your battles."

"Oh, get a room," Nori said without opening her eyes. Mason snuck another kiss. I pushed him away. No need to make Nori uncomfortable. Not when she was putting herself in danger for my benefit.

Saving Jacoby was Nori's settlement of our debt. In a minor fit of jealousy, she'd given information to Polina's agents—information that led to my abduction. I should have hated her for that. But in the month since then, she'd gone above and beyond by keeping Jacoby alive. Her debt to me was already paid, though she didn't see it that way. She'd made a promise to her grandfather before his passing. Her kitsune honor demanded that she see this through.

Princess pedaled her legs, chasing some dream rodent. Lying on her back, her lips flapped back, revealing finger-length canines. A muted woof escaped her dream.

"That mutt is going to get restless before too long," Mason muttered, without taking his eyes off the screens. The car was moving at a steady forty kilometers. We were heading northeast until we met the railroad. Then it would be a straight shot south and, if the tracks were indeed clear, we'd pick up speed.

After an hour of watching the endlessly unchanging forest on the screens, I rose and stretched. Nori was sleeping. I tucked two fingers under Jacoby's chin and scratched his soft fur. He was unchanged—unchanged and slipping away every second.

Mason saw me frowning and said, "You must change your mind of things."

Most days, I forgot English wasn't his first language. Then he'd mess up a saying, and I'd be reminded that he wasn't just French. He was French-Revolution French.

"You mean I should take my mind off things?" I teased.

"That's what I said." He arched one eyebrow at me, as if I would dare to contradict him.

"Okay. Tell me what's going on with Angus."

"I sent him away to sort out his business."

"That sounds harsh. Did he do something wrong?"

Mason glowered and leaned into the screen, as if he saw something in the forest. After a moment, he sat back, but his expression hadn't improved.

"Not wrong. Just awkward. It has to do with Naomi."

"Oh."

Most ghosts were mere reflections of spirits, like videos stuck on repeat. Naomi was one of the few ghosts I'd ever met powerful enough to keep her psyche intact. If she worked at it, she could even interact with the physical world. She could also jump into other bodies and inhabit them for a time. During our little tête-à-tête with Polina, Naomi had jumped into Angus, and now she was stuck.

"He's gone to see the witches at Sanctuary Ward."

"That's risky." I'd heard good and bad things about the Sanctuary witches. They lived in a secluded ward north of Montreal and were ruled by a prophetess. The witches worshiped her like a living patron saint for wronged women. She had real power, but she rarely helped men. "Do you think she'll even see him?"

"He felt that he had to try—"

The rest of his thought was cut off. The car lurched.

"We hit something!" Mason pounded on the controls and the car jerked to a stop.

Nori tumbled off the bench. I caught Jacoby before he hit the floor. Princess woke, flipped, and landed on her feet, ready to take on whatever had disturbed her sleep. A growl simmered in her throat, and her ears pricked toward the door.

"Why aren't we moving?" I asked.

Mason worked the console. "I don't know. Something's blocking the wheels. I can't see from here."

On the wall of screens, one camera view was suddenly filled by an eye.

CHAPTER

5

The eye disappeared. I stared at the screen, willing it to give up its secrets. All we could see was the brushy foliage beside the road. Then a shiny, bald dome, more like an egg than a head, trundled by on the lower limit of the lens.

Oh, no.

"Put it in park," I said. "We've got a problem."

Nori was awake now, watching the screens with wide eyes.

Mason adjusted the camera angles, revealing the dozens of creatures surrounding the car. They were pink-skinned and headless, with eyes, flat nose holes, and wide mouths in the middle of their chests below a bald hump. Long, bony arms waved about in frantic and meaningless gestures.

"What in the hells?" Mason powered down the car, rather than force it through the headless bodies. "We've been caught by a pack of Humpty Dumpties?"

"Blennys," I said.

"You know them?"

"Not these guys in particular. The forest around my grandmother's city is full of them. They're mostly harmless. But in a mob they can do some damage."

"What do we do?" Nori asked. "Should we go out there and talk to them?"

"Definitely not. I don't speak their language, and anyway, they're not that intelligent. I don't think I could reason with them."

The car shook again, followed by piggy squeals. Blennys pounded on the metal walls. The sound echoed like we were inside a drum. Nori groaned and grabbed her head. Princess paced and whined. The hair on her back stood up like a brush.

"So we wait it out?" Mason asked.

I nodded. "Wait til they get tired of their new plaything and move on."

"Terrific." He scowled at the screens. The blennys were now standing one on top of another, trying to mount onto the roof of the car. Clarence had taken flight when we first stopped. The cameras didn't pick him up, but he wouldn't be far away.

The car tipped, then landed upright again.

"We can't wait them out," Mason said. "If they knock us over, we'll be stuck out here."

Something scraped across the roof with a grating sound.

What now?

A flash of red and yellow tore through the blennys. They screamed like little girls.

Clarence!

Princess was barking and jumping at the door. I cracked it open, and she tore outside. I grabbed my sword and followed her into the mob of blennys. Their pale heads-that-weren't-quite-heads reached my shoulder, but their eyes were much lower, at my bellybutton level. Because they had no necks, their field of vision was limited. This caused a lot of stumbling and bumping into things. One blenny let out a garbled cry and reached for me. I shoved him aside before his fingers latched onto me.

"Don't hurt them!" I shouted after Princess. She'd already knocked a bunch down and trampled them under her overgrown paws. The blennys scattered, not exactly running away, just hithering and thithering. One ran face-first into the door hatch and knocked himself out. Another backed into Princess. She whipped around with a snarl and chased him, sending the others into a squealing, spinning, arm-flailing frenzy. A mob of them ran over Mason.

"Tabernak!" he shouted as he fell. I lost sight of him in the crush of little egg men.

Right. Enough with the niceties. I dove into the melee, using my sword like a baseball bat. Thwack! A blenny screamed. Thwack! I spanked another on the butt. He jumped up and grabbed his backside with both hands. His eyes went wide, and his fat lips pursed in a surprised pout. I conked him again, and he ran off, arms flailing like an enraged chimpanzee. From the pile of bodies on Mason, I yanked at a spindly arm. A blenny fell away from the pack, scrambled to his feet and disappeared into the trees. I continued to grapple with the little buggers until a stone arm punched through the pile. I grabbed it and hauled Mason up from the jumble of bodies.

"Damn thing bit me!" His flesh arm showed a red welt. He rubbed it against his pants. The tangled blennys were sorting themselves out.

"Get behind me," I said and jumped in front of him.

"What?" Mason turned and saw what I saw.

The blennys had lost their endearing befuddlement. Those that were left—about a half dozen—stood ready to fight.

Blennys were omnivorous scavengers. Their teeth weren't meant for tearing flesh or killing prey. But their snarling lips revealed broken and blackened teeth that could do a good deal of damage. And I didn't even want to think about the infection rate of that bite.

I grabbed Mason's arm and pulled him behind me. My sword hummed with anticipation. It was just getting warmed up for the fight. The blennys scuffed the dirt like bulls ready to charge. They bowed their egg-heads and bolted forward. One caught me in the gut with enough force to send air rushing from my lungs and slam us both against the car. I twisted as we hit and kicked out at a second blenny battering ram. My sword came up as the first creature opened his maw to take a chunk out of my thigh. His teeth clashed with my blade. I yanked it back, slicing his grin a little wider. He shrieked and fell. Blood spattered my feet, but I was already turning to face the next attack.

Clarence swooped down and grabbed a blenny in his talons. He flew away, skimming the ground until he dropped the creature about fifty meters away. It scrambled to its feet and disappeared into the brush. Clarence plunged into the fight again and yanked another one skyward. The other blennys decided that they'd made their point—whatever that was—and ran away, hooting and yammering and pounding fists on their bald domes.

"Unbelievable." Mason shook his head and let his stone arm drop.

"Still better than berserkers," I said, remembering our last trip through the Inbetween and the Sasquatch-like creatures that had nearly captured us.

"Do you think they'll come back?"

"Probably not." I reached for his arm. "You should let me clean that bite." He scowled and pulled away.

"It'll be fine. Didn't break the skin." He bent to inspect the car and kicked away stones the blennys had lodged under the tires. "We'll have to talk to Oscar about fitting this thing with weaponry. For next time."

I liked that he was optimistic enough to believe we'd survive this trip and fatalistic enough to know we'd probably find an excuse to do it again.

Clarence landed on the roof and ruffled his wings, settling himself after the fight.

"Thanks, buddy." I reached up to pet his soft feathers.

A caw echoed from deep in the trees. Clarence's head whipped around. The cry came again, and he answered it, a deep, throaty sound I'd never heard from him.

The trees came alive. Dozens of brilliant rocs perched in the uppermost branches. One bird flapped his massive wings and called out in that deep song. The others watched silently. Clarence hopped across the roof. His head cocked to one side as he considered the new arrivals. He'd never seen a flock of his own kind before. The colorful plumage made the tree they rested on look like a giant flower. A blossom of rocs, I thought. But each petal of that blossom had talons as long as my fingers and a beak capable of ripping my arm off.

"We should keep moving." I shoved Princess back toward the door.

"Agreed." Mason didn't take his eyes off the flock.

"Clarence, come inside," I said. Clarence flicked a glance at me but made no move to leave his post. I shut the door, and we continued our journey. On the interior screens, I could see Clarence poised like the figurehead on a great ship. The blossom of rocs watched us pass with silent, predatory stares.

CHAPTER

6

We made it to the railroad just after dark. I stood outside, directing Mason while he worked the controls to line up the car so the train gears would engage with the track. Princess paced beside me.

"It's okay girl." I ran my hand along her neck and felt a growl vibrate in her chest. She didn't like being exposed out here any more than I did.

A warm wind blew up from the south. Fifty paces on either side of the track, the forest loomed. The clearing would give us enough time to spot anything coming from the trees, but not enough for us to mount a defense.

"A little to the left." I pointed with a thumb and Mason turned the car. "A little more. Okay, stop!" He cut the engine and a minute later, the fat rubber tires receded, leaving the car sitting on the train wheel set. It was perfectly balanced on the track.

Princess and I hopped back in the car. Mason engaged the new system. With a squeal of metal on metal, we started slowly, but soon picked up speed.

And then we stopped. A barricade of branches blocked the track.

"Ciboire," Mason swore. I noticed him rubbing the blenny bite on his arm as he peered at the screens.

"Are you sure that bite is all right?"

"It's fine," he snapped. Without another word, he opened the hatch and went outside to check the blockage.

"All right then." Something more than the delays had irked him.

Princess cocked her head at me, trying to decide if I spoke to her.

"Come on. Let's go see what the problem is."

"I'll help." Nori started to rise from the bench, using her arms for leverage as if she were heavily pregnant. I gently pushed her back down.

"You stay and rest. Try to eat something."

She didn't fight me. Instead, she leaned against the bench's headrest and closed her eyes.

I ignored the knot of worry in my gut and called Princess again to follow me outside.

The sun was setting, and in the dim light, Mason was inspecting a bramble of debris that flooding or wind had deposited on the track. A broken pole was caught up in the mess and the dormant wire that had once been a live ward line draped across it.

Mason reached for the line.

"Wait!"

The ley-line ward that ran along the tracks protecting it from attacks by beasts and marauders had been Gerard Golovin's crowning achievement. It had enabled the first rail line between two wards—Montreal and New Manhattan. And for his obsessive love of Polina, he'd blown it to pieces. That didn't mean this wire was inert.

"It could be linked to a local ley-line," I said.

Mason glowered at me under his dark lashes and grabbed the wire.

I grabbed his sleeve and jerked his hand away.

"What is wrong with you!"

"Nothing." He dropped the wire and rounded on me. "Look. I'm fine. I didn't explode or suddenly burst into flame. See?" He held up his hands and swiveled them back and forth to show me his unburned skin.

"But you could have! You didn't know if that wire was dangerous or not. You didn't even ask."

"Why? Because you could have sleuthed it out with your superhuman keening?"

"Yes!" I could feel the anger pressing against my eyes, hot and scratchy.

"And then what? You'd push me behind you and tackle it yourself? Oh, don't let the poor frail human get hurt!"

He paced around the bramble, kicked a rock, swore when he hurt his foot, then kept limping onward. He stopped on the edge of the trees. I could hear him muttering in French. At least he had enough sense not to go blundering into the forest.

Now what did I do? I could wrangle a two-headed cerastes or take down an angry were-bear, but this relationship stuff was...*hard*. I'd done something to piss him off. Should I cave and say I'm sorry, even if I didn't know what I was sorry for? Or should I let him spin his wheels until he calmed down?

"What do you think?" I whispered to Princess. She'd hunkered down to crack open the skull of a rodent that had been hiding in the brambles. She raised her muzzle when I spoke and sniffed the air before going back to her meal. At least one of us was relaxed enough to eat. My stomach felt like it was inhabited by a den of snakes.

The sun sank below the treetops and all the color drained from the world. Mason returned from his tree-line vigil.

"I'm sorry," he said. His eyes held a storm of emotions.

"Um, me too?"

He laughed, the kind of laugh that held no joy. It was a sound you made when the world seemed determined to spank you at every turn.

"You don't even know why I'm mad."

"No. But I know whatever I did, I didn't mean it."

He reached for my hand and tugged me toward him. I let myself be tugged.

"I really am sorry. Those blenny creatures were ridiculous. I shouldn't have let them get the drop on me." He rubbed his palms up and down my arms, a nervous gesture that told me he had more to say.

"Go on. Say it."

He stepped back, putting distance between us again, and rubbed a hand over his head, making his hair spike.

"I don't like it when you have to rescue me. There. I said it. Happy now?"

I sighed. If that was all this was—a bruised male ego—then yes, I was happy. Bruises healed.

I crossed the few steps separating us, but didn't touch him.

"And how many times have you rescued me?" I started counting on my fingers. "Let's see, there was the time you took a bullet meant for me, and the time we fell through the floor in the warehouse and you dragged me to safety. Oh, and let's not forget the time you scoured the St. Lawrence seaway until you found me stranded on an island."

"Those don't count."

"They do count. I'm not some spoiled princess stuck in a tower. I don't need rescuing either. Except when I do. And you're the one who is always quick to point that out. So let's stop counting and just have each other's back. Deal?" I held out my hand for him to shake.

He watched me for a long moment. I could see the anger and frustration drain from his eyes. They were replaced with exhaustion and resignation, but it was a start.

"Deal." He took my hand and pulled me in for a hug.

A howl from the darkening forest reminded us that this wasn't the time or place for hugging.

"Let's get this mess cleared and get out of here," I said.

It took us an hour to pull the branches aside. It was full dark by the time we returned to the car. We needed food and sleep and decided to stop for a few hours. Princess, already fed, curled up under the console to sleep. Nori slept on her bench.

"Should I wake her to make her eat?" I said as Mason doled out dried fruit and jerky from our rations.

"Let her sleep. I'll set the alarm for three hours. We'll wake her then."

I choked down the dry meal. Mason made up a bedroll, and we huddled under a blanket on the hard floor.

I was drifting off when I felt a surge of magic. I sat up.

"It's just me," Nori whispered. Her hand glowed with the magic she'd pumped into Jacoby. "He needed a boost."

I nodded. Nori looked tired. She couldn't keep feeding Jacoby.

"I'm sorry I got you into this," I said.

"I got myself into this." She smiled and laid back down on the bench.

I'd thought Mason was asleep, but he pulled me close against him and murmured incoherently in my ear. I guessed I was forgiven for saving him from the blennys. Princess was asleep on my other side, twitching as she dreamed. I felt like I was in a cocoon of family. And despite all the worries about Jacoby, Nori, and the long track ahead, I slept.

"MASON, WAKE UP! We overslept." I shook him. He rolled and threw one arm over his eyes. I shook him again. "Come on! We've got to get moving."

He dropped his arm and stared at me, bleary-eyed.

"What?"

"The alarm didn't go off."

"Shit." He sat up and threw off the blanket. Princess was already snuffling at the door to go out. My bladder was near bursting too.

We all shuffled outside. Dawn was perking up the sky. Birds were busting out the good-morning arias all around us. We'd slept for over six hours. My head felt heavy and full of wool. I could easily lay it down and sleep for six more.

Princess dashed into the trees to do her business. I wouldn't go that far, but I didn't want to squat in the gravel beside Mason either. I didn't care if he'd seen me covered in dragon poop or heaving my brains out. We definitely weren't at the open-door bathroom policy stage of the relationship yet. There were some things that just killed the romance.

I spotted Clarence sitting in the higher branches of a nearby tree and headed over to him. The forest was unusually quiet here. Clarence was scary enough to keep smaller birds away, but my eyes scoured every shadow, looking for something to jump out at me. Not far inside the tree line, a root wheel from a fallen tree gave me privacy. I squatted there, feeling exposed. As I was choosing leaves to wipe with—and desperately hoping they weren't poison ivy, poison oak or some other mutated and deadly vegetation—Clarence let out a caw and launched into the air, leaving me alone in the forest.

A moment later, Mason called out, "Kyra, you better come see this."

I zipped up my pants and jogged back, feeling about four liters lighter. Clarence stood on the roof of the car. His feathers puffed up like a lion's mane. On the other side of the tracks, the trees were filled with red and yellow.

The blossom of rocs had returned.

CHAPTER

7

The alpha roc screamed a warning that sliced through the quiet morning. He spread his wings and soared toward the car. It was a gently arcing flight, but as he flew overhead, he plunged into a dive. Clarence shrieked as the roc's claws scraped across his back. The others stood as silent witnesses.

Clarence shot upward, and the roc followed him. As the sun burst over the trees, the alpha roc's wings pumped, and he overtook Clarence. He was so fast! I gripped Mason's arm hard, expecting the birds to crash and plummet to the ground. At the last second, the roc wheeled left. His powerful talons snagged Clarence's feet, and he swung the smaller bird around like a counter-balance.

In an eerie but beautiful ballet, the rocs spun around the axis of their locked feet in three great loops, the last one dangerously close to the ground. Then the alpha roc cawed out in triumph and let go.

Clarence hit the gravel with a sickening thud.

The alpha roc flew back to his flock. Feathers ruffled all down the line as he took his top perch on the tree. They settled and watched the downed bird with fierce, cold eyes.

Clarence rolled, got one leg under himself, and tried to rise.

Get up, get up, get up!

He fell forward, but his beak planted in the dirt kept him upright. Wings spread and he got two legs under himself now. He stood and shook out his feathers. Fluffs of down filled the air like snow.

I expected Clarence to fly away, or at least keep his distance, but that showed how little I knew about rocs.

He rose into the air, circled once as if testing his bruised wings, and flew straight toward the resting flock. He landed on a branch near the alpha, but low enough that Clarence had to look up at him.

I held my breath. Would the other rocs accept him? Or would they tear him to pieces for invading their territory?

The alpha roc considered this new young male. He tilted his head from side to side and looked down his impressive beak. Clarence bowed his head. The alpha flexed his wings and cawed. The flock took to the air with a great whomping of wings and flew off over the treetops.

Clarence went with them.

I watched them soar and bank left, like they were of one mind. I watched until they were lost in the shadows of the rising sun. And then I watched the empty sky.

"You okay?" Mason's arm snaked around my shoulder.

"Yep." That was all I could say. If I let out more, I'd break into a million pieces.

Clarence was gone. And this time, I knew he wouldn't be coming back. The frail little chick that hatched from a lost egg and stole my heart with his gobble-gobble antics had finally grown up and left the nest.

I should have been proud.

Mason didn't give me any platitudes about how he'd be better off with his own kind, and I was thankful for that. It was true, of course. But platitudes wouldn't fill the new gorge in my heart.

"Come on." He steered me toward the car. "We should get moving before we attract the attention of something worse."

He whistled and Princess came tearing out of the trees with a rabbit the size of a wolverine dangling from her jaws. It had been dead for some time and stank like rotten garbage.

"You're not bringing that inside." Mason crossed his arms and blocked the door. Princess dropped the carcass at his feet and nudged it with her toe. "Not inside."

"Princess, leave it!" I snarled. The hound whined. I sniffled, and she tucked her muzzle under my hand to lick my fingers. "I'm sorry." I hugged her, not caring that she smelled like she'd just climbed out from a mass grave.

Clarence was gone. Jacoby was gone. At least I could hang onto my hell hound for a bit longer.

CHAPTER

8

nce we got going, the car rolled at a decent sixty clicks until we hit the next blockage. And the next. We stopped a dozen times to clear debris. By late afternoon, we hadn't even made it to Junction Point, the halfway marker where Golovin had staged his coup.

I stared at yet another tumble of branches lying across the track and sighed. It was piled higher that my head. And it wasn't just a fallen tree. The blockage looked more like tangled driftwood left after a receding flood. It would take us hours to cut it away. Hours that would keep us from finding Jacoby.

"I'll get the saw." Mason turned back to the car.

Stretching the kinks from my back and shoulders, I watched Princess sniffing at the brambles. The scurry of a small critter caught her attention, and she dug frantically. Maybe I could repurpose her energy.

"Princess, get the stick!"

The hound pulled her head out of the hole she was making. Dirt crusted her nose.

"The stick! Come on, you love to chase sticks!" In our walks at home, she was always grabbing sticks and thrusting them at me in hopes of enticing me into a game. Often those sticks were as thick as my wrist, and if I wasn't careful, she could take me out at the knees as she ran by gripping one in her mouth.

Princess sniffed the pile, unconvinced.

"That's right. Take it." I jerked on a branch, but it was stuck in the tangle. The hound caught on and grabbed it in her powerful jaws, tugging until she dislodged it. She pranced around like a puppy, exuberant about her new toy, then saw a shiny new squirrel and ran off into the trees.

Some help.

Mason returned with a small emergency axe and a handsaw.

"Pick your weapon."

I reached for the saw. He could do a lot more damage with the axe than I could.

Nori stepped out of the car. Her hair was mussed and clothes wrinkled. She blinked in the bright afternoon sunlight with eyes rimmed in dark smudges. Her hair had lost its luster and hung like limp noodles around her face. She still looked like a runway model, just a runway model who'd survived a drug overdose.

"Do you need help?" she asked.

I held up my saw. "Only one saw and one axe. Go get some rest. We'll clear it and be on our way soon."

She nodded absently and returned to her bench.

"I don't know how much longer she can sustain Jacoby and keep going," I said.

"I'm worried too." Mason's frown etched lines into his cheeks. I knew he felt responsible for Nori. He was the one who'd brought her to Montreal. Now she was alone in a strange country, and the first thing she did was sacrifice her health for my dervish.

"I'm also worried about you," he said.

"I'm fine."

"I mean about Clarence." He watched me with his signature Mason intensity, the kind of scrutiny that made me feel like my soul was bared to the sky and about to get sunburned.

"I know." I dug my saw blade into a branch and gave a half-hearted tug. A silent minute passed. I could feel the weight of his stare.

I sighed. "I'm fine, really. Being with his own kind is the best thing for Clarence. Letting them go is all part of the rescue process."

"Doesn't make it any easier though, does it?"

I shook my head. He squeezed my hand, and I pushed back the tears that seemed too close to the surface these days.

"Let's just get this track cleared." I dug the blade into another branch and started sawing. The only way we could help Nori was to help Jacoby. And the only way to help Jacoby was to get the car moving again.

At the far end of the blockade, Mason began pulling branches and hammering at the mess with the axe if they didn't budge. Princess dashed around, blessing us with her particular brand of helpfulness—worrying at branches, growling at shadows and generally being a nuisance.

We worked for over an hour, sawing, cutting, and tossing branches aside. I stopped for a sip of water and watched the sun dip into the tree line. To the west, the sky was clear, but the setting sun lit dark clouds in glaring reds and purples over our heads.

Mason leaned against the bramble pile that didn't seem any smaller. My right arm ached from the repetitive sawing motion.

"Do you think we'll get this cleared before dark?" I wiped sweat from my forehead with my sleeve.

He glanced up at the churning clouds. "I'm more worried about that storm."

Another hour of chopping, sawing, and dragging away logs brought us to the brink of night. The setting sun had given the clouds permission to mount an attack. Wind blustered down the funnel created by the rail line. It pulled at my clothes and dried my damp hair. Debris from our work scattered, sending sharp bits of wood through the air like shrapnel.

We'd almost cleared the track. Another fifteen minutes of chopping and we'd be ready to roll again. The muscles in my arms hummed from the constant sawing. I wanted to finish the job so we could move on. Sitting through a storm here didn't seem like a good idea.

Lightning crackled across the sky. After a beat, thunder rumbled like a sleeping giant.

"Should we stop?" I asked.

"Another few minutes," Mason shouted over a second crack of thunder. We redoubled our efforts. Most of the big logs were already cut away. Now we scrambled to pull off smaller branches. Princess barked at the dust devils that swirled up on the open ground.

"Princess! *Hael*!" I called her to me. Dust devils could be more than they seemed in the Inbetween. The last thing I needed was to have my hound pulled through a portal to another world.

We were clearing the last branches when hail fell like ice daggers.

"Ow!" An ice pellet grazed my cheek. There was a moment's lull when everything stopped—wind and hail. Then lightning hit a ley-line pole with an atom-splitting BANG! The heavens opened, and the gods pelted us with golf ball-sized hail.

"Run!" Mason yelled. I was already dashing for the car. Nori held the door open and Princess leaped inside. Mason followed me in and slammed the door shut, cranking the hatch to lock it. The noise of ice hitting the metal roof was deafening. Nori sat beside Jacoby, her dark eyes wide and scared.

Mason threw himself in to the console chair and fiddled with the controls.

A noise like a metal grate falling into place shook the car, and all the screens went black except for two. The cameras at the front of the car and over the door still projected the apocalyptic storm. The pounding of hail against the roof dimmed, but not by much.

"What did you do?" I rubbed the back of my head where a lump was forming. I must have taken a hit from the ice, but I hadn't felt it until now.

"I put us into panic mode. Nothing short of a nuclear bomb could penetrate these defenses. But we also can't drive like this. We'll have to wait out the storm."

We hunkered down. After the hours of hard labor, my limbs felt like rubber. I fed Princess and then flopped on the floor, leaving Nori and Jacoby undisturbed on the bench. I replenished my energy from our small store of food and water.

Mason sat beside me. We were wet and dirty and tired. The storm continued to batter the car, the sound like a thousand-man firing squad opening up on us. I hoped the armor held.

I leaned my head on Mason's shoulder. "Oscar won't lend us his toys again. This is the second time we've mangled one of his vehicles."

"Not our fault." Mason pulled the elastic from the end of my braid and trailed his fingers through my tangled hair. He planted a kiss on the tip of my nose. A voracious gleam lit his eyes, and his grin suggested that his thoughts weren't on storms or armored cars.

"What?" I patted my hair, suddenly feeling self-conscious.

"Why do I always want you the most when you're sopping wet and caked in dirt?" He leaned in and kissed me again, just beside my mouth, then nibbled along the line of my lips.

"Tease." I turned to meet his kiss. Stubble from his two-day beard raked my chin, sending my nerve endings into high alert. Kissing Mason was amazing. Every time felt like the first time, with that little zing of electric desire that went right to my groin. But it also felt familiar, like coming home. I never thought the two sensations could exist in the same space. Not until I met Mason. But now I understood the truth. Desire and familiarity were the yin and yang of intimacy.

I didn't need to put on lacy underwear or paint over my flaws with make-up. Mason saw me as I was, blemishes and all. And he still looked at me with fire in his eyes. That assured me that when I got old, chubby and wrinkly—*if* I got old, chubby and wrinkly—he would look at me the same way.

I shot a glance at Nori. She was asleep, but could wake up at any time. I sighed and tucked my head under his chin, taking comfort from the slow beat of his heart.

"I wish we had time to be alone." We hadn't been truly alone since that one night on the island. After that, we'd been chasing Gerard and Polina, then he'd been healing from the wound I'd inflicted on him. And now we were on the run again.

"Never enough time," he murmured against my ear. "We should do something about that when we get home."

Home seemed a long way away.

The hammering hail trailed off, and soon I dozed with my head tucked against Mason's chest.

I'd been listening to the silence for a while in my groggy, almost-dream state before I realized that my keening was picking up something else.

I sat up, pushing damp hair from my face.

"What…?"

Mason caught my hand. "Shh." He pointed to the screen that showed the world outside the door.

While I slept, the storm had tapered off and dawn was lighting the track ahead. A few branches remained from the blockade and a few more had fallen during the storm.

Princess was awake, her ears pricked forward as she stared at the door hatch.

Something dark ran across the screen.

My keening pinged like a radar. Nausea swept over me. I pressed fingers to my temples.

Whatever was out there was magically huge or it was bleeding, leaking its life-magic at an alarming rate. Those were the only two reasons for my keening bell to ring.

Mason knew the signs of my magic sensitivity. He rubbed my back while I fought nausea. Both of us were fixated on the screen.

Again, the shadow ran by, closer this time. I got an impression of a man dressed in a cloak made of icicles standing near the burned ley-line pole. But that couldn't be right. He was impossibly big to be that far away.

My stomach churned. I leaned in and squinted at the screen.

"Can you make it bigger?" I asked.

Mason punched in commands and the screen zoomed in on the creature. It wasn't wearing a cloak of ice. The beast was covered in metal blades like the feathers of a Stymphalian bird. Long limbs, more wing-like than arm-like, hung at its sides. Blue eyes glowed from a face hidden in steel-gray fur. It stalked forward like a raptor, and far too soon, its chest blocked the entire view. That thing was colossal.

My keening buzzed like I'd drunk a dozen pots of coffee. I swallowed hard and repeatedly to hold down the acid that threatened to erupt from my gut. I couldn't boost my personal wards fast enough.

"What is that?" Mason asked. I could only shrug, not trusting my voice to come out without spewing vomit. I might be the resident critter expert, but there were things in the Inbetween that no one had ever seen. Or at least things that no one had ever lived to tell about.

The beast hugged the side of the car with the scraping sound of metal on metal. The car interior dimmed as it blackened the camera's view. What was it doing out there?

A low moan came through the speakers. The magic tripping my keening took on a more agitated note. I squirmed in my seat as it washed over me in waves of…

Was that sexual desire?

The car shook.

Nori woke and sat up, bleary-eyed. The creature's moan escalated. The shrieking grate of metal burned my ears.

"What's going on?"

"Some beast is trying to shag our car," Mason said with a grin.

"It's not funny!" I doubled over.

Mason handed me a canvas sack. A barf bag. Aw. He knew me so well.

The creature's magic pounded us. The car rattled and bounced with a Bang! Bang! Bang! as the wheels lifted and smacked down on the track. The moaning and shaking increased until the creature climaxed in a nerve-shredding explosion of magic. The car tipped. Everyone slid sideways. Princess yelped as she was thrown against the console and landed on me. A canteen fell off the table with a crash. I gripped Mason's hand as the car teetered. If it fell over, that would be it for us. Mason and I might make it on foot, but not carrying Jacoby and Nori. Not through five-hundred miles of the Inbetween.

The car righted itself with a slam. I let out a long, half-choked breath.

The creature's agitated magic calmed. We waited in silence. Finally, it moved away, and sunlight filled the view screen.

"I feel like I need a shower." I pushed Princess off my legs.

Mason grinned. "Or a smoke."

CHAPTER

9

The next morning, Mason and I cleared the track three more times. As we drove between stops, Nori seemed alert, so I thought it was a good time to question her about what was to come.

I handed her a cup of water, wishing we had a small hot-plate to make tea. Another update to suggest to Oscar.

"When we get to Iona Park, how will I make the connection to the Life Tree?" I asked. This whole trip depended on me being able to use Timberfoot's Life Tree as an anchor while my astral body went off to find Jacoby. But Nori had been vague about the details.

"You'll have to petition the spirit of the tree for his help. But that shouldn't be hard for you. He's your father."

"Dad and I weren't exactly close."

She shrugged. "The connection is there. You'll just have to figure out a way to tap into it."

Terrific. We could be making this entire journey for nothing.

"And after that? What happens if he accepts and becomes my anchor? Will he take me to Jacoby?"

Nori chewed on the end of her hair. It was a nasty habit she'd taken up recently. "The Life Tree will only open the door for you."

"The door to the Nether."

"That's right." She smiled, as if it all made perfect sense. It didn't. The way forward was a big, blurry abstraction to me. Thinking about it gave me a hollow feeling in my stomach. I stood and paced the full three paces that the car allowed, stretching and fisting my fingers.

"It won't be that bad," Nori said. "I promise. When you get to the Nether, you'll find a guide to help you."

"What kind of guide?"

"I can't say. It's different for everyone."

"So I've got to find a park in the middle of the dryad forest, connect to a father I've never met to get to a realm called the Nether where I'll find an unknown guide to lead me to Jacoby. Any other good news? Will there be fireworks and marching bands too?"

She frowned and held open her hands, as if to say, "You get what you get."

The car slowed, and I had no more time to agonize over the inevitable.

"Another roadblock," Mason said as he scrutinized the forward screen.

We jumped out to look at the mess of debris across the track.

"It doesn't look too bad," he said. "We should be able to clear it quickly."

Thank the gods for small favors. Dozens of cuts covered my hands, and my shoulder muscles burned from the unusual exercise of sawing. But we put our backs into it one more time, and fifteen minutes later, we were ready to roll again.

"Hold on." Mason jumped onto the roof of the car and squinted into the distance. "There's a pair of binoculars in the trunk," he called down to me. "Can you get them?"

I scrounged through the trunk until I found his fancy alchemist binos and passed them up. After scouting the track ahead, he jumped down with a frown wrinkling his brow.

"Is it that bad?" I couldn't face another day of breaking up branches.

"It's not that. The track is clear as far as I can see."

"Something else then?" My mind conjured up the carnivorous bison herd we'd encountered last time. Or it could be berserkers, manticores, marauders, vampires....There was no end to the fun to be had in the Inbetween.

"I'm not sure. There's activity ahead. Could be a caravan."

Homesteaders often traveled in packs for safety. A caravan was the best-case scenario, but I could tell that Mason had only mentioned it for my benefit.

"We'd better find out what it is," he said, "unless you want to travel off track again."

I really didn't. The railroad was the most direct route to Manhattan, even with the blockages. Out in the forest, we'd encounter worse than dams of tree branches.

Mason was right. The track ahead was surprisingly clear, like someone had already been through this way. But who? No trains were running between the cities and Oscar's little hybrid car was the only one of its kind.

A few minutes later, we had our answer when our car was stopped by a new kind of blockade. Two armored vehicles sat on the tracks. Beside these, a dozen men and women in military uniforms waited with blasters pointed our way.

"Get out!" The senior officer banged on the side of our car. Princess snarled and threw herself at the door, but the rest of us froze.

"Who are they?" Nori asked.

"Should we get out?" I said at the same time. Mason was studying the console screen. I peered over his shoulder. The officer was unarmed, but the others hadn't relaxed their stance. A dozen blasters focused on our only exit point.

"They're not making a great case for opening that door," I said.

"What other choice do we have? Wait here until we run out of food and water?" Mason stood and pushed Princess away from the door. "Hold her back."

"You can't go out there! Not until we know who they are."

"I'm going to play my Kester card. Don't come out until I signal."

He reached for the hatch. I jumped in front of him, blocking the door.

"They could shoot you on sight. You have no idea if these people are working for Kester, and you're not...I mean..."

He ran his fingers along my jaw and tucked my braid behind my shoulder. His eyes were soft and dark and sad.

"You can finish that sentence. I'm not what? Immortal anymore. I'm not bullet proof? Neither are you, and yet I can't ever stop you from running into the fight."

He was right. But ever since I'd taken away his gargoyle curse—the curse that had kept him alive for three hundred years—I couldn't help worrying that I'd lose him.

He leaned his forehead against mine and I breathed him in, filled myself with his magic, as if trying to commit it to memory.

"I'll be fine." He ran a thumb along my jaw and smiled.

I nodded.

The officer pounded on the door again. I grabbed Princess around the neck and held her back. Her lip curled and a string of drool dripped onto my arm.

Mason opened the hatch and stepped out with his hands up. Nori shut the door behind him and engaged the lock. I smiled at her, grateful. I wasn't sure I could have sealed Mason's fate so easily.

On the screens, I watched as the soldiers surrounded Mason. They patted him down, looking for weapons, then they marched him toward the waiting trucks, where they none-too-gently shoved him into the back of an armored van. The door shut and the soldiers fell into place behind the van. A wall of guns.

I slumped into my seat. Now what? Were they going to take him away?

I eyed Nori, who was sitting in the corner with her arms clasped around her drawn-up knees.

"You should get ready to shift." I'd seen her shift within seconds, her human form melting into the fox like water. As a fox, she'd be a smaller target and faster. "If Mason doesn't come back, you and Princess run for the trees. They won't follow."

"And then what? Live in the Inbetween, hunting rodents for the rest of my life?" Her tone had a sharp edge to it. I didn't have any answers, so I wrapped my arms around Princess's fluffy neck and watched the screen.

A soldier standing by the vans shouted. He blasted a round of fire into the trees and took three steps in that direction before his comrades pulled him back. Our cameras didn't pick up whatever had spooked him. He went back to the van, arguing with the others. After that, they were all on high alert.

We waited for five minutes. Five minutes that felt like five hours.

Mason emerged from the truck. The soldiers surrounded him, but they no longer pushed him along like a captive. He walked back to our car, and I cracked the hatch.

"We're fine." Mason smiled. "Just keep the hound on a tight leash. These guys are jumpy."

"No kidding."

The soldiers scanned the forest. The officer followed Mason and greeted me.

"I need to see the other passengers." He was a tall, pale man with a crooked nose and sunken eyes.

"I'm Kyra Greene." I stepped outside to greet him. He nodded, then peered inside the car.

"That's Nori Ogawa."

"And that?" He pointed to Princess, who was crouched low, ready to spring.

"Princess! Enough!" I snapped. The hound dropped her belly to the ground, but didn't relax her snarl.

"That's my dog."

The officer's face went even whiter, but to his credit, he didn't step back. "Anyone else on board?"

Mason spoke up. "Just the dervish I told you about. We're heading to Pennsylvania to find a cure for him."

"And what's in Pennsylvania?" the officer asked.

Mason leaned casually against the car. "I believe that Kester Owens told you to extend us every courtesy. I don't find your questions courteous." His tone was light, but his eyes were flint hard.

"I'm just doing my job."

"Your job is whatever Kester says it is, or should we call him back to confirm that?" Mason held up his widget. Was it a bluff? Or had he really been able to call Kester? That would mean that the ward was up and running. I turned to scan the rail tracks that led south, sending out my keening. Yes. There it was. The faint magical hum of a ward. Kester was working hard to reestablish the trains.

The officer waved to the soldiers standing with the vans, and the vehicles backed off the tracks. He leaned in and spoke slowly, as if we might be dim-witted.

"You're clear to go through, but we'll escort you to Manhattan. That's the deal."

"We'll take it."

10

The forest skimmed by on the screens as we whisked along the tracks. With a direct road and no more barricades, we made it to Manhattan Ward an hour after sundown. Despite all Gerard Golovin's faults—and there had been many—this railroad was a gift to human and fae kind. For the first time in over fifty years, travel between wards could be safe and even pleasurable.

The world was changing. Again.

The train tracks ended at a newly-built station. We shifted our wheel set back to rubber tires, and then the soldiers escorted our car to the North Gate on the shore of the Hudson River. It wasn't like the gates at home. There were no inns lining the street, no beggars, refugees or pickpockets. Instead, the fields beside the road leading to the gate were planted with corn, already half as tall as me thanks to the warm June weather. Soldiers patrolled the area. Spotlights mounted on trucks scanned the dark fields, looking for vegetable poachers. The only buildings we passed were a barracks for those soldiers and a military base where we parked.

Kester Owens was waiting for us.

Mason jumped out of the car to meet his old friend. They did that guy thing, where they shook hands and clapped each other on the shoulder at the same time. I held back, fussing with Jacoby's backpack.

"Let me have him," Nori said, taking the sling from me. "You deal with the hound."

"Right." I snapped a colar and leash onto Princess. They were just for show.

There was no way I could hold her back if she decided to bolt. But people tended to trust dogs on leashes. I thought about asking her to transform into her chihuahua form, but she hadn't willingly done so since Polina died, and I didn't want her to take a shape that made her uncomfortable. I suspected Polina had forced it on her as a way of controlling her. I wouldn't do that if I could help it.

I helped Nori slip Jacoby's sling on her back and made sure he was settled, giving him a scratch under the chin. He looked like a sleeping, poodle-furred baby. His magic was so faint, like an echo of a dream.

I stepped from the car. Princess bounded after me, hit the ground, and headed right for Kester.

"Heel!" I tugged on the leash, but didn't push magic into the command. The hound side-eyed me, then shook her head, flinging drool at my pants. "Fine. At least stay close. And don't bite anybody unless I say."

I took a moment to watch Mason and Kester chatting. Then Kester saw me watching and smiled. He was one scary looking dude. Tall and whip thin, his bald head seemed overlarge for his body. He had big blunt features—hatchet nose, round, almost lidless dark brown eyes. He was too skinny to be handsome and his skin seemed stretched too tightly over his bones. His smile did not invoke any feeling of friendliness. It was toothy and menacing. A shark's smile.

"Kyra Greene, welcome." He didn't offer his hand. Demons were touchy about being touched. A good sorcerer could bind a demon, but they needed to be in contact for the binding to work. It probably became habit to a demon to forego the handshake ritual. That he'd done so with Mason spoke of a deep mutual trust. I wondered how he managed in the business world where handshakes could turn into alpha-male pissing contests. Did he cultivate an aloof mystique or pretend to be a germophobe to hide his demon-ness from others?

Whatever he did, he couldn't hide it from me. His magic burned darkly and it had the faint tang of brimstone.

"Hello Kester. It's good to see you again." It really wasn't. Seeing the demon congressman again brought up a visceral reaction in me. I could suddenly feel Gerard's blood on my hands again. And though Kester hadn't been part of the plot to overthrow the Montreal Triumvirate, he would always be linked to it in my mind.

After getting the VIP treatment through the North Gate, Kester led us to a wharf that ran along the shore.

The Flood Wars reshaped the landscape of New York, eroding a chunk of land between the Long Island Sound and the Hudson River. When the waters receded, Manhattan became a more isolated island. Like Montreal, the founders of the new ward used the natural enchantment of the water to reinforce the man-made barrier they erected around the island. Unlike Montreal, the first New Manhattanites had acted in an overabundance of precaution and destroyed the Lincoln Tunnel and most of the pre-war bridges off the island.

We strolled down the wharf, passing military crafts and a few luxury yachts. On the other side of the river, the lights of Manhattan glittered like another galaxy in the night sky. The leviathan skeleton of the old George Washington Bridge jutted from the water to the north. But Kester was quick to point out recent improvements like the train station and the pilings that were the beginnings of a new bridge.

"It's all to accommodate the expected traffic coming this way once the train is running."

"You think the rail line will bring that much traffic?" Mason asked.

Kester pinched his already thin lips. "If the Montreal Triumvirate can get their heads out of their asses and make some decisions about the future of commerce in your ward, then yes. I believe we'll need the new bridge, and maybe even a second train station."

Mason grunted a noncommittal response. Kester raised one eyebrow at him, then let out a deep laugh.

"Come, my friend. You look like you need a drink. We'll talk business later."

He stopped us at his private boat, a forty footer that would have been a prize in pre-war times. Now? It was priceless. And expensive to run on ley-line batteries.

Kester conferred with the captain and led us into the cabin where we all settled on three plush couches. Princess prowled the cabin like a caged beast, sniffing every corner. Her eyes glowed red, a sure sign of her agitation.

Kester fixed us drinks and watched the hound. "I haven't seen one of those in a long time. A gate keeper?"

"Yes." Hell hounds were the guardians to the underworld, like security dogs for the inhabitants of hell, though I was never sure if they were meant to keep people in or out.

"Fascinating." Kester snapped his fingers and Princess trotted over to sit at his feet. She looked up at him with adoration shining from her eyes.

Not cool. She wasn't really my dog, and I knew I'd have to re-home her when we returned to Montreal, but I didn't like a demon having that kind of power over her.

Kester scratched Princess behind one ear, and the mutt sank into it, her tongue lolling and dripping drool.

"Who's a good doggie?" His deep-voiced baby talk didn't fit with his grim appearance. He found a treat of mystery jerky in the cupboard of the small kitchen next to the lounge and tossed it to the hound. Then he handed out drinks, something like gin and tonic. Carbonated drinks were a luxury I hadn't tasted in years. So good. I sipped it and felt myself sinking into the couch like my bones were softening.

Mason cleared his throat. "I didn't expect to see you, but now that we're here, we could really use your help."

Kester sipped his drink and threw him a skeleton smile.

"My help doesn't come cheap. You know that."

Mason squinted. "What's your price?"

Kester leaned back and studied him. "All in good time, my friend. The walls have ears." He lifted his glass to the ceiling. "Enjoy your rest. We'll talk when we reach my home."

Mason raised an eyebrow but didn't protest. Why would Kester have crew on board he couldn't trust? Or did he think his boat was bugged? Neither option left me feeling safe. It spoke of either a deep paranoia or a deep animosity among the New Manhattan leaders.

The boat ride to the island was short, and I had just dozed off when we docked. I carried Jacoby off the boat. Mason tried to hang onto Princess, but she tore away from his grip and ran down the dock. In a moment, she was lost in the wild gardens around Kester's mansion. I started to run after her.

"Let her go," Kester said. "My property is secluded. She'll be fine."

"If you're sure." I wasn't. Princess could do a lot of damage in a very short amount of time.

Kester texted something on his widget. "I'll ask my groundskeeper to keep an eye on her."

We followed a path toward the big house that was barely visible through the trees. Another small cottage suddenly appeared in the darkness when someone turned on the porch light. An ogre stepped out the door, scratching his round belly. Kester spoke to him quietly and pointed into the trees where Princess had disappeared. The ogre yawned, nodded and trundled off into the woods.

"That's your groundskeeper?" I asked.

The light reflected Kester's bright smile. "Wainright. He has a way with beasts. Now please, don't worry. You're safe here."

Reluctantly, I let Princess go. Ogres *were* good with animals. And I was kind of relieved to let down one of my burdens, even if only for one night.

Kester's home was grand and Gothic. It looked like something from a fairytale—maybe one of the original dark and broody tales from the Grimm brothers. The front facade was made of three square towers fitted together in a semi-circle with a wide staircase leading up to tall black doors flanked by arched windows. It would be hard to make an inconspicuous entrance through those doors.

Inside the vaulted foyer, a tiny, wizened fae woman greeted us.

Kester made introductions. "This is Havia, my housekeeper. Havia, this is Mason, my old friend and his companions, Kyra, Nori and…I'm sorry I don't know the dervish's name."

"Jacoby." I shifted him in my grip. "He's the reason we're here."

"Is he ill? Poor wee thing." Havia cooed and brushed his fur from his eyes. Her magic hummed like a warm summer day, and I instantly felt calmer. She was the godmother kind of fae, the kind that drew energy by caring for others.

"Let me take the poor fella. I'll see he's comfortable." She held out her arms. I glanced at Nori, but she seemed asleep on her feet. Mason gave me a slight nod. I didn't trust Kester, but I trusted Mason. I handed over Jacoby. Havia headed deeper into the house, cuddling him against her bony chest and singing a soft lullaby.

My feet lurched me forward, ready to follow.

Kester reached out a hand, stopping short of touching me. "Havia is a true mother. She's never happier than when she has someone to care for. Let go of your burdens for a while, Valkyrie."

It was so close to the thought I'd had outside that I squinted at him, wondering if he was an empath. He winked.

The dining room had been plucked from the Victorian era, with damask wallpaper in a busy pattern of deep burgundy and black. The furnishings were heavy dark wood and the only lighting came from an elaborate chandelier fitted with modern gleams that looked like candles.

We sat at one end of a table that could have seated twenty people. Two servants brought in plates, platters, and glasses and set them before us. I was almost too tired to eat, but as soon as the smell of roasted fish and dill hit me, I dug into it.

"How did you manage all this?" Mason asked. "You didn't even know we were coming until a couple of hours ago."

"I entertain a lot," Kester said. "It's the only way to get anything done in this town."

Manhattan was ruled by a Congress, similar to the Senate in Montreal, but they had no over-arching Triumvirate. No one to cut through the politics and make executive decisions. Congressional representatives like Kester would have to manipulate the political arena to get what they wanted. Somehow, I suspected Kester was very good at his job.

Nori ate only a few bites, then pushed her plate away.

"If you'll excuse me. I must see to Jacoby."

Kester called to one of his servants to lead her out.

"She needs to eat more," I said.

"Let it go for now," Mason said.

Kester watched the exchange with frank curiosity, and I explained, "Nori is going to feed some of her magic to Jacoby. She's keeping him alive. But if she starves herself, she won't be helping anyone."

"Ah." Kester snapped his fingers, and a servant appeared like magic.

"Please see that rooms are ready for our guests. And bring a bowl of broth and some bread up to Miss Nori's room. See that she has everything she needs." The servant nodded and left.

"Thank you," I said, though I wasn't sure Nori would eat it.

"I want to know all about your dervish friend and what brings you south," Kester said, "but first tell me what in the hells is going on in Montreal?" He addressed Mason, who frowned.

"What do you mean?"

"I mean that ever since that bastard Golovin destroyed the pact between our wards, I haven't been able to get in touch with the Triumvirate. We're ready to re-establish relations, to connect the rail line and finish the job. We want to bring peace and prosperity to both wards."

"Sounds like a good plan." Mason chewed and swallowed, not taking his eyes off Kester.

"You'd think so." Kester puffed out a little snort. "But I can't get a straight answer from any of my contacts in Montreal. It's like no one is at the helm up there."

"That's because no one *is* at the helm," Mason said. "I don't know how much you heard, but Golovin blowing up the train wasn't the worst thing that happened recently."

"Tell me." Kester set down his fork and leaned back in his chair.

"You know Leighna was killed?"

Kester nodded, his expression solemn.

"Her death left a void. The humans lost their party leader, too. And the alchemists have been running with Oscar Lewis as Prime Minister since Golovin stepped down."

"But Merrow Farsigh took over as interim Prime Minister of the fae, no?" Mason nodded.

"And I heard the humans are ready to name Eugene McIlroy as their new Prime Minister. So what's the problem?"

Mason weighed his words before answering. "Merrow is a no-nonsense leader. She gets things done. But she lacks Leighna's…diplomatic grace. She attacks every project with a blunt hammer. She's already made many enemies. And now the godlings are all stirred up again, demanding recognition as the fourth official party. Merrow's opponents will side with them just to force an election."

The godlings were descendants of various pantheons, like the Olympians and the Hindu gods. They didn't fit into any of the three existing political parties and had been making noise for years about forming their own. The only reason they hadn't done so yet was because the different pantheons despised each other and couldn't come to an agreement about who should lead this new party.

Kester frowned, and a deep, low rumble came from his chest. "That worries me. I've met McIlroy. He doesn't know his ass from his earlobe. And with the rail project stalled, I planned to appeal to Prime Minister Farsigh next. I will have to consider my options. It's too bad the alchemists don't have a strong minister in place. Seems like there's a vacuum that needs filling." He looked pointedly at Mason.

"Don't you start with me, too. Oscar has already outlined all the reasons I should run for office. I can't even think about it until we get this business with the dervish settled."

Kester watched him for a long minute. Mason watched him right back.

The demon sipped his wine and said, "Well then, you'd better tell me how I can help so we can get back to business."

I TOLD KESTER everything about the bloodstone and how Polina's ex-lover had used Jacoby's fire magic to finally break it and set the witch free. I told him about Polina's plans to "save" Montreal after she was the one who destroyed the ward in the first place. And since he seemed touched by Leighna's death, I explained how she died. I finished with Nori's exceptional healing talent and how Jacoby was lost between worlds.

"You think you can find him?" Kester asked. "Walking between worlds isn't easy." He spoke like someone who knew.

"I'm the only one who has a chance of finding him, of bringing him home. But I need a Life Tree to use as an anchor, or I'll end up as lost as Jacoby."

He chuckled and shook his head. "You really are a magnet for mayhem." Then he winked. "Mason always did like a woman with a bit of darkness at the core." His eyes were a deep fathomless brown, so dark they seemed black. "That doesn't explain what you're doing in New Manhattan."

I ignored my pique at his assessment of me. As long as I sat at Kester's table, I'd be polite.

"Iona Park is about two hours west of here. There's a Life Tree in the middle of the park."

Kester made that soft rumbling noise again. "I know the place. Some lunatic with too much money and too much time on his hands built a stone henge there, sometime in the late seventies."

I nodded, knowing he meant the nineteen-seventies. The park was over a hundred years old. But I didn't think the man who built it was a lunatic. Iona park sat on a conjunction of ley-lines. The man probably had a deep connection to magic. He most likely didn't understand his driving need to set up a circle of two-ton stones, or that his chosen site was sacred to the Underhill fae and a place where the veils between worlds thinned.

"This Life Tree," Kester said. "You're talking about Timberfoot Greenleaf, the dryad who sacrificed himself to close the last door to Underhill."

"Yes." I met his gaze. My heart was thudding, and when he squinted at me, I wondered if he could hear it.

"How will you get there?" he said finally. "Even if you get past the marauder gangs—and there are plenty of those—that tree is deep in dryad territory. There are no roads going in."

"There is one. The Dryad Highway."

Kester barked out a laugh. "The dryads will never let you use their roadway. Lisobet Greenleaf is Ranger of that canopy. She's fiercely protective of her trees and especially that one. What makes you think she'll let you near it?"

"Because she's my grandmother," I said quietly.

It was satisfying to see Kester's eyes pop out of his head.

CHAPTER

11

Kester let out a booming laugh, accompanied by a blast of magic that shook my bones. Demons. They could never keep their magic in their pants.

"This day keeps getting better and better." His eyes were wet as if he squeezed mirth out of them. He leaned into me. "Do you realize what kinds of concessions I could get from those damned dryads if they knew you were a *guest* in my home." He emphasized the word *guest* like he meant something darker. Mason kicked his chair back and stood, gripping the table edge in both hands. I keened his magic surging, and the skin on his left hand turned to stone.

"Easy, old friend." Kester held out his hands like a magician, proving he had nothing hidden up his sleeves. "I'm not threatening your woman. Lisobet Greenleaf and I share, shall we say, a history. Most of it friendly." A smile crept across his face. "I'm not saying that I would use your presence as barter. I'm saying, I could." His expression darkened. "And others will, so you should keep that bit of information to yourself."

Mason relaxed.

Kester downed the last of his wine and stood. "We'll take my car."

"What? Where?" I said.

"To Iona Park, of course. Or at least as far as the road will take us. We'll hike the rest of the way."

"Who said you're coming?" Mason growled.

"You might have an in with the ranger, but getting to the Dryad Highway won't be easy. Marauders have been attacking the West Gate. Rumor says they're planning something big. Besides, the militia won't let you through without me."

"And you're willing to come all that way with us…why?" I was standing now too, with my arms crossed. The three of us were at a stand-off.

"Like I said. Lisobet and I have a history. I wouldn't mind seeing the old acorn again."

Acorn? Oh, wow. It was bad enough when I had to picture Queen Leighna getting it on with my dad. Now Kester Owens with Nana Timberfoot? There wasn't enough soap in the world to scrub that image from my mind's eye.

"I'd suggest we leave at first light, but with our gargoyle friend here," Kester nodded toward Mason, "we'd better move out now. With any luck, we'll make it to the dryad highway by sunrise."

"Actually, we could use a few hours of sleep. And my curse won't be a problem." Mason looked away, like he was embarrassed. "Kyra broke it."

Kester looked from me to Mason and back again. "Now, that's another story I'd like to hear." When neither of us offered a comment, he sighed. "Fine. Keep your secrets. For now. I'll let you get some rest, and we'll leave at dawn. The raiders are less active during the day. Shall I have one room made up for you, or two?"

"One room is fine," Mason said.

"Excellent. I'll wake you in a few hours."

I peeked in at Nori and Jacoby on the way to our room. She'd fallen asleep with her hand on his chest, no doubt after giving him a dose of magic. Charcoal circles outlined her eyes, and her cheekbones were sharp enough to cut diamonds. I turned off the light and let her sleep.

Our room continued with the Gothic theme, though it was done in cherry wood and a blue that was almost turquoise. The bed was set on a dais, and I had to climb stairs to flop onto it.

"You can have the bathroom first." Now that I was lying down, I didn't want to move, not even to brush my teeth. I listened to the water run as Mason washed up. A few minutes later, he was shaking me awake.

"Get under the covers." He pulled back the blanket on the other side to make room for me.

"S'ok," I slurred. "Gonna wash first." I stumbled from the bed, forgetting about the stairs and fell down them.

"Stealthy," Mason said.

I stuck out my tongue and tottered to the bathroom. The bright light gleamed off every shiny surface to stab my sleepy eyes. I shut it off and suffered through my ablutions in the dark. By the time I made it back to bed, I was wide awake. Mason lay on his back, staring at the ornate canopy over the bed.

"What are you thinking?" I asked.

"Just worried about these constant delays."

"Me too. But if Kester is right, we should be at Timberfoot's tree tomorrow. I hope that's soon enough."

Mason turned and propped his head up with one hand, leaning on his elbow.

"How come you always refer to him as Timberfoot instead of Dad or Father?"

"Do I?" My feet were cold, and I tucked them between Mason's thighs.

He grunted. "It's a hundred degrees outside. How are your feet cold?"

"It's a talent." I stuck my ice cubes against his warm skin. He wrapped his hands around them, instantly filling me with warmth from the toes up.

"I don't mean to call him anything. I have no concept of my father in my head. He was just a thing that happened to my mom a long time ago. They had a brief affair, then he disappeared. I think he forgot I even existed."

Mason searched my face. "And that doesn't bother you?"

"Not at all." I spoke without thinking, then considered those words. I didn't want to lie to him. So, I poked at the scarred-over wound.

As a child, I had nagged my mother endlessly about my father. She evaded my questions until I wore her down. In a fit of exasperation, she finally said, "He wants nothing to do with us, so leave it be." That was the last time I asked.

"I guess it does bother me." I tucked my head into the crook of his neck and shoulder so I wouldn't have to see the concern on his face. He stroked my hair. "Or it did once. Father is an abstract idea to me, though. The Timberfoot that Leighna told me about, the one who sacrificed himself to close the last door to Underhill because he loved her…that man seems more real to me."

"Are you nervous about seeing his tree?"

"No." I sighed. "Yes. I'm just glad my grandmother won't be there. The last time I visited, we didn't leave things on a good note." Silence followed as he waited for me to elaborate. Instead, I sucker-punched him with a change of subject.

"Do you regret that I broke your gargoyle curse?"

"What? Why would you think that?" He leaned back so he could see my face.

"Because you seemed hesitant to tell Kester about it."

Mason rested my head against his chest again, and I listened to the slow tolling of his heart.

"Don't think like that. Whatever I gave up…it's worth it." He snugged me closer and suddenly all thought of absent fathers and broken curses left me. His lips found mine, and I stretched, feeling my body fit against his like it was meant to be there.

We wasted our few precious hours of sleep, but it was worth it.

12

We headed into the city in three armored cars. Kester drove with Mason, Nori and I in the back seat of the middle car and Princess rode shotgun. Jacoby lay across Nori's lap. She refused to let him go. He was colorless, as if his body were fading from this plane of existence.

Kester wasn't kidding about needing extra security. Once we left his gated community, the streets thronged with people. They watched our black cars pass with unveiled hostility.

We stopped at an intersection waiting for a group of school children to cross the road with their teachers. Six young men pushed away from the guardrail as if they'd been waiting for us. One gripped a piece of metal rebar. Another clenched a small blade in his fist.

"Come on, come on." Kester beeped the horn to urge the kids to walk faster, but that only startled them and they stalled while the teacher scowled at us. The gang of thugs was almost at the car. The one in the lead swung his bar like he was warming up to bat.

I leaned forward. "Roll down the window."

"What?" Kester frowned back at me, then saw what I meant. Princess had her snout pressed against the glass, teeth bared. The window slid down.

"Princess, guard." I laced the command with a touch of magic.

The hound's magic swelled, and she visibly grew. Her shoulders filled the window space. She thrust her head outside and growled loud enough to be heard over the traffic. A string of drool hung from one of her fangs. I couldn't see them, but I knew her eyes would be glowing red.

The batter skidded to a halt and backed up a step. Princess let out a deep, bone-shaking woof.

The light changed and we shot through the intersection. Princess's drool slapped against my window. Nice. Kester tried to close the front window, but Princess was enjoying the wind in her fur. Her lips peeled back as she caught all the city scents.

"I didn't realize Manhattan was so…" I couldn't find the right word.

"Gang-ridden?" Mason supplied.

Kester squeezed the steering wheel, his face grim. "We've spent too much money on militia and not enough on food and housing. It's something that I hope to rectify, but we need an influx of funds."

I nodded. "Like the tariffs from the new rail line."

"Exactly."

People who could afford it would pay decent money to travel to another ward. Not to mention the tax on freight. For the first time in over fifty years, trade between wards would be safe and fast.

"The only thing standing in our way is the bunch of babies on the Montreal Senate who can't agree on a lunch menu, let alone a trade agreement." He turned to glare at Mason.

Mason held up his hands in surrender. "Message received. You want better leadership in Montreal. But I can't do anything about it from here. So let's focus on this mission."

Kester grumbled something under his breath, but didn't push it.

On the west end of the island, the ancient Lincoln Tunnel had been replaced by the Josephina Wolfe Bridge in honor of the alchemist who built the ward. It led traffic from the West Gate into the wilds of what was once New Jersey. As the magic of the ward boundary rippled through me, I distracted myself from the discomfort by turning to look back at the Manhattan skyline. It was a city from another age, with its cluster of skyscrapers. I couldn't help but marvel at the engineering of a ward built big enough to encompass those towers. The Josephina Wolfe Bridge was longer and higher than any in Montreal and the view was stunning. Below us, the Hudson River was a glossy blue ribbon rolling through thick greenery as far as my eye could see.

Armed militia stopped us at the far shore. Kester pulled ahead of the lead car and rolled down his window. A guard scanned his face, then scowled at the scanning device.

"Representative Owens. I have no notice that you planned to leave the ward."

"I don't need permission."

"No, but it's…irregular."

"Life if full of surprises, son. Get used to it." Kester pointed to the cars behind us. "I'll be perfectly safe. They're with me."

The guard nodded and waved us through. This gate had a bigger settlement built beside it, but still military in style. We passed through it to find more crop fields and more militia guarding them.

"With all these farms, Manhattanites must be well fed at least," I said.

"You'd think," Kester said. "The fields are too big for us to patrol properly. Raiders and wildlife take a good share every year."

The fields ended abruptly, and we drove into a thick forest. Kester tapped the console and spoke to the other cars. "We don't stop for anything until we reach Bangor. Understood?"

"Copy," came the replies.

"What's in Bangor?" Mason asked.

"It's where the road ends. We walk from there. If we make it that far."

We drove in silence after that, each of us lost in private thoughts and worries. The vibrations of the car lulled me, and I felt myself sliding toward sleep.

Something jolted me awake.

"How long have I been out?" I stretched a kink from my neck.

"About an hour," Mason said.

The car had stopped. That's what woke me. Ahead of us was another bridge over a smaller river. The forest grew right to its edge, but ahead, the sky was clear and blue, reflecting on the water.

Two vehicles blocked the road just before the bridge, and two dozen men and women were arrayed behind them. These were not the well-dressed, well-armed militia we'd seen at the gate and patrolling the fields. These were marauders, dressed in dust colored clothes, carrying an assortment of weapons from pre-war rifles to crossbows. Their eyes were hard and unyielding as they leveled their sights on us.

"What do they want?" I asked.

"A toll for using the bridge," Kester said.

"Are we going to pay it?"

"Not in this lifetime." He tapped the console again. "Do you have your trackers on?"

"Yes, boss."

"Good. If this goes bad, use it to follow my lead car. Don't stop. Don't get left behind."

"Copy."

"What are you going to do?" Mason leaned forward between the front seats.

"What I do best."

Some people have deep-set eyes. Kester had eye-hollows. And when he turned and grinned at us, those dark hollows seemed to blur and spin. Crazy eyes, I called that. They were the eyes of someone who was about to do something spectacular and unpredictable.

Kester turned back to face the marauders. They were waiting for us to make the first move.

I keened power building in Kester. It had that sulphuric zest of demon magic. A shadow leaked from him, spreading like black ink dropped in water. Princess barked and whined. I wrapped my arms around her seat and jammed my hands into her ruff, taking as much comfort as I gave.

Kester rolled the car forward. The blackness thickened. It shot forward, smothering the marauders. Someone screamed. A blaster fired wildly into the trees. The shadow grew, spreading across the bridge. It expanded until it blotted out the trees, the road, and the sun. I couldn't see the marauders anymore, but I heard their gunfire and screams of terror like a nightmare that I couldn't run from.

We drove onward. It was like driving through tar. Arrows, bullets and blaster fire pelted the car, but they pinged off the reinforced body. Kester accelerated, and we rammed the bumper of one of the blockade trucks. It spun away enough to let us through. As we passed the marauders in the inky darkness, I caught shadow glimpses of them fighting each other. They'd dropped guns and bows in favor of fists. Like primordial apes, they bashed each other with a ferocity that left all reason behind. Faces were bloody and twisted in savage grins. Bodies sprawled on the ground and over truck beds like puppets with cut strings. One man grabbed his opponent's arm, locked the elbow with his other hand and twisted, popping the joint and nearly tearing the limb off. He beat his chest and roared. Blood coated his teeth.

And then we were through the darkness, passing over the bridge under a beautiful, sunny sky.

Mason hissed through his teeth.

"That's your superpower?" I asked.

"Among other things." The edges of Kester's grin were ragged. Creating the shadow had aged him.

"Remind me to stay on your good side." I threw myself back into my seat. My hands were shaking. Kester had brought his demon magic to bear. I could taste it. It wasn't just the darkness. That was bad enough. But somehow, he'd infected those marauders with a killing mania.

My bloodless fingers squeezed Mason's hand. He offered me a smile that was meant to be reassuring, but I knew his magic signature well enough to know that he was as freaked out as me.

Kester was Mason's friend, so I'd accepted his unusual origins. What did I know about demons, anyway? The last one on Terra (so the histories read) had been expelled at the end of the Flood Wars at great cost. I'd seen one in Asgard, a minor demon who fought with the giants before my grandfather's treaty went into effect. He'd also tried to use fear and mania to make his enemies kill for him, but it didn't work so well on the descendants of gods. Aaric squashed him like a bug with Thor's hammer.

My sword was purring in its sheath by my feet. Kester's burst of dark magic delighted it. I lifted it to my lap, taking comfort from its vibrating energy.

We drove for another hour through the forest. The road ended at a wall of brambles. We parked and got out. Kester's soldiers stood in a circle around us, blasters pointing into the dense foliage.

"You and your men should stay here," I said. Dryads were pacifists. They wouldn't welcome the armed guards into their domain.

"They'll wait here, but I'm coming," Kester said. "I have unfinished business with your grandmother."

Right.

"We won't be seeing Lisobet," I said. "We've no time to waste on social calls."

Kester nodded toward the trees. "We'd better get moving then. How do you plan to find the dryads in that?"

"We won't. They'll find us."

CHAPTER

13

bout half an hour after we left the cars, the forest changed. At first, it was subtle. The thick brambles and underbrush thinned, and the trees became sturdier. There were fewer pines and more oak, maple and ash. Their upper branches tangled into a roof of foliage that blocked all sunlight. We passed trunks wider than cars. The lack of sunlight deadened ground cover, so we walked on a spongy bed made from decades of rotting leaves. The only color among the shadows were flashes of moss and clusters of red or yellow mushrooms.

Princess spotted something moving in the forest. Her ears perked up, her legs bunched and tensed under her and then, with a burst of speed, she pounced. The shadows swallowed her.

"Princess!"

Princess's fate had been weighing on me. I had already resolved to find her a new home, but I'd been thinking of a nice young hedge witch or an alchemist, someone who could handle her peculiar brand of magic. Someone who had acres of land for her to run in. Letting her loose in the wilds of the Inbetween to fend for herself was not on my agenda. But she seemed to have other ideas.

I waited a full minute, scanning the underbrush for my hell hound. We were bringing up the rear of our party and the others had already disappeared on the winding deer path ahead. The forest was dead silent except for my pounding heart.

"Princess, *hael!*" I sent magic with my voice this time. It was a dangerous tactic in the Inbetween. I risked attracting any number of beasties looking for a crunchy snack. I found my sword in my hand without even being conscious of unsheathing it. Nothing moved in the shadows.

I waited.

Mason appeared on the path ahead. He'd come back to see what was keeping us.

"Princess took off after a squirrel or something." It was the "or something," that worried me.

He took in my rigid stance, my expression and the knuckles turning white on my sword grip. Not saying a word, he rummaged in his pack, found a bag of trail mix and handed it to me. I lowered my sword to take it. He relaxed against a tree trunk.

"What are you doing?" I asked.

"Waiting." He sipped from his canteen. "Nori and Kester are taking a break, too. Nori needs it. We have a few minutes."

I nodded. A few minutes. What if she didn't come back by then? Would I leave her out here? What about Jacoby? Every minute we delayed put his life at risk.

"I hate this."

Mason quirked his eyebrow, letting me know he needed more context, so I added, "I hate making decisions for others."

"You're good at it."

"Doesn't mean I don't hate it."

He gently tugged on the braid that hung over my shoulder. "If you liked it, you wouldn't be good at it."

A black figure stepped from the bushes.

"Princess! You scared me!" I hugged her neck even though a something dead and furry hung from her jaws. The bone armor on her face was smeared with blood. I didn't care. "Don't run away again or I'll put you on a leash."

She sneezed and shook her head, dropping the rodent.

"You have two minutes to eat that, and then we have to get moving." But she was already into the meaty bits. I turned away, not needing to witness it.

Mason looked relaxed, but he studied the thick canopy above. "We've got to be in dryad territory by now,"

"We are."

The highway was above us. I was sure of it. These great oaks were my grandmother's domain, the Lekythoi Clan's territory. But, so far, we'd had no luck finding one of the few stairways that led up to the treetops. Dryads would have no need of a pathway to the canopy, of course. The stairs were for visitors only, and since dryads didn't encourage contact with the outside world, there were only a few of these.

Shadows moved between the great trees. Not dryads. We would never see those. But the forest was full of life, big and small. The skin on the back of my neck itched as I felt eyes watching us. Nothing had confronted us so far, but until we found the dryad highway, we were vulnerable.

The last time I'd come this way was over ten years ago, when I first returned from Asgard and spent the summer with Lisobet. That time, I'd simply stumbled around in the forest until a dryad dropped from the trees to confront me. When I explained who I was, she'd taken me along the highway to Bosk, the dryad capital city.

I'd hoped that a dryad guide would find us again, but despite our noisy bumbling around, none had appeared. We were heading in the general direction of Iona Park where my father's tree stood, but without their help, I had little hope that we'd find it.

"Ready to move on?" Mason asked.

I swallowed another gulp of water and nodded. Princess had finished her meal and rolled on the bloody carcass. She rose and her legs splayed to take the weight of her hulking body as she shook the bits of dirt and bone from her fur. It was the hound equivalent of "I'm good to go."

We moved off in silence, each of us scanning the shadows between the trees.

Nori was asleep with Jacoby in her lap when we found them. Her gaze met mine. Tracks of dried tears marked her cheeks.

"He's fading." She bent her head, and her long black hair fell around Jacoby like a curtain.

"He's getting weaker?"

"No, he's actually fading. Look." She held up one of his skinny arms. The poodle fur on his knuckles seemed blurred, like it was misting away. I held his tiny hand. His gray fingers were dry and cold.

"What does it mean?"

"It means we're running out of time. Wherever he is, he's dying. If he dies there…" She let the thought trickle off. I didn't push her to confirm my fears.

Kester stood with his back to us, staring into the upper reaches of forest.

"See anyone?" I asked.

He shook his head. "No, but they're up there. I can feel them."

Me too. So why weren't the dryads coming down to stop us from trespassing in their territory?

I lifted Jacoby from Nori's lap. She protested weakly, but I ignored her and started to strap his baby sling across by back. Mason stopped me.

"It's my turn." He took the pack.

"He's my burden."

He leaned in and whispered, "Your burdens are mine, remember? At least, I hope they are." His breath tickled my ear, and his warm, steady magic soothed my jangled nerves. I held onto Jacoby a second longer, then released him.

"At least let me help you," I said.

Mason leaned in for a quick kiss, then turned. I strapped the pack to his back and adjusted Jacoby's head so it lay snug between Mason's shoulder blades. And I took a moment to ruffle his furry ears and keen the faint bit of life still clinging to him.

Hang on, buddy. Just hang on.

We walked for another hour, then stopped for a water break. It was hard to tell under the dense canopy, but the sun was setting. The shadows deepened and soon we'd be stumbling around in complete darkness.

"This isn't working," I said finally. "The dryads should have come for us by now." I turned to Kester. "You said you had dealings with my grandmother before. How did you get to Bosk?"

"I didn't. She came into the city as part of a delegation. Many years ago, when we first starting cultivating land outside the ward."

That was no help. I studied the trees. Something howled in the distance. Princess's ears swiveled, tracking the sound as it circled us.

"Don't you dare." I dug my fingers into her fur. An answering howl came from another direction. Princess tensed under my hand. "It's just wolves. Ignore them."

The howl turned into a yip, more like a coyote. No telling what weird blend of canines hunted in this forest. The calls became more frantic, and closer. The pack of whatevers was closing in on their prey. I hoped that prey wasn't us.

"We need to climb." I turned my gaze upward. If the dryads wouldn't come to us, we'd go to them.

Mason understood immediately what I meant. He pulled out a gleam, shook it and tossed it up so it floated overhead. The light would announce us to anything hunting in the wood, but we needed it. Mason studied the nearby trees. "This one." He tapped the trunk of a younger oak. "We should be able to reach the lowest branch."

I peered up at the dense branches. The first branch was five meters above our heads.

"Can you manage?" I asked Kester.

Teeth shone in the gloom as he grinned. He held out his hands and claws bloomed from his fingertips. "Not a problem."

Mason and I could use our knives as climbing picks until we reached the first branches. But Nori...she wasn't strong enough and none of us could climb and carry her.

The kitsune saw me considering her. "Don't worry about me. Just take my pack. I hate walking around naked after a shift."

One moment she was a pale, rumpled woman. The next, she melted into the form of a red fox. Her clothes vanished with the change. I'd never figured out how she did that. After a good shake to acclimatize herself to her new form, she scampered up the tree and was soon staring down at us from the lowest branch.

That left Princess.

She sat at my feet, her eyes big pools of trust. It would never occur to her that I might abandon her here. I glanced up at the immense trunk. It would be a hard climb with only a knife and rope as climbing tools. Could Princess follow us on the ground?

Another symphony of howls echoed through the night, canceling that idea. Princess had to make it into the treetops, or we all stayed behind.

I knelt and wrapped my arms around her fluffiness, not caring about the dirt and less savory things embedded in her fur.

"You have to come with us." I charged my words with magic, just as my grandfather taught me. Dogs could understand vocabulary on par with a human toddler. Hell hounds were a step above that. But they understood magic even better than words.

"Remember when you were a little dog. So cute, with a bow in your hair." I filled my mind with images of a chihuahua and hoped she understood. "Can you do that again? Can you be a chihuahua?"

She cocked her head. Her eyes were alert and interested, but her magic was steady, not the magic of a beast about to transform.

"Chihuahua." I'd never forced her to take another form, but I could. A little push of magic into the right command...I didn't want to force the change on her. Polina had often paraded her around as the harmless toy breed with bows in her hair. The fact that she hadn't once tried to take that form since coming to stay with me spoke volumes about how she felt about it.

"Come on, girl, I know you don't want to. But I promise, it will only be for a little while."

I laid my hands on her and let my magic flow into her, not forcing the change, but definitely nudging her in the right direction.

She whined. Her wet nose jabbed my cheek and she licked me.

The howling predator took up its song again, answered by another, and another. We were surrounded.

I nudged with a little more magic, feeling like a total heel for pushing her to be something she didn't want to be.

And suddenly, like breaking through a membrane, I felt her understand. In the span of a heartbeat, my smelly giant hound transformed into a smelly tiny hound.

She yipped and turned in a circle.

"Thank you." I dumped out my extra sweater to make room, tucked her into my backpack, and zipped it up enough to secure her in place.

Kester had already joined Nori on the branch. He threw down a rope.

"You first," I said to Mason.

He hesitated only a moment. I knew his old-fashioned, chivalrous side was fighting with his modern-man side.

I cut through his dilemma. "Get Jacoby up there."

The wolves howled again. Closer now. "Go!" I gave Mason a little push, and he grabbed the rope. By the time he was halfway up, I keened a pack of at least a dozen beasts around us. The light from the gleam caught their eyes.

I couldn't wait for Mason to finish his climb. I only hoped the rope could hold us as I grabbed it in both hands. My feet braced against the oak's trunk.

Hand over hand, I started the ascent. The rope burned my palms, but I had no time to worry about that. A beast jumped from the forest floor into the light, teeth snapping at my legs. I kicked it in the muzzle. It snarled and fell back. Princess barked furiously and squirmed to get loose from my pack. I jerked my feet up and pulled with my arms.

More beasts broke from the shadows. They were more panther than wolf, with long sinewy bodies and powerful shoulders. Teeth flashed as a canine muzzle snapped at the air only inches below me. The others paced, hoping their prey would fall and make an easy meal.

Climb. Climb.

My heart thrashed in my chest like a fox in a snare.

Climb. Climb!

My shoulders burned from the effort. Princess was a lopsided weight as she continued to wriggle and bark. My hands became slick. Not sweat. Blood. The rough rope had cut me.

And just when I thought my muscles couldn't forge ahead one more inch, hands grabbed my jacket and hauled me up.

I sat panting and shaking on a branch that was wider than the deer path we'd been traveling on. Below us, the panther-wolves howled their loss and ran around the base of the tree.

"Let's hope they can't climb like mountain lions," Mason said.

"Everyone all right?" I asked between gulps of air. Nori, still in her fox form, darted over to sniff Princess, then scampered a few feet up the great trunk and froze.

I looked up.

An arrow pointed at the spot right between my eyes.

An arrow that was notched in a bow held by a very angry-looking dryad.

CHAPTER

14

ason stepped in front of me. The dryad didn't waver except to aim his arrow at Mason's heart.

"What are you doing?"

"Just take Jacoby and stay behind me." Mason's voice was laced with something gravelly. Anger? Fear? Bravado?

He was still thinking like a gargoyle, like he could take an arrow to the chest and survive it. I tried to shuffle him out of my way. He wouldn't budge. I hopped over to a nearby branch and eased along until it dipped dangerously under my weight, then I flailed and latched onto a higher branch to steady myself. The ground seemed impossibly far away. My heart pounded, and I shifted my eyes away from the long drop. The light of the gleam caught two more dryads perched on nearby branches, weapons drawn and ready. Others would be hiding in the leaves.

"I thought you said they were pacifists." Mason's voice came through clenched teeth.

"Mostly. They'll fight to protect their trees if pushed." I spoke quietly, but I knew the dryad facing us could hear me.

I raised my voice for the others hiding nearby.

"We mean no harm to you or the Canopy. I am Kyra Greene, Lisobet Greenleaf's granddaughter." This brought the slightest ruffling of leaves like an uneasy wind blew through them. "I swear it. Test my magic."

The lead dryad's bow lowered a fraction. I keened his gentle magic probe and tried not to shrink from it. He nodded and one of the other dryads slipped away.

Seconds passed. Minutes. No one moved. The nocked bows pinned us in place. Behind Mason, Nori perched on a smaller branch, her copper tail wrapped around her toes. Kester was almost lost in the shadows. I hoped he didn't do anything stupid.

I stared at the lead dryad and he held my gaze. There was no fear in his eyes, only steady confidence.

"You're from the Birchhold clan." I wasn't really asking, just trying to open a dialogue. I could tell his clan from the scars notching his bare biceps like the lines on birch bark. The dryad bent his neck in what could have been a nod. Green hair curled around his face. His features were elfin and youthful. But dryads never grew beards, and they aged slowly. If he was in charge of this scouting party, he had to be a senior officer. His fingers didn't relax their hold on the bowstring, which took strength, and his lithe arms didn't shake with the effort. He was a dryad in his prime.

"What are we waiting for?" Kester shifted on the branch, and a dryad swung his bow around. Kester raised his hands in surrender. "Don't panic. Just shifting my ass. This branch could use padding."

"Your ass could use padding," Mason growled. Kester's teeth flashed white in the dim light.

"We're waiting for approval to travel through the trees," I said.

I keened the new arrival before he appeared. The dryad dropped from above and landed on the branch beside me.

"Hello, Kyra."

I startled. The dryad grabbed my arm before I plummeted to the ground.

"Thorn!" I gripped my cousin's arm. He grinned at me. That was all the greeting I'd get. Dryads didn't hug.

Thorn was from the Lekythoi clan, like me. Put him in a suit and he could pass for human. But standing on a branch, ten meters up and dressed in nothing but the soft green tunic of our clan, he was all dryad. His hair was the color of wheat chaff, and it hung in messy curls to bare muscled shoulders.

"Your grandmother will be pleased to see you." He gripped my arm one more time, then stood back.

I shook my head. "I have no time for a visit. My friend is sick." I pointed to Jacoby lying limply across Mason's back. "He's dying. I need to get to Iona Park to heal him. Can we have permission to travel the Canopy Trail?"

Thorn's eyes flicked to Jacoby, then over the rest of my motley crew, resting for a long moment on Kester.

He nodded once. "Of course. I will lead you."

"Thank you." I didn't want an escort, but I hadn't really believed the dryads would let us roam in their territory alone.

Nori stayed in her fox form. We climbed another dozen meters and came to a platform built in the spread of trees.

I let Princess out of my pack and she transformed back to her usual hell hound form.

Thorn didn't even blink at the change. "I see you're still taking in strays."

"It's a sickness." I grinned. "Don't worry, she's perfectly tame."

Princess, happy to be released from the constricting chihuahua form, squatted and peed. We listened to it patter down the leaves like rain.

Thorn wrinkled his nose. "Lovely."

A BRIDGE WOVEN from thick hemp stretched from the platform we stood on to the next tree. Vines and branches were trained to weave through the bridge—under foot and along the rope handrail. I knew from previous adventures on the dryad highway that these interlocking branches made the bridge more sturdy, but it would still sway with each step. Thorn bounded along with a rolling gait that matched the swaying bridge like they were parts of the same beast. I followed with none of his grace. The road lurched sideways under me. I grabbed the rope rail, but that gave me as much reassurance and support as grabbing a leaf blowing in the wind.

"Steady." Mason stepped up behind me. His weight balanced the rocking motion. Nori scampered by us to wait with Thorn on the other side. Princess growled at the tilting bridge. I turned back, squeezing by Mason to coax the hound onto the bridge.

"Come on. You can do it." I used my "Hey, here's a fun game" voice. Princess whined and pawed the platform. "Do you want to be a chihuahua again? Don't make me stick you in my backpack. Come on, girl." I got behind her and nudged her big, fluffy butt forward.

Step by slow step, Mason led. I prodded, cajoled, and sweet-talked Princess to follow. Behind us, Kester swore in multiple languages as the bridge lurched and swayed. The gleam hovered above our heads, throwing enough light to make lurid shadows. When we finally made it to the next platform, Thorn waited with amusement glinting in his eyes.

"You're out of practice, cousin."

I waved my hand forward. "Keep going." It would get easier. In the summer I spent with my grandmother, I traveled the Canopy every day. I'd find my leaf legs soon.

The second bridge took half the time. Princess bounded across the third bridge like a puppy. By the fifth bridge, even Kester had stopped complaining. The muscles in my calves burned from the constant pressure on them to keep my balance, but we moved at a good pace.

We took turns carrying Jacoby. Nori eventually tired of being a fox. We rested while she shifted and found clothes from her pack to change into. When she reached for Jacoby's sling, I hesitated to hand him over.

"You're exhausted. Let me carry him for a while."

The kitsune shook her head. "I need him close. He will need to be fed soon." She took the leather sling from me and cradled him against her chest like a baby. Except he wasn't a baby. And she wouldn't be feeding him mother's milk.

"You need to slow down with the magic output," I said. "You can't keep up this pace and feed him too."

Over Jacoby's fuzzy head, she looked at me with haunted eyes.

"Just get me to that damned Life Tree, and then I will stop."

I left her to him and caught up to Thorn. "Can we make it to Iona before first light?"

"If we hurry."

We'd been traveling since daybreak. We were all tired, achy, and grumpy. But so close to our goal, none of us would give up.

Thorn set off for the next platform and I followed.

"How's your mother?" I asked. Thorn's mother was my great-aunt, Gladiris. Lisobet's younger sister.

"She's nesting." Thorn spoke over his shoulder. "The healers say this will be her last fledgling, so she is taking great care."

"You're going to be a big brother! That's wonderful" Dryads produced few offspring. They cherished each child like a miracle. We chatted about mutual friends and family. I was surprised at how good it felt to reconnect. I'd been an outsider when I lived with the dryads, but that was my doing, not theirs. Everyone had welcomed me to Bosk. And if my grandmother had never been the warm, gentle granny who plied me with hugs and cookies, at least she had given me a haven to lick my wounds after leaving Asgard.

I was so taken with chatting that I didn't notice the change in the Canopy road until we stood on a larger platform with an arching gateway.

Two guards stepped out of the branches.

"Thornbane!" snapped one of the guards. "What strangers do you bring to Bosk?"

Bosk? That couldn't be right. The dryad capital was well south of Iona Park. I turned to glare at Thorn, but he only shrugged, as if to say, "What did you expect?"

"Not strangers," he said. "I bring home Kyra Greenleaf, granddaughter of Ranger Lisobet Greenleaf."

Sigh. There would be no getting out of a visit with granny now.

From the Archives:

ON THE ORIGIN OF DRYAD NYMPHS

April 22, 2078

Edit (April 23, 2078): Nymph is not an abbreviation of nymphomaniac! It refers to a spirit (once believed to be mythical) that inhabits forests, streams and mountains. Comments have been closed.

Over two millennia ago, the Greeks discovered the nymph communities and suggested there were thousands of them living unseen in the wilds. But they rarely made contact with humans because dryads and most of their nymph cousins were uncommonly shy.

This was one of the eras in history when the veil between worlds thinned enough to let magic creatures from other worlds break through. The Greeks might have been right. The ancient forests could have hidden entire dryad civilizations. What they got wrong was believing that dryads were minor deities. They're not. It's time to set that record straight.

This article focuses on dryads, a type of nymph known for their affinity to forests and trees. Other nymphs include naiads (water nymphs) and oreads (mountain nymphs). Subscribe to the blog for upcoming articles on those.

Dryads are beings from Drys, a world with much more magic than ours. And when Terra's magic dried up, the dryads went home or went into a kind of stasis or died.

There are many dryad clans, including the Bircholds, the Graywoods, and the Alderas, but the Lekythoi—sometimes called the oak clan—were the first to return to Terra. Of all the dryads, they could most easily pass as humans. In the mid-twentieth century, they found a crack in the veil and left Drys to make a new home among the humans, who were still blind to the magic burgeoning in their world. The Lekythoi are perhaps a little too graceful, a little too willowy for the average human. But their skin tones range from birch bark white to oak bark gray, close enough to Caucasian to mingle freely in most Western cities. Only the delicate green veining at their ankles and wrists set them apart as anything other than human, and these could be explained as elaborate tattoos.

Other dryad clans didn't blend so well. The Hornbeam Clan is taller with pointed elf ears, leaf green skin and hair that curls like new alfalfa greens. The Hunnewell Clan is gnome-short, but still has that signature dryad grace. They are covered in spongy green fur that lets them camouflage against moss, and they sport long curving tails used for everything from combat to cultivating to traveling like monkeys through the canopies.

All these clans and the other races of nymphs—naiads and oreads—have found homes on Terra now. I'd like to say they found homes and a welcome on Terra, but that isn't true. There is a great stigma against fae who look too much like "others." And though some dryads can manage a decent glamor, most of the clans prefer to keep their green curls and dryad ways. For this reason, you almost never see them within the wards, but I have it on good authority that dryads have set up their own fortified cities in the treetops of the Inbetween.

Tell me your dryad tales! Have you seen a dryad, naiad or oread inside your ward? Let me know in the comments.

COMMENTS (8)

Keep your nymph whores out of our wards!
TheHappyPlace14 (April 22, 2078)

——•——

There's a tribe of dryads living in the mountains near our homestead. They don't live in the trees though. Maybe some kind of rock-dwelling nymph? Or something else entirely?
CarabinerCabin (April 22, 2078)

Do they have bark-like protrusions on their heads, almost like horns?

Valkyrie367 (April 22, 2078)

Yes!

CarabinerCabin (April 22, 2078)

Those are probably oreads. Be wary. They tend to be more warlike than other nymphs.

Valkyrie367 (April 22, 2078)

Thanks for the heads up

CarabinerCabin (April 22, 2078)

———•———

Nymphs? Like in nymphomaniac? I want to visit that town!

CurtWad (April 22, 2078)

———•———

A nymphomaniac "rack" will look great next to the other trophies on my wall!

BigGameGuy (April 23, 2078)

CHAPTER

15

I turned to Thorn, not bothering to hide my irritation and snapped, "You promised to take us to Iona Park." Thorn made that understated shrug that dryads used to communicate anything from agreement to displeasure.

"And I will. But Ranger Greenleaf would crack my skull like a ripe acorn if I didn't bring you home first."

I glanced at the gate. Made of solid oak, it framed the only road into Bosk like an arching arbor. The whole thing was elaborately carved with a vine motif. Realistic forest creatures were half-hidden among the leaves. A black burn spread from the apex of the arch, but instead of letting it mar the art, the artist had incorporated it into the carving, so the blackness spread like a storm cloud over the rest of the scene. The burn was significant. Dryads would never cut down a healthy tree. The wood for this gate had come from a tree felled by lightning. It was considered a gift from the gods. Fashioning it into the lintel that watched over their city to greet guests and foes was an appropriate reverence.

The gate appeared unguarded, but there would be archers in the branches overhead with arrows trained on us. No one could come upon the dryad capital unseen. In fact, scouts had probably been watching us for some time.

I'd been foolish to think that our trek through the canopy would go unnoticed.

"We don't have time for social calls," I said, but Thorn was already heading through the gate. I turned to Mason.

"What do you want to do?" he asked.

I ground my teeth. "I want to end this day at Iona Park. But that's not going to happen. What my grandmother wants, my grandmother gets."

"She sounds like one tough old bird." He reached for my hand. Normally his touch soothed me, but my back was up, and I pulled away.

"She is a tough bird," said a voice behind me. "About as tough a winter bramble bush and just as thorny."

I plastered a smile on my face, turned and stepped through the gate. "Hello, Grandmother."

She stood on the wide platform that served as the first square in a vast city of platforms and treehouses connected by bridges. She looked no older than the last time I saw her, but she'd been ancient then. Dryads aged gracefully. Her pure white hair hung to her waist. Fine lines marked her mouth and eyes, but she stood as straight as an oak sapling. An unstrung longbow hung from a holster on her back. I'd have trouble with the draw on that thing, but Nana Greenleaf could nock an arrow and let it fly before I could even draw my blade. I'd seen her do it. The bow was as old as she was. After hundreds of years, its grip had molded to her hand. No one else could—or would—use the weapon, and when Nana died, it would be buried at the foot of her Life Tree.

"Nana, I'd like to introduce you to my friend Henry Mason." I stepped aside to present him. Nana slitted her eyes and didn't disguise the fact that she appraised him from head to toe.

"I am honored to be welcomed to your home." Mason gave her one of his easy smiles. He pulled his sheathed knife from his belt and handed it to Thorn, then left his hands hanging at his sides, as if to say, "Look at me. I'm a harmless, unarmed human." Smart man. I wouldn't disarm myself in Bosk. But, of course, I couldn't turn my arm to a stone cudgel at will.

Nana inclined her head at Mason, and the hint of a smile flickered across her lips. Wow. That was high praise by Nana Greenleaf standards. Mason was such a charmer.

I tugged on Nori's arm, and she stumbled forward. "This is Nori, another friend."

Nana nodded to Nori, and the kitsune smiled wanly. Her hair had curled in the humidity, and her face was pale with purple shadows under her eyes.

Lisobet frowned. "And what is that?" She pointed to Jacoby, who hung like a wet rag doll in the sling across Nori's back.

"That's Jacoby, the friend we're all trying to save, and the reason we need quick passage to Iona Park. Please, grandmother we must hurry—"

She cut me off with one sharply raised hand. Her eyes were no longer focused on Jacoby. They were latched onto something behind me.

"You bring that beast into my city?"

Princess was pressed against the back of my legs. A low growl rumbled through her. I sunk my fingers into her fur, willing her to behave.

"Princess is mine. She comes with me or we'll leave Bosk now."

Nana had never agreed with my need to collect strays. But I was a grown woman now, not the child I'd been the first time I visited her, nor the lost young woman I'd been when I sought refuge here the summer I came back from Asgard. She would have to accept me with all my friends, or I'd find my own way to Iona Park.

"Not the hound." Nana pressed her lips into a moue of disgust. "That beast."

I turned. She was pointing at Kester.

Kester, who had been doing his whole demon thing and fading into the shadows, now pushed past Nori and swooped up Nana's hand. He bowed over it in a courtly manner and planted a kiss on her knuckles.

Nana squeezed her hand into a fist and punched him in his nose. Kester's head jerked back. He grinned as he wiped a trickle of blood from his lip.

"My lady. I'm sure I deserved that." From his squat, he gazed up at her. The hard angles of his face softened. His eyes, which were usually flinty and guarded, became liquid. From a pocket of his jacket, he produced a sparkly tiara thingy made from gold leaves and vines and held it out on his two flat palms.

"I come to you with a gift, my lady."

Oh, by Thor's horny hammer. Kester had a hard-on for my grandmother. Nana didn't look impressed. Her normal cool resolve broke like lightning striking a calm lake. Her lips pressed to a thin line and her long, silver hair seemed to puff up on some fey wind.

Nana plucked the tiara from his hand and gave it a cursory once-over before handing it off to the young dryad who attended her.

"See that our guests are fed and given quarters to rest," she said to the attendant, then turned to us. "Make yourselves comfortable. Eat. Rest. I have urgent matters to attend to."

I grabbed her elbow. "Nana, I need to talk to you now."

Nana looked down at my hand. The dryad who fluttered around her at all times blanched. I removed my fingers but fisted them. "We have no time for R and R."

"If you want passage through my trees, you will make time." She scoured my face with her gaze. "Really child. You look worn out. You have your mother's genes. You can't go go go, without expecting it to wear on your face." She *tsked*. My jaw hurt from the constant grinding of my teeth. "I will be back by fern hour. Poppy will see to your needs." She shoved the dryad attendant toward me. "Go now and get cleaned up. We will meet for breakfast and you can tell me what kind of trouble you find yourself in this time."

I bowed my head. "Yes, Grandmother."

CHAPTER

16

Poppy, our new dryad guide, led us over a rope bridge away from the gate and toward the heart of Bosk. We'd arrived at sage hour, the hour before sunrise when color slowly leaks back into the Canopy leaves. Gleams perched on poles lined the walkways, but their glow began to fade as the day lightened.

Despite the appearance of abandonment, the treetop city housed over a thousand dryads. During the day, they would all be busy with their assigned tasks, whether that was cultivating and gathering food, crafting clothes, tools or housewares, or guarding the city's many gates. Right now, only a few dryads walked the narrow boulevards between platforms, and these hurried on their way after a brief nod of greeting. From somewhere deeper in the trees came the lilting sound of a flute as someone welcomed the day with music. We passed a gathering of dryad children sleeping on an open-air platform under the watchful eyes of their guardians.

Poppy led us through a main square lined with pods made from woven reeds. Each pod contained a shop displaying wares, such as knives, pottery, or clothing. Dryads of all clans worked or shopped in the market. No two clans shared the same DNA, and they rarely mated outside their own race. Children from such unions didn't survive into adulthood. But despite their differences, clans lived and worked together in harmony. I thought of the warring factions in Montreal—how the godlings were vying for more power, the humans were fighting among themselves, and the fae couldn't seem to get it together to choose a new leader. We could learn a lot from watching a dryad market for a day.

Many eyes watched us as we made our clumsy way across the suspended boulevard. It was a thriving marketplace, even at sage hour, but unlike any in the human cities. No money would change hands. Dryads gifted each other with any product needed. And no dryad would insult another by taking more than they needed. It was a cooperative community that thrived on mutual respect, and this, more than the treetop residences or the green tinted skin tones, set them apart from humanity.

It was also the reason that dryads kept apart from other races. Visitors were rare and kept under close scrutiny. Dryad hosts encouraged their guests to take anything they needed from the market or even from the host's home. But a savvy visitor would never take more than they could offer in return. Unsavvy visitors found themselves quickly ushered on their way and not welcomed back.

After we left the market, we came to a small platform circled by pods designated as guest quarters. A cozy sitting area with a fire pot on a low table surrounded by cushions filled the space between the pods.

"I hope your stay with us will bring you comfort," Poppy said. She was one of the rare Aldera Clan with bushy orange hair and freckles covering all exposed skin.

"I'm sure we will be very comfortable." I touched her elbow and lowered my voice. "I didn't expect to be visiting Bosk, and I didn't bring anything to trade for your hospitality. Please tell my grandmother that I will make amends for this slight when I return home."

Poppy's eyes sparkled. "Dear cousin, this is your home as much as mine. There is no need for amends. Besides, your friend's generosity reflects well on all of you." She glanced at Kester as she spoke. He lounged on a cushion before the fire pot, his eyes closed and legs stretched out. Kester, at least, had expected this detour, unless he always packed a gold tiara when he traveled.

Poppy patted my arm. "Ranger Lisobet will be here by fern hour. Now, may I bring you food and drink?"

"Thank you. That will be welcome." Unlike the fae, it wasn't dangerous to thank a dryad. They were an overly polite society that found comfort in small niceties and conventions.

Poppy dashed away in that peculiar dryad gait that was somewhere between a loping giraffe and a blowing willow tree.

Nori had already flopped down among the cushions and fallen asleep with Jacoby on her lap. Princess twitched on the wood floor, deep in puppy dreams. We could use a rest, but I chafed at the delay.

"What is fern hour?" Mason asked.

"The dryads tell the time by the shading of the leaves. Fern is two hours past dawn, when the sun has risen enough to lighten the leaves."

Mason rubbed the back of his neck as he peered upward. The sky was completely invisible under the thick canopy. "So what? We have an hour to discuss how we deal with your overbearing grandmother?"

"A queen cannot be overbearing," Kester said without opening his eyes. "Ranger Lisobet is strong but not rigid, as she needs to be."

I side-eyed him. "What's between you two, anyway? You seem pretty down with dryad customs. One would think you've been to Bosk before. One might even think you and my grandmother have a history."

He opened one eye. "One might consider minding one's own business."

"Whatever." I flopped on a pillow. "I don't want to know."

Poppy returned with tea which she left warming beside the fire, and a bowl of water for the hound. A second attendant followed her, bringing a tray of nuts and fruit.

"Do you require anything more?" Poppy asked.

I smiled. "No, thank you. We will rest here until the ranger has time for us."

Poppy dipped her head, and the two dryads loped away.

"Kyra!" A familiar voice made me turn my head. I groaned inwardly, but kept my expression strictly pleasant.

"Lyle. So nice to see you again." I rose to meet my former lover-wannabe. Lyle took my hands in his and kissed both my cheeks. Lyle was from the Grayswood Clan and had the silvery coloring they favored. In another age, an artist could have sculpted him from marble and called him a god. Wide cheekbones highlighted vivid green eyes and a straight, thin nose. His lips were full and always quirked in a half-smile as if he went through the world with only entertaining thoughts. Silver and green veining ran up the sides of his face like tattoos and they enhanced his handsome features. He was tall, even for a dryad with long arms and legs, and when he leaned down to hug me, I felt like I was being enveloped by a giant squid. When I disentangled myself, he held onto my hands.

"I didn't believe it when Poppy told me you'd arrived. I had to see you with my own eyes."

Thanks, Poppy.

"I won't be staying long." I pulled my hands from his grasp. "We're on an urgent mission."

Mason seemed amused by Lyle's obvious attentions. I wondered what it would be like to be so comfortable in one's own skin that jealousy wasn't even a thing. I remembered the way Marcella, the innkeeper at Pack Station, had looked at Mason as if she could taste him. Even now, the memory made me squirm.

Not that Mason had any reason to be jealous. Lyle might be handsome, but he was also a brown-noser. His affection for me was directly proportionate to my closeness to the real authority of Bosk: my grandmother.

Kester also watched Lyle with a knowing smile. His eyes darted from me to Lyle to Mason and back again, while the rest of us muddled through the niceties of pouring tea and making small talk. Luckily, I didn't have to endure that introvert's nightmare for long.

Kester suddenly jumped to his feet. His amused smile was replaced by a beaming grin as he bowed to my grandmother.

"My lady." He offered her the seat beside his cushion. "It is a pleasure to be welcomed into your amazing city. And may I say, you look even more beautiful than the last time we met." Wow. He was laying it on thick.

Lisobet eyed him with her lips pulled back slightly. I couldn't tell if the expression hinted at anger or distaste. Either way, it didn't bode well for Kester's attentions.

"Lyle, I wish to speak to my granddaughter and Mr. Mason alone. Will you please escort Mr. Owens to the market. He has a fine eye for weaponry, so be sure to show him old Tanta's knife shop."

Lyle nodded and held out a hand so that Kester could precede him. Kester opened and closed his mouth a couple of times like a fish out of water, then sighed and followed the dryad.

Lisobet took Kester's vacant seat and turned to Mason. "Now tell me why I am so lucky as to have a visit with my granddaughter. You know she is my *only* granddaughter. The only one I will ever have."

If I could have turned green and faded into the foliage, I would have.

Mason, the stinkin' charmer, said, "She's lucky to have such a wise and formidable grandmother, but I suspect she knows that." He winked at me. "Family is very important to Kyra."

"Not important enough to visit more than once a decade." Lisobet crossed her arms. She was too dignified to humph, but it was implied.

"I've been busy building up my business," I mumbled. "Not much time to visit when you're the boss and only employee." Not to mention that travel through the Inbetween could kill you a million different ways. How did she always manage to make me feel like an errant child?

Lisobet's eyes flashed. I could feel her building to a tirade about the importance of family ties. And she'd be right. I had let my familial obligations slack. I steeled myself for the scolding, but she sighed and wilted onto the cushion beside me.

For the first time in my life, my grandmother looked old.

"Tell me why you're here. What do you need?"

So I told her everything, starting with the dragons and the bloodstone and ending with Leighna's death at Polina's hand and my killing of the witch in return.

Lisobet listened with her eyes closed, nodding once in a while. When I finally stopped speaking, my mouth was dry. I sucked back a gulp of tea. Lisobet opened her eyes and smiled faintly.

"Sounds like you won out in the end."

Was that pride lacing her words? Dryads were a peaceful race, mostly. But pushed into a corner, they would come out fighting until the last dryad was left standing. Polina had threatened my clan, and I'd made her pay. It was fitting.

Then Lisobet shook her head. "Though I am sorry to learn of Leighna's death. She was a Queen in the true spirit."

"She'll be hard to replace," Mason said. "Montreal is rudderless without her."

"Maybe you should do something about that." Lisobet raked him with a sharp glance.

Mason smiled. "People keep telling me that." With his hair messed and falling over his forehead, he looked boyish, but his eyes were as hard as Lisobet's.

She leaned forward on the cushion and studied us.

"So you fought a battle and won the day. I don't see the problem."

I nodded my chin toward Nori, who slept with Jacoby curled like an infant in her arms. "Jacoby saved me more than once. He saved our friend Errol by jumping into that machine to protect him." I thought of Pierre's madness, of Gerard's brutality, and Polina's utter disregard for life, human or otherwise. There were bad people out there. That's what clans were for. Strength in numbers to defend against those who would do us harm.

"Now Jacoby needs me. He's in some place called the Nether. I want to go to him, but I need an anchor in this world."

"And you want Timberfoot to be that anchor." It wasn't a question, so I didn't answer it. Grandmother poured herself a cup of tea. She sipped it for several moments without looking at me, and I didn't press her. She was thinking. Thinking of the ramifications to the clans and to herself. Timberfoot's Life Tree was a national treasure to the dryads. Sure, many of the Lekythoi Clan turned into trees after death, but only two in all their history had become Life Trees—trees so big, they crossed the veil between worlds, trees so magical, they could give life to the dying.

"And what shall you give me in return for access to Timberfoot?" Lisobet asked.

I squirmed in my seat. "I have nothing to barter. I'd hoped to get in, find the door to the Nether and be done with this before you knew I was here."

Lisobet arched one silver eyebrow at me.

"That was wrong of me, I know. But my only thought was for speed. We have so little time. Please, Grandmother, Jacoby is already fading." I held my hands open in front of me to show her that I was not hiding from the truth. "I can barter my time. My promise to spend more of it in Bosk."

Lisobet waved away my suggestion. "Your attention is not something I will barter for. That is my due. No, I have another request." Her lips pressed into a thin, reptilian smile. I was no longer dealing with my grandmother. I was now dealing with the ranger of the largest dryad tribe on the continent. She could ask me for anything and I would be hard pressed to deny her. We might have seemed alone in this little pod on a secluded platform, high in the canopy of Bosk, but with one shout, Lisobet could have dozens of armed guards at her side. Anything she wanted, I'd have to give her, if I wanted to leave Bosk at all.

"I want access to Montreal."

That wasn't the demand I'd expected.

"What do you mean? You can come to Montreal any time you want."

"I said I want access, not a tourist visa. You and your boyfriend here seem to know those who are in charge. I want a seat at the table."

"I don't understand."

"You might have noticed some changes in Bosk." She looked toward the boulevard that passed by our platform and collection of guest pods. It was much busier now as dryads went about their morning chores.

"We've grown. We're a proper ward now, with our own magical protections, our own militia. Our own government. We want to be recognized by the other wards. We want trading rights too."

"I can't promise all that," I said.

"I don't expect you to. I just want introductions to the proper authorities and your support as a dryad when I send our ambassadors."

I glanced at Mason. He was the one with the real connections in Montreal politics. He nodded.

"Okay. We connect you to the Triumvirate and for that you will let the Life Tree be my anchor?"

Lisobet smiled. "For that, I will let you travel through our ward. I will even give you an armed escort in case you encounter trouble. For the rest?" She pressed her lips together in a smug frown. "You'll have to ask your father."

CHAPTER

17

estled in a valley at the base of the Pocono Mountains stood a henge of stones—eight megaliths, all taller than me. Two were capped with a lintel stone to make an impressive gate. Unlike the henges of the old country, Iona Park wasn't built by some mysterious race thousands of years ago. Connor MacDonald erected it in the nineteen-seventies, taking inspiration from the sacred oak groves and standing stones on the Scottish Isle, Iona. Friends and family thought he was mad.

Standing among the stones now and sensing the ley-lines running through this valley, I suspected that MacDonald had a bit of the keening that compelled him to build this monument, to harness the ley-lines in a way that only he could understand at the time.

As impressive as they were, the megaliths were no longer the most imposing thing about the park. That honor went to the Life Tree growing in the center of the henge. It was an oak, easily thirty meters tall, with a trunk wide enough to carve a house into. Its branches formed a perfect arch, an umbrella of foliage to shade the standing stones. Light glinted through the dense leaves—a spot here, a dappling there—a song being sung with sunlight and wind.

My father was as magnificent and forbidding as I'd feared.

Like the beautiful diversity of humans, dryads weren't a homogeneous race either. They were as varied in looks, habits, and beliefs as the trees they revered. Some clans were tied to their trees, living and dying as the tree did. Others revered specific trees as deities. The Lekythoi clan—my father's clan— transformed into trees upon their death.

That's what my father had done, but the roots of his great oak pierced the veil between Terra and Underhill, keeping the possibility of travel between the worlds alive even as he'd blocked the way for a murderous demon to come through. He'd sacrificed himself for his true love, Leighna Icewolf, Queen of the Winter Court.

I wanted to admire him for that, but a small, childish part of me hated him for it. All my life, my father had been this vague idea in my mind, a presence that only became real in my imagination. My mother wouldn't talk about him. I only knew that he disappeared shortly after I was born. She never heard from him again.

During the summer I spent with the dryads, Lisobet had urged me to visit my father's tree, thinking I would find comfort or connection there. I resisted. Not because I was afraid I wouldn't find my father, but because I was afraid I would. How could a tree make up for not having a father my entire life?

Now I stood before him, and his presence was still a vague idea. I was staring at an oak, not a man.

"You ready for this?" Mason's voice was a calming rumble. He stood at my back and wrapped his arms around me. I didn't realize how much I needed his touch until I sank into his embrace.

"No." I glanced at Nori as she laid Jacoby on the ground beneath the tree. I wasn't ready, but Jacoby needed me.

Mason brushed stray hair from my ear with his lips. "I wish I could come with you." His laugh was bitter. "I swore I would never let you go into battle alone again. And yet, here we are."

"I wish you could come too. But I'm glad you'll be here."

"Right by your side."

"I know. It's the only thing keeping me going." Timberfoot's tree was supposed to be my anchor, the line that would keep me tethered to this world as I sent out my spirit. But I knew the truth. Mason was my anchor. Mason and Princess. Gita and Errol waiting at home for me. And even Nori, who had come all this way and given so much of herself to keep Jacoby alive. They were my tethers. Timberfoot was just an oak tree, prettier than most, but just a tree.

"Come now." Nori beckoned me. "Put this on."

I pushed away from Mason, but he squeezed me one last time before letting go. I held onto the tips of his fingers with the tips of mine, looking back even as I stepped away.

"I'll be right here." His smile was generous, but his eyes spoke of worry.

Nori held out a white gauzy robe. Lisobet had made the journey with me. She waited outside the ring stones along with Kester and a dozen dryads that included healers, in case things went very wrong. Now that I had to undress, I was glad only Princess, Nori, and Mason were with me. When I stood naked, with the soft moss squishing between my toes, Nori helped me put on the robe. It fell against my skin like a breath of wind.

"What's the purpose of this?" I fingered the diaphanous material.

"Regular clothes constrict the flow. For the best connection, there needs to be nothing between you and the earth. You should be sky-clad, but most people are shy about nakedness, and that's counterproductive. The robe is for modesty. Now sit here." She pointed to a spot beside Jacoby. She picked up the pile of my discarded clothes and was about to toss them aside.

"Wait. I need something from my pocket." I reached for my jeans and pulled out Leighna's necklace. The enameled pendant was shaped like an oak tree with a silver ring around it. Timberfoot had given it to her before his transformation. She had once offered it to me, but I'd declined. After her death, I took the necklace but had never worn it. Now I slipped the chain over my head. The pendant was a solid weight against my chest. I settled cross-legged on the mossy ground. Nori draped Jacoby across my lap. She wove a ring of leaves and twigs around us, tweaking it until she was satisfied.

"Right. That ought to do it." She stood and stretched out her back.

Princess bounded over, kicked the leaves aside and dropped a dead squirrel on my lap. She sat back on her haunches with tongue lolling.

"Thanks. But I'm not hungry."

"Damned hound!" Nori pushed her out of the way and began resetting the ring of leaves.

Princess curled in a ball at my feet and dropped her armored head in my lap.

"Uh, Nori? Maybe Mason should take Princess away before you reset that."

Nori eyed Princess, then turned to Mason. Her gaze was thoughtful. "No. Leave the beast where she is. She'll be less trouble. Mason, you should join them too."

He nodded and stepped carefully over the leaves.

"Sit there." Nori pointed to a bare spot beside me and a little behind. "From there, you shouldn't distract her. But if things go wrong, it might be good to have you close."

"Things better not go wrong." He scowled.

Nori shrugged. "I'm working from ancient lore here. Nothing is certain."

"Let's just do this," I said. Jacoby had waited long enough. "How do I start?"

"Do you meditate?" Nori crouched outside the ring. Her face was pale against dark hair.

"Yes. Some."

"Okay. It should be easy here. The ley-lines are strong. I want you to sink into yourself, find your balance first and then reach for this." She held up a crystal orb mounted on a long metal spike. She drove the spike into the ground in front of me. "You can use it as your focus, if you need. From what I read, the spirit of the Life Tree will lead you to the Nether, the space between worlds. That's where Jacoby is lost."

"Okay. Focus. Connect to the tree. Find the Nether. Then what?"

"A guide will be waiting for you. Trust your guide."

"That's it?"

"That's all I can provide. You must do the rest. Now center yourself."

I closed my eyes. My nerves jangled like sleigh bells. The pendant was warm against my chest and seemed to enhance the beat of my heart so that I could hear my pulse in my own ears. Moss prickled under my legs. Princess whined and stretched, nudging me with her nose. I dug fingers into her fur and stole some of her calm. This was how I would find my center. My hand roamed across her shoulder, and I keened the lifeblood flowing through her sturdy frame. Mason's magic was another slow rise and fall at my back. I sank into the moss, making myself heavier with every thought.

When I felt calm, I opened my eyes and latched them onto Nori's crystal orb. Sunlight glinted off it. I squinted, but held my gaze. The orb reflected the oak behind me. A gust of wind tossed branches, and the orb sparked like green fire. My eyes felt hot. Tears leaked down my cheeks, and I let them run undisturbed. I stared at the sparkling, shifting, dazzling light until the world around me faded.

Then the orb exploded outward.

Or I was drawn into it.

The edges of my vision blurred like I was being pulled through a tunnel of liquid color, and I landed barefoot on mossy ground. Nausea made my head spin as I got my bearings. I pressed two fingers into my waist, feeling a stitch there like I'd just run a six-minute mile. Everything was the same—the standing stones, the great oak tree. But everything was different.

Mason and the others were gone. No, not gone. They had...shifted. I could see us sitting a few meters away. Princess stuck her nose in the air as if she scented prey. I could see myself sitting in the same spot, staring at Nori's crystal. Jacoby lay in my lap and Mason crouched at my back. But we were all gauzy and insubstantial,

The air felt heavy with a coming storm. A sound like a distant train rumbled in my ears. I looked down at myself. I still wore the white gown. I was still me. Looking at the other me was disorienting, as if I watched a flickering film through a soap bubble.

I turned to the Life Tree. It was the only constant thing in the two visions before me. The sun was a white-hot eye, glaring through its leaves. No matter how I turned or shielded my eyes, I couldn't look directly into the highest branches.

I couldn't look at him.

My father.

For the first time, I keened his presence. His gaze swept over me the way a storm sweeps over a valley and moves on.

"Timberfoot?" My voice sounded small and insignificant in this strange place. I cleared my throat and spoke louder. "I have come to ask for your help."

I waited. Nothing.

"You don't know me. You never had the chance to. But I'm your daughter." I stepped closer to lay my hand on the trunk. Rough bark grated against my fingertips. Wind ruffled the leaves, but I got no other response.

How was I supposed to connect with a man I never knew? We had no shared memories. He'd never made me pancakes with smiling faces. He'd never cheered me from the sidelines of a soccer match. We had no emotional history. He'd never scolded me for getting a C on a math quiz or consoled me over one of my many childhood traumas. I'd never found him waiting up for me with a frown on his face when I came home after curfew. Even the father I'd made up in my head as a child—the one who came out every time we had to create a family tree in school, or when other dads volunteered to coach our t-ball team—even that dad had no bearing on this solid, staid, silent oak tree.

But if I couldn't connect with him, I couldn't save Jacoby.

I sucked in all my hurt and abandonment and squashed it into a tiny ball in the corner of my mind.

"I have something for you." I pulled off the silver chain. Leighna's pendant glittered in the sunlight. I hung it on the lowest branch.

The ground rumbled. Wind lashed the oak like a shudder. The sun turned. The *eye* turned to look at me.

"Hi." I flapped a hand at him. I felt his gaze. This time, it didn't wash over me, but stayed to inspect the insignificant being standing under his canopy. Wind ruffled his branches, obscuring the pendant with his leaves. And when they shifted again, the necklace was gone.

What do you want?

The voice boomed in my head. I winced. Clearly, it had been a long time since Timberfoot spoke to anyone.

"I need your help. My dervish is very sick." I pointed to where Jacoby lay in my world, and his figure shimmered inside the circle of leaves.

"That's him. He's lost in the Nether and I have to find him. My friends and I came a long way."

Princess flickered for an instant too, and I could feel the weight of Mason's hand on my arm. Timberfoot was drawing them into his space, taking their measure. Would he find us acceptable? Worthy of his time and notice?

"I need you to be my anchor."

I wanted to lash out at this tree that was once a man who had given me nothing. Instead, I bit down on the bitterness roiling in my gut and waited.

An age passed while he considered my request.

I sat on the mossy ground, waiting for him to pass judgment.

Something tickled the underside of my thigh. A thin, white tendril poked up from the moss and wrapped around my leg. A second circled my other leg. Soon dozens of tiny roots wrapped my legs and hips in their gentle embrace. I keened life coursing through them. Pure life energy—beautiful, boundless, brazen energy.

Timberfoot wasn't just anchoring me. He was sharing his unique perspective. His roots dug deep into the earth, touching other roots that, in turn, touched others. I threw back my head and laughed for the sheer joy radiating from this interrelation.

Everything was connected.

And now, so was I.

Jacoby, Mason and Princess were glimmering halos beside me.

All connected. All one.

"Thank you." I smiled into my father's leafy face.

A door appeared in the oak's trunk. It was faded blue-gray, weathered by time like the door of an old barn left to the elements. A brass knob in the center of the door was its only feature.

I rose and walked toward it before realizing that I shouldn't have been able to stand, not with my legs wrapped in roots. I turned back to see myself sitting on the grass, eyes closed, legs cocooned in white tendrils, and a small, secretive smile on my lips.

And in the other bubble, I sat inside a ring of sticks and leaves, holding Jacoby on my lap.

Freaky.

I faced the door again. I wasn't ready to dig into the implications of seeing this stereoscopic view of myself. I could examine the existential divide of body and soul at a later date. Right now, I had a job to do.

Here's goes nothing. I reached for the knob. It was icy under my grip, but it turned easily. I shoved the door open and stepped through.

hree worlds collided. The dryad forest spun and melted. The other me, anchored by Timberfoot's roots, faded to nothing. I fell onto a brighter, grassier ground and held my head until the disorientation passed. Then I rose to survey this new world.

A vast grassland spread before me in undulating waves of hills and valleys. A pale sun glittered in a uniform blue sky—not the blue of Terra, but a robin's-egg blue. The difference was slight, but enough to drive home that I wasn't in Kansas anymore. Behind me, the door stood open in the trunk of the Life Tree. The oak looked the same here. Its trunk was wider than my outstretched arms. The branches were silhouetted against the sky and no wind tossed the leaves. I laid my hand on the rough bark, trying to keen the life that coursed through its roots, penetrating the worlds.

I faced the door. Shifting mist filled the open frame. If I stepped through again, would I find myself sitting rooted to Timberfoot? Would I be back with Nori, Mason and the others? Or would the doorway hurtle me into another world altogether?

I wasn't ready to try those possibilities. But looking over the empty waste in front of me, I wasn't ready to move forward either. I stood under the odd sky and hugged my arms around myself.

For an astral spirit, I felt pretty solid. I tapped my legs with my hands. I wore my usual work clothes—jeans, boots, cotton button-down shirt in an indiscriminate plaid that hid dirt and blood. But I carried nothing with me. No tool belt. No sword.

A beast hurled through the door and knocked me sideways. A big pink tongue assaulted me and lashed my face.

"Princess! Stop!" I laughed and pushed the hound away, ruffling the fur at her neck, before realizing what was wrong.

"You shouldn't be here!"

Was it even Princess? This hound stood taller, nearly as tall as my shoulder. She had the same bone plating on her muzzle, but her fur was fluffier, more like puppy fur. I gently keened her magic. It had that familiar cinnamon sweet signature that I knew so well. It was definitely Princess.

"How did you find me?" I ran my fingers over her soft ears.

"Just like I did." Mason stepped through the door and caught me in his arms.

"You're here!"

His lips found mine and for a long moment, I forgot everything else. There was just me and Mason. Then the hound head-butted my elbow. I stood back, not ready to let go.

"I told you I wouldn't let you fight your battles alone again." In the strange light, his eyes sparkled with bits of gold.

I leaned my forehead against his chest and laughed, a rough sound of need and relief. I should have known he'd come.

"But how?"

Mason shrugged. "No idea. But I'm here now. We'll worry about the logistics later. Let's find Jacoby and take him home."

He turned to survey the landscape as I had done, and I took that moment to examine him. Like Princess, he was Mason, but not Mason. He had the same dark, intense eyes, the same soft curve to his smile. But his hair didn't fall in its normal unruly mess across his forehead. It was perfectly coiffed. Like it was carved in stone.

"You look strange." I ran my finger along his cheek. It was warm and pliable, but his skin tone was pale and lustrous, like marble.

"You're a gargoyle again!"

"Am I?" Mason rolled his shoulders as if testing his body. "Pretty spry for stone."

"Something about this place makes you different. Look at Princess. She's like a puppy on steroids."

Mason glanced at Princess, who was busy digging a hole in the new world. He turned to me, took my chin between his forefinger and thumb, and tipped my head from side to side.

"Do I look the same?" I ran my hands along my thighs. Everything felt in order.

"Something's different, but I can't put my finger on it."

"I don't feel different."

"Nor do I."

Princess bounded by us. Red dirt stained her face and paws, but she'd grown bored with digging and now chased a butterfly the size of a dinner plate. She topped a rise and disappeared into the next valley.

"Princess!" Worry spiked through my heart. I didn't want to lose sight of her in this strange place. "Princess, *hael!*" A moment later, she dashed back and rubbed herself against my leg. I gripped her thick ruff, wishing she wore a collar and a leash.

"You stay close."

She whined, and I let her go.

My father's tree was the only feature rising out of the landscape. The air was hot and humid and clung to me like a second skin. A swarm of insects had gathered above the tree. They morphed and flowed like a murmuration of starlings. I swatted my arm as one landed on me. It was as big as a dragonfly, and I shuddered as I flicked its squashed carcass off my arm. I wouldn't want to get caught in that swarm.

"Now what do we do?" I turned in circles. There was no clear path to follow.

"I don't know." Mason shaded his eyes to peer at the horizon. "Didn't Nori say you'll find a guide?"

"Yes, but do we go looking for him or her? Or it?"

Princess growled and I turned to find her ready to pounce.

I touched Mason's arm. "Look."

At the base of the oak tree sat a gray cat. His tail was wrapped around his feet like a fluffy feather boa, and he watched us with that calm disdain perfected by cats everywhere. The tail tip curled and thumped against the grass—curl, thump, curl, thump. A mane of silver fur sprouted from his shoulders, crested to a point on his chest and blended to black at his ears, feet and tail. His charcoal face was an understated backdrop for startling green eyes that shimmered with sparks, and I had the irrational feeling that they weren't really eyes but tiny galaxies full of stars. Then he slow blinked, and they were just eyes again.

Princess's growl rolled on like summer thunder. She lifted a paw and carefully laid it one step closer to this new creature.

"Stay where you are, hound." The cat spoke with perfect English diction.

Princess's lip vibrated. She took a step forward.

"I mean it. Keep your distance."

One canine paw stretched forward, closing the distance. I held my breath. The cat didn't move.

Princess crawled closer, placing herself an inch from the cat's tail.

The cat puffed up his chest and sighed. "Fine. Have at it." He turned and offered his back end, tail straight in the air.

Princess stuck her muzzle into the cat's rump, snuffling him all over. Then another butterfly caught her attention and she dashed after it.

The cat sat down again and shook his fur into place like a little old man straightening his tie and suit-coat.

"Dogs. Disgusting creatures. No manners."

"You can speak!" I said.

"So can you. Congratulations." The cat turned his back and washed a paw.

I stepped closer. His ears flicked backward, assessing my movement. He was bigger than any house cat, even a Maine Coon, and rosettes dappled the fur along his back.

"Are you our guide?"

"Maybe." He turned to watch me with half-closed eyes. "First, we do the interview. Then I decide."

"Fine. Ask me anything."

"It doesn't work that way. You are the Seeker. You do the asking. Three questions. No more."

"Seriously? Why is it always three? What if I have four questions? Will the ground open up and swallow me?" I didn't want to play games. I wanted to find Jacoby and get home.

"You're babbling," Mason murmured.

I shot him an angry look. "Maybe, but I still want to know."

The cat's tail swished in the grass.

"Are those your questions, then?"

I drew in a deep breath and exhaled. Mason was right. I babbled when I was nervous. And this situation was putting me on edge. But I thought I deserved a bit of slack considering I stood in an alien world in an alien dimension. The cat's steady glare told me he didn't agree. So I put on my big-girl pants and tried again.

"No." My dealings with the fae had taught me never to look a gift question in the mouth.

"Okay. First question. Where are we?"

The cat rolled his eyes. "So predictable. You are in the Nether."

I waited for him to expand on that, but he simply lifted one leg to lick the underside of his thigh. I couldn't decide if he was very patient or the most infuriating creature I'd ever met. His answer jived with what Nori had told us, but I'd needed confirmation. I trusted Nori, but spells could easily go awry and we could have been flung into any dimension. I glanced back at the door in the tree trunk, still open and enticing with the invitation to go home.

"Our friend, Jacoby, is lost somewhere here. In the Nether. Can you help…" I stopped myself. I'd bargained with too many brownies to make that colossal mistake. I. "*Will* you help us find him?"

The cat watched me for a long minute. His viridescent eyes shimmered, and he favored me with one slow blink.

"I suppose I will show you the way, but only so that you can leave and take that beast with you." He flicked a glance at Princess, who lay in the deep grass, waggling her feet in the air as she satisfied an itch on her back.

"And your last question?"

The pest controller in me couldn't resist. "What are you?"

The cat rose on all four paws. The tips of his ears reached my waist. "I am a grimalkin." He bowed his head.

"I'm Kyra. This is Mason. And you already met Princess. What should we call you?"

His whiskers twitched. "You may call me Grim."

"That's a bit on the nose, isn't it?" Mason said. "Like calling a cat, kitty."

"Says the gargoyle, named Mason."

"Touché." Mason nodded. He didn't ask how the grimalkin knew his history. There was a lot going on here that we didn't yet understand.

The cat's tail twined around my knee as he paced forward to glare at Mason. "I have many names. Grim is the only one you are worthy of knowing. Before we begin, there is paperwork to fill out."

Grim drew a claw across the empty space between us. A scroll appeared and unrolled in midair.

"The rules. For your safety, please read them over carefully and sign at the bottom."

Red letters glowed and shifted on the parchment-like surface. The magic leaking from it made me nauseous as I read.

No teleporting, except by permission from the Birdies.
Do not go through any door uninvited.
Do not delay the Messengers.
Do not disturb ki stones.
Do not take anything from the Nether back to your home world.

All disputes between Seekers and Birdies will be heard by the Tribunal of Stewards.

A golden quill appeared beside the scroll.

"Do you understand the rules as they are laid out?" Grim asked.

"Some of it. Take only pictures, leave only footprints. I get that. But who are the messengers and birdies?"

"Let's hope we don't have to find out." The cat stretched as if this whole procedure bored him.

"And that other thing. Tribunal of Stewards?"

"Sounds ominous," Mason said. "Should we be worried?"

"Just do what I say, when I say, and you won't need to worry. Sign here." The cat pointed to the last line of the scroll. I took the quill in my right hand.

"What if I don't sign it?"

"Then our business is concluded, and I will escort you back through your door."

He held my gaze, unmoving. The letters of the contract squirmed on the page. A dozen flying insects landed on the parchment. I turned to look back at my father's tree. The door to Terra stood open, but home seemed very far away.

"You shouldn't sign it." Mason's eyes had gone dark, and his shoulders were as rigid as an uncut slab of stone.

"Do I have a choice?" I wasn't going home without Jacoby.

I scribbled my name across the bottom of the page.

Behind me, the door to Terra slammed shut and disappeared.

"How will we get home?"

The cat was already walking away through a swarm of buzzing insects, his tail curled like a question mark and the fur on his back legs like fluffy pantaloons.

"You are now officially a seeker. When your quest is complete, your door will appear to you. Now come. We have a long way to go."

"Go where?" I asked. Something tickled my cheek, and I raised my hand to swat away another fly. Gods, the insects in this place were unbelievable.

"To First City. Everyone who travels the Nether ends up there sooner or later. If we are going to find your friend before it's too late, we must fly." Wings sprouted from Grim's back. They were pearlescent gray, shading to inky black on the tips. He launched into the air and hovered near the upper branches of the Life Tree.

"Come on!" he shouted and flew higher.

I turned to Mason "Any idea what he's talking about?"

He flexed his shoulders. Wings fanned from his back and spread wide. He turned to gape at them. "Those are new."

Huh.

His were pure white with long feathers, the way I imagined angel wings. He flared them, testing their strength. His grin was the grin of a child with the new toy he'd been wanting forever. Mason had led the gargoyles but always stood apart from them. Now he too had wings. Angus would be proud. He jumped into the air, fanned his wings, and fell, landing lightly. After another couple of attempts, he was airborne. Princess barked and ran in circles below him.

Grim fluttered down to me.

"What are you waiting for?"

"I don't have wings." The heat was stifling, and I pulled my damp shirt away from my back.

"Of course you do, Valkyrie. Your kind was meant to fly."

Putting aside the fact that once again Grim knew our histories, I said, "Valkyries fly on winged horses."

"Don't you get it yet? In the Nether, you appear as you see yourself. You can have wings or scales or horns. You just have to see yourself that way."

I glowered at him. "If you can be whatever you want, why are you a cat?"

"Wouldn't you be a cat if you could be?"

Fair point.

"It isn't that simple. I can't be something I'm not."

"It is that simple. Try it."

"Fine." I closed my eyes. If I had wings, what kind would I want? An image of Ollie's stubby dragon wings came to mind. Cute, but not practical. Clarence had impressive wings too, but too flashy for my tastes. I thought of Ruby, the red queen dragon. Her wings had been elegant and tough all at once. If I had wings, I'd want those. I opened my eyes and flexed my shoulders.

My wingless shoulders. My weak, lackluster, human shoulders.

The cat hovered over me like a furry cupid. "You're not trying."

"Really? And what does trying to grow wings look like?" I stuck my thumb in my mouth and pretended to inflate a balloon. "Gosh that didn't work either."

I crossed my arms over my chest and could feel my heart battering against them.

Grim dropped to the ground. His wings disappeared.

"I guess we're walking."

19

The cute, fluffy kitten turned out to be a relentless taskmaster. After what seemed like hours of trying to manifest wings from my all-too-human back, I flopped to the ground.

"I can't do it."

"Try again." Grim's tail flicked like a whip.

I was already dizzy from trying to wrap my head around the idea of wings. I lay back in the grass as stared at the green-blue sky.

"I'm sorry. I want to fly. I really do."

"Do you?"

"Yes!"

"Then you're not trying hard enough."

Grim leaned over me, blocking my view of the sky with his green eyes and button nose. His ears were tufted with silver fur. A charcoal beard made his heart-shaped face taper to a point. It was hard to take his dour expression seriously when it was nestled among such cuteness.

Mason landed beside us. He reached out a hand. I grabbed it and he hauled me upright.

"Don't interfere," Grim said.

Mason stared down the cat. "If she says she can't fly, she can't fly. We'll walk."

Competing emotions stormed in my gut. I was grateful for his backup, but ashamed that my incompetence would put us in more danger than necessary.

"Do you know what waits for us out there?" Grim pointed a paw into the grasslands. "Death. That's what. A million possible deaths. The sooner we get to First City, the more of those possibilities we avoid."

Mason crossed his arms over his chest. His wings furled against his back and disappeared. Grim's gaze shifted from my sweaty face to Mason's determined stare.

"Fine." Our guide turned and headed into the grassy field, away from the Life Tree and my only anchor to my world.

"Are we following?" Mason asked.

"I guess we'd better."

The grimalkin kept a fast pace. Mason and I walked behind him, up one slope and down another. Princess ran twice as far as the rest of us because she darted forward, scouting with her nose pressed to the ground, then retraced her footsteps to be sure we followed. She'd bound to the left about a hundred meters and run back. Then forward. And to the right. And back again. It was exhausting to watch.

The cat's fluffy pantaloons swished unrelentingly as he pranced over hill and dale and hill again. I was still sulking over my lack of wings, more so because Grim's chosen path seemed endless and I was hot, tired and thirsty. Mason, too, had fallen into a broody silence until he stopped me with one hand on my arm.

"Kyra, don't move. There's something on your face." His voice was low and steady, but it shot a jolt of panic into me. As soon as he spoke, I spotted something blue from the corner of my eye—as big as my nose—crawling across my cheek. It had the sticky feel of caterpillar feet.

"Gah!" I swatted it away without thinking. My back arched, and I flailed, suddenly sure there were hundreds of bugs crawling all over me.

"Are there more?" I patted down my arms and hair.

"No, you're fine." Mason's silver eyes sparkled. He was enjoying this way too much.

Then a blue slug crawled out of his ear.

"Get it!" I pointed and hopped around like a ninny. Bugs didn't faze me. I'd walked through tents of spider webs and uncovered nests of termites that would keep most people from sleeping for the rest of their lives. But bugs coming from my ears? That spiked even my heebie-jeebie-o-meter.

Mason scraped it from his face and threw it to the ground.

I crouched to examine the creatures. About as long as my little finger, they were a deep indigo, shot through with glittery silver bits. They had segmented bodies and no legs, but a ribbed underside that oozed across the ground like a snail's foot. Tiny blue pearls lined their backs like spikes. I saw no eyes or orifices. If they weren't slowly wriggling, I would have thought they were just pretty stones.

As I examined them, one tried to climb onto my shoe. I scooted backward. It followed like a bluetick hound on the scent of a coon. I let it crawl into my hand and keened it, but could sense no magic. A strange longing welled up inside me, like I'd found a favorite toy I'd lost as a child.

"I have a very bad feeling about this." I put the slug down beside the other that was inching toward Mason's shoe.

Grim glanced over his fluffy shoulder to see what was delaying us.

"What are they?"

"Those are your ki." Grim glided back toward us. His eyes were hard and angry.

"Wha—?"

Princess made a sound halfway between a grunt and a whine. I turned in time to see her swipe at another blue slug crawling across her muzzle. It landed on the ground, and she pounded it flat with one paw. Then she hunkered down to eat it.

"Princess, no!" I ran to stop her, but the slug was gone in one bite.

"Did she just eat what I think she ate?" I asked Grim.

"She did. She ate her soul." He stretched one leg straight up so he could wash the puff of fur on his back end.

"Really? You're going to tell me that my hound ate the physical manifestation of her soul, then you're gonna wash your ass?"

Grim looked up from his task. The tip of his tongue stuck out like a pink jewel. He straightened and smoothed back his whiskers with a paw.

"Tell us what's going on!" I stomped one foot, then backed up when I realized that I almost squashed my ki.

"Strictly speaking, it's not part of a guide's duties. I lead, you follow. That's the deal."

"I don't care."

Grim flattened his ears. I held his gaze until he looked away.

"Fine. Those are ki stones." He pointed to the creatures undulating at my feet. "Or at least they'll become stones. Right now they are more or less alive, but the longer you stay in the Nether, the more they will petrify. Eventually they will stop moving…and you will stop breathing."

"More or less alive?" Mason's expression was flat. He was having the same trouble as me, wrapping his mind around this.

"Animated by your spirit. You are linked. I suggest you don't lose them."

My gorge rose. I picked up the stones, one in each hand, and closed my fingers around them. Now I could keen the difference. The one in my left hand emitted a wave of warm magic up my arm, and I couldn't stop the smile that spread across my face. Mason. I was holding Mason in my hand. How many times, when we were making love, had I wanted to embrace all of him at once. And now I could.

"Here." I handed him the stone. For the first time since we'd met, I saw uncertainty on his face. But he held out his hand like a trooper and I deposited the ki in his palm. His eyes shot open, then his face softened into that little kid grin that I was sure I wore, too.

I turned my attention to the stone in my right hand. Other than that strange feeling of nostalgia it gave off, I sensed no magic coming from it. But that made sense, too. I'd never been able to keen my own magic, just like I couldn't smell my own scent or hear my own accent.

"How did this happen?" Mason asked.

"The door," Grim said. "Crossing the boundary into the Nether separates the astral body from the physical body. It takes a while for the ki to crawl out of your core."

Ugh. Amazing or not, I didn't like the thought of the ki crawling around inside me.

"So where's your ki stone?" I asked. Grim didn't seem to have any pockets on his fluffiness to hide a stone.

He watched me with a half-hooded, steady gaze but said nothing.

Fine. I would learn his secrets another way.

"What about when we leave the Nether?" I asked.

"Most people don't." His tone implied there was no alternative.

"But when we do?"

His whiskers twitched. "When you do, you must find a way to reincorporate the soul. The hound might be a dumb beast, but her instincts are correct. Keep your soul close, as I always say."

Mason stared at the grimalkin for a long moment. His dark eyes guarded his thoughts. Then he popped the slug in his mouth and swallowed.

"Tastes like chicken." His smile was only a little green around the edges. He waved a hand toward my ki. "Your turn."

"Nuh-uh." I backed up and closed my fist around the stone. "No way. No how."

"Come on. Don't tell me the pest controller is afraid of a little slug."

I stink-eyed him. Sure, I'd eaten bugs before. Candy coated mealworms were one of Nesi's specialties and a good source of protein in a world where protein could be scarce. But this wasn't a bug. It was my soul. I couldn't be more freaked out if you asked me to eat my own hand.

"We have to get moving. We're too exposed here." Grim studied the sky as if expecting an army to fall from it. "If you're not going to eat it, keep it close. You lose it and you won't be going home." He trotted off. The tall grasses parted and seemed to swallow him. Only the fluff of his tail and the tips of his ears could be seen above it.

I tucked the little beastie into my shirt pocket next to my heart.

CHAPTER

20

The hills rose and fell with a fatiguing monotony. Mounting one hilltop, we could look over the vast prairie. Down the backside, our world shrunk to a cage of green. Then back up another hill. It seemed endless.

We topped a rise and spied a caravan edging along the next hilltop. Bulky beasts, more like bulls than horses, pulled four carts with at least a dozen people walking alongside. The sun was behind them, and they were too far away for me to make out any features, but they were definitely not human. They moved more like apes. With each step, their long arms reached forward. Knuckles pressed against the ground while their legs leap-frogged through them.

Princess's hackles rose, and she stared at the strangers, her lip quivering.

"Stand down," I said. "They won't hurt us." In fact, the strange caravan of travelers seemed not to notice us.

"Keep that hound close," Grim snapped. "If she disturbs other seekers, she'll bring down the wrath of the birdies."

"Who are they?" I was intrigued to find other seekers here.

"Who knows? People come to the Nether for many reasons. They could be merchants seeking a quick way into another world. They could be assassins, crusaders, or pilgrims. It's none of our business."

We walked for hours until the grass gave way to rocky terrain dotted with scraggly shrubs. The heat was oppressive. My tongue stuck to the roof of my mouth. The only reprieve from thinking about how thirsty I was came when we walked through clouds of winged insects that hovered around the bits of vegetation. I swatted them and shook out my hair. The insects didn't seem intent on biting, but they were thick enough to choke on. Mason slapped my back when one landed on my shoulder.

"Thanks," I said, and he nodded, his expression stony. Neither of us spoke about our lack of water, but he had to be feeling it, too.

We kept plodding forward, one foot in front of the next. Grim seemed to know where he was going, and I had no choice but to trust him.

I paused at the top of a hill that looked exactly like the last one. Ahead, the ground leveled into a vast, featureless plain. A sprawling city was silhouetted against the horizon to our left. It was the first sign of civilization we'd seen, but our guide headed away from it.

I called after him. "I need to rest."

Grim turned, saw me flagging with fatigue and rolled his eyes. Then he sat in his regal pose with tail curled around toes, closed his eyes and tipped his face toward the sun.

I gazed over the featureless landscape. My vision blurred around the edges. The glaring sun leeched color from everything. Thirst was becoming a real threat now.

"Isn't there a faster way to travel? By truck or beast of burden?" My voice was ragged.

The grimalkin cracked his eyes open. "We could fly."

I waved my arms. "No wings, remember?"

"That wasn't there a moment ago either." He tilted his head toward a jumble of rocks sticking up from the grass. A clump of scraggly bushes surrounded it. Water burbled over the rocks and fell into a rudely carved basin. A spring.

"How the…?" I was too thirsty to question it further. I cupped my hands in the basin and drank.

"In the Nether, you get what you want. You're thirsty. Bling! Water appears." He licked one paw and smoothed back his whiskers. "But only if you really want it."

"Then why isn't it vodka? I could really use something stronger right now."

Grim didn't dignify my complaint with an answer. "You have five minutes, then we move out." He gave one disdainful look at Princess, who was chomping down on a giant winged thing, and stalked off.

Mason took his turn at the spring. Then we tried to entice Princess to drink, but she was more interested in the insects that seemed to keep her hydrated as well as fed.

I sat on the grass, took my ki stone from my pocket, and inspected it while we rested. It was kind of pretty now that my initial shock had passed. The blue shell glittered with silver bits, and it was smooth to the touch. It didn't move much and its weight was somehow reassuring in my hand.

Mason sat beside me. He raised an eyebrow when he saw me fiddling with the ki. I wondered what it would feel like if he touched it. I almost asked him to, but that seemed strangely intimate, like asking him to make love to me right here in the open. I glanced at Grim, who waited for us only a hundred meters away and tucked the ki back in my pocket.

Princess was busy with another mammoth dragonfly, and Mason leaned back in the grass, resting on his elbows. His eyes dipped closed as caught a few moments of rest. I should have done the same, but my mind was racing.

Even through the long journey, Mason hadn't lost his rock solid looks. His hair was still swept back, and he'd barely broken a sweat. I missed the old, slightly mussed Mason with a scruffy beard and and hair falling into his eyes. Was this put-together Mason how he envisioned himself? Is that why he appeared like that?

I patted down my hair. Normally, by halfway through the day, I looked like a dandelion gone to seed with loose ends poking from my braids. Not today. The braids were neat and tidy. Aunt Dana couldn't even find fault with them. I thought of how disgusted she'd been with me when I first arrived in Asgard and she found out I couldn't braid my own hair. Even Aesir toddlers can braid. Luckily, my cousin Gunora had taken pity on me and taught me the fine art. By the time I was ready to ride with the Valkyries, I could braid a passable plait.

And here in the Nether, where I could be whatever I wanted, I had turned myself out like the perfect little Valkyrie. I tried not to brood over that idea.

Princess had exhausted the stock of insects and flopped down to sleep. Mason was watching her with a frown.

"She's going to hate going back to your little apartment after this adventure."

I nodded, though he was facing away and wouldn't see. "I've been thinking about finding her a new home. It won't be easy."

Mason turned to me and smiled. It changed his countenance completely, and I spied that old, mischievous Mason. "She should come live with me."

"You would take her?" That was brave. Princess was a handful.

"And you." He rolled onto his side and took my hand. "You should come live with me too."

I opened my mouth to say something, then closed it again.

He sat back with a frown. "Don't look so surprised."

"You want me to move in with you?"

"I do."

A hundred reasons why I couldn't live with him came to mind. Most of them had tiny clawed feet. Some were scaled. Others had feathers. All of them were a ton of work and responsibility. Mason didn't understand what he was asking. I wasn't like other women who could hook up with a guy, pack my undies and a toothbrush, and move in. I came with a lot of baggage.

I wished I could say yes, but that was like wishing away Errol and Kur and Jacoby. And Gita. No, I would never wish for that.

"That's a big decision to make so lightly." I stared at my feet, looking for inspiration there. Was there any easy way to reject the man you loved?

"Big decision, yes. But I didn't make it lightly." He tipped my chin up, forcing me to meet his eyes. Gods, they were so beautiful. Silver like the edge of a storm cloud and lit with a bit of humor.

"I've been considering it for a while," he said. "Why do you think Arriz is renovating the barn?"

"For me?"

"For your menagerie. For *our* menagerie."

My eyes grew hot and my heart turned into a solid lump that threatened to choke me.

"You really did that for me?"

He tugged gently on one of my braids, and let his knuckles slide down the side of my jaw. Then he leaned in and pressed one gentle but firm kiss on my lips.

"For you. Now that I can, I want to wake up every morning with you beside me. I want to give you everything you want, even if that everything is a fire-breathing, slime covered, venom spitting manticore. I want you to fill my house with creatures and life. Will you do that?"

A hiss from ahead told me Princess was awake and harassing Grim again.

"Just think about it." Mason squeezed my hand and rose, dusting off his pants. He called Princess to his side. The hound came running, with Grim not far behind.

"Hide! Now!" Grim said as he dashed by.

"What?"

The cat hissed and ducked behind the spring.

When I paused, Grim shouted, "Get down!"

CHAPTER

21

We huddled between two smallish boulders. The bush was spare camouflage. Grim scanned the sky for some threat I couldn't see. Princess's butt stuck out from the blind, but I hoped from above it would look like a black boulder among the other gray ones.

"What are we hiding from?" I whispered.

"Birdies," Grim said. "Now be quiet."

Mason had draped himself over me in the cramped space. I didn't know what was coming, but I wouldn't let him shield me with his body. Since this trip began, he'd been too quick to put himself in the line of fire. He needed reminding that he was no longer the invincible gargoyle captain. We all had the same chance of dying out here.

A loud cawing told me that whatever Grim feared, it was coming closer. I tried to free myself from under Mason's stifling protection.

"Stop squirming," he whispered.

"Stop trying to be the hero."

Grim snarled like a pissed off alley cat. "Both of you shut up!"

The caw resounded again. I shoved Mason's arm aside and peered through the pitifully thin branches that were supposed to shield us.

A bird the size of a truck flew overhead. It was back-lit by the sunlight, and all I could see was its impressive wingspan and sharply taloned feet. It circled the valley and passed over our little nest again. Was it looking for prey? Were we prey? It called out once more, but the sound was fading.

We hid for several minutes longer, until Grim deemed it safe, and then began our walk again.

"What was that thing?" I asked.

"Birdie," Grim said over his shoulder without stopping.

"I got that. But why'd we have to hide?"

The cat flicked one ear and looked away. Oh, no. He was going to answer me this time. There was something he wasn't telling us. I could feel it in my bones. I ran forward and tweaked his tail. I was pretty sure Grim was cat enough to find this an egregious insult. He rounded on me and hissed.

"Very scary," I said. "Now tell me. Would that thing have eaten us?"

Grim twitched his shoulders to smooth down his ruffled fur. "Eaten you? No. Killed you? Yes."

I closed my fist around his tail again. His eyes went wide and wild.

"I am a guide!" he sputtered. "You can't just…just manhandle me like that?"

I yanked, just a bit.

"Talk. Why was that birdie thing looking for us?"

Grim's lips pulled back. In a human, it could have been a smile, but animals don't show their teeth when they're happy.

"It might be looking for you. Or rather for that hound."

We all turned to look at Princess, who perked up and said, "Aroo?" One spindly insect leg poked from the side of her muzzle. She decided we weren't worth the distraction and went back to her meal.

"The birdies don't like it when their messengers are disrupted," Grim said.

"The bugs? They're the messengers? Why didn't you say so before?"

"You didn't ask."

By the One-eyed Father, I wanted to strangle that cat.

I was squeezing his tail too tight, and Grim slashed a claw across my hand. I let go, and he scrambled away with another hiss. I pulled out my hair tie and re-braided my hair. It was a nervous gesture that helped me think. My hand hurt where he'd clawed me, but no blood welled from the scratch. I rubbed it as I tried to remember back to the rules. What had they said about the messengers? Don't disturb them or don't detain them? Either way, I figured eating them covered all the bases.

Mason and I conferred while Grim tried to restore his dignity by washing his toes.

"What do you want to do now?" Mason asked.

I sighed. "We keep going. But we keep an eye out for those birds."

"I think our guide will do that for us. He seemed pretty terrified of them."

I nodded. "That's one canary the cat doesn't want to catch." But there was more to it. I couldn't shake the idea that Grim was holding out on us.

As we continued, I kept one eye on the sky and the other on our dodgy guide.

I just wished I had a third eye to keep track of Princess.

THE HILLS LEVELED out, and we walked across flat ground. In the distance, a forest loomed, backed by the gray smudge of a mountain range. Grim changed his course, heading us toward the nearest edge of the forest.

"Does the sun ever set here?" I asked.

"It will," Grim said. "And then you'll have something else to complain about—the cold."

Right about now, with sweat drenching my collar, cold sounded good.

Other seekers had passed this way and, for the first time, we walked on something resembling a road. It was hard packed dirt, with deep ruts that would stop any carriage, but it was faster than slogging through the grass.

Two more caravans moved slowly across the valley, one heading toward the forest and one away. I hoped that before this adventure ended, I'd have a chance to meet some of those alien seekers. Wouldn't that be a story for the blog!

"Get down!" Grim flattened himself to the ground. I followed his direction and pulled Princess down. Mason hit the dirt beside me.

"Birdies?" he asked.

I nodded toward the caravan we'd been watching. A flock of birds descended on them. From this distance, they looked like nothing worse than seagulls. Then one of them landed on a wagon to give me perspective. It picked up the wagon and tossed it aside. People scattered like ants from a nest. One birdie caught a seeker in its great talons. The bird rose into the air, then opened its grip and dropped the poor seeker. He or she landed with a small puff of dust and didn't get up. I rolled onto my side and hid my eyes against Mason's shoulder. I didn't want to see anymore.

"Why are they doing that?" I groaned.

"Rules." Grim said. "The seekers broke them, and now they're paying for it."

"Where's Princess," Mason asked at the same moment that I realized the hound was gone from my side. I rolled to see her a few meters away, digging furiously. Dirt sprayed up behind her as she worked her excavation with furious intent.

"She found something," I said. When Princess scented something interesting, there was no way to deter her. I hoped those birdies didn't see the spray of dirt.

"Make her stop!" Grim's eyes were wide and his fur stuck up on his back like a brush.

"Princess, *hael*."

The hound's head swung out of the hole. Her muzzle was covered with dirt, and she held a blue stone in her mouth.

"No!" I cried out as she swallowed it.

Grim groaned beside me.

I slid over the dirt and looked into the hole. It was littered with glittering blue stones. Princess had disturbed a grave site. That was two strikes against her.

Wispy trails of bluish smoke rose from the dirt to hover over the grave. Ghosts. Dozens of them and more appearing every minute.

"Oh, crap!" I skittered back from the hole, dragging a whining hound with me.

"What is it?" Mason asked. He couldn't see ghosts, and I thought he was the lucky one. The specters weren't human. Their bodies were too tall and thin, their heads too bulbous. But they all wore lost expressions. They turned pleading eyes on us, as if we could answer for why they were stuck in this alien world.

"Ghosts," I said. "A lot of ghosts."

A raucous "CAW!" hit me like an echo of a gunshot. I turned back to the massacre that was still happening on the plains. One black silhouette had broken off from the flock. The birdie was flying right toward us.

Grim road-runnered for the trees. Halfway across the open plain, wings burst from his back and he took flight.

"Now what do we do?"

Mason's mouth set in a stark line. "Now we fight."

HARPIES: WINGED GODS OR DEMONS?

June 30, 2081

Harpies have been called everything from evil child snatchers to seductive maidens. So what's the real deal with harpies? Do they even exist?

Yes, they do.

Here's what I know about them.

They stand about 2.5 meters tall on feathered legs that end in vicious talons. Their torsos are bare and show off a generous buxomness. They are graced with both wings and arms. Oddly, while their wings span nearly 3 meters, their arms are stubby, almost stunted looking.

And harpies are ugly.

I know, I know, beauty is in the eye of the beholder and everything. But unlike beauty, ugliness is more than skin deep (how's that for a bag of mixed metaphors?). With harpies, the ugliness radiates from angry, twisted souls.

It's hard to say if their temperaments are more hag-like or more bird-like. Certainly, a predatory gleam lights their yellow eyes. But I have not observed any typical avian behaviors from them.

Stories of harpies have been around since the time of the ancient Greeks. I suspect that like dryads, centaurs, gorgons, and other mythical beings, harpies were once more plentiful on Terra. Magic is in their arsenal of weapons, so perhaps they disappeared when magic waned from the world. I might even be so bold as to hypothesize that there is an entire world of harpies somewhere, and the few we have seen have come through cracks in the veil.

Here's what Virgil had to say about harpies in the *Aeneid,* some time in the first century BCE (taken from the John Dryden translation):

When from the mountain-tops, with a hideous cry,
And clattering wings, the hungry Harpies fly;
They snatch the meat, defiling all they find.
And, parting, leave a loathsome stench behind.

He also describes them as abominable, haggard, and insatiably hungry. Definitely not seductress material. But it's easy to see why early civilizations might have thought these formidable beings were gods or demons.

What is your experience with harpies? Are they nasty old crones or beautiful winged goddesses?

COMMENTS (5)

I have never met a harpy, but I have a grimoire from the renowned Aisling Abernathy with a recipe for curing twisted gut syndrome in horses. One of the ingredients is a feather from a harpy's tail. Abernathy was the real deal. If she believed they exist, then so do I.
cchedgewitch (June 30, 2081)

> I'd like to have that recipe.
> *Valkyrie367 (June 30, 2081)*

>> Sending now.
>> *cchedgewitch (June 30, 2081)*

———•———

What a dumpster fire of human waste this blog is. There's no such thing as a harpy and you know it. You should be ashamed of yourself for inciting fear.
PercivalPapa (July 1, 2081)

> You know if you don't like my blog, you could just scroll on past.
> *Valkyrie367 (July 1, 2081)*

CHAPTER

22

ason grabbed my hand and we ran. Princess thought it was a game, and she gamboled along at our side. There was no way we could make it to the sanctuary of the forest in time, but we could pick our battleground. The terrain was flat and bare except for a lump of something in the not-too-far distance. As we approached, it resolved into a wagon tipped on its side. The torn canvas awning flapped in the wind. It wouldn't provide cover, but at least we could have something solid at our backs. Mason had the same idea, and we skidded to a stop. I bent and pressed a fist into my waist.

"I need…breath." Princess joined us.

Mason was breathing hard, but not nearly as winded as me. Princess flopped at my feet. A shadow fell on us. I looked up to find the "birdie" passing overhead.

By the One-eyed Father. Those weren't birds.

"Harpy," I gasped. The beast swooped down, claws extended to rake across my back. I dropped to the ground and rolled. Mason roared. He swung his stone arm and connected with the harpy's raptor leg. It shrieked and lurched out of the way. Its wings, wider than any eagle's, buffeted the air, sending up whirls of dust as it rose into the sky again. Its back end was all bird of prey with brindled feathers on stout legs and three-toed feet that ended in talons as long as daggers. It wheeled around for another pass, and I saw its face—a wrinkled hag with long gray hair streaming behind her and bare breasts dangling like basketballs in skin socks. She dove and hissed, flaunting blackened teeth sharpened to points.

Princess jumped, snarling and spitting. Mason beat her to it and swung again. This time, the harpy was ready. She knocked him flat with the swoosh of one wing, then grabbed his leg in her talons and wrenched him upward.

Oh, no! Not on my watch. Mason was too heavy for the harpy to fly away with, but his leg was caught in her vise-grip and his head bounced as she dragged him across the hard ground. I swung my sword and slashed the harpy's foot.

Mason fell to the ground, but he wasn't down for long. He jumped up again as I was marveling at the blade in my hand.

My sword!

I gripped its hilt. It was solid and real. I'd wanted it and it appeared.

"Kyra, watch out!" He pushed me aside and screamed as the harpy's talons raked his leg.

"Stay down," I said, a bit too roughly. "I've got this."

The harpy dove again. This time her talons grabbed for Princess's scruff, but the hound snarled and twisted away, smashing into the wagon. The harpy screeched as she missed her target and rose into the air.

"Dammit, Kyra! Get out of the way." Mason was crawling back onto his knees, but the effort cost him. He favored his right leg. His pants were torn, and his calf was scored with long red lines.

"No, *you* stay out of the way. I'm the one with the sword."

Mason growled out a curse in French and pulled himself up, using the wagon as leverage. But the wagon already balanced precariously. It tipped over and slammed to the ground. When the dust cleared, we found Grim hiding in the shadows of a wagon wheel. Even with wings, the grimalkin had decided that the forest was too far away.

"You two are hilarious," he said. "You spend more energy fighting yourselves than your opponent."

"Shut up," Mason and I said in unison.

The harpy circled above, preparing for another attack. I put Princess between us. Mason and I stood back to back. He raised his stone arm like a club, and I held my sword, ready to strike.

The harpy dove. Grim squeaked and bolted onto the open ground. He didn't get far. At the last moment, the harpy checked her dive and took off after the cat. He was so terrified, he forgot about his wings. The harpy struck.

Grim flattened himself to the ground. Her talons missed him by a hair. As she rose for another assault, I leaped over the wagon and launched myself through the air, swinging my sword with every inch of effort I had in me. The blade glinted in the sunlight as it sheared off a taloned foot.

A scream of pain laced with pure rage assaulted me as I landed on the rough ground. My knee buckled, and I rolled, taking a face full of dust. The harpy screeched again. Blood poured from her severed leg. Leathery wings beat furiously, and in a moment she was just a speck on the horizon.

"WHAT WERE YOU thinking?" Mason's eyes flashed with dark fire and his eyebrows scrunched so low, I thought they might fall off his head.

I cleaned his wound with a piece of his ripped pants.

"I thought I was saving your ass," I said, dabbing at the talon marks. Remarkably, there was no blood, but the skin gaped open in a long gash.

"You're not an immortal gargoyle anymore, remember?" I ripped another piece off his pant leg and tied it around his shin with a jerk.

"Ow! That doesn't mean I can't take care of myself."

I tied off the bandage a little more roughly than necessary.

"You're lucky. It's just a scratch. She could have taken your head off."

Mason grumbled and flexed his knee, testing the muscle. "Feels worse than a scratch."

"That's because you're…Not. Immortal. Anymore. Get that through your thick head."

"Actually," Grim piped up, "Wounds don't usually bleed in the Nether. Doesn't mean it won't be fatal. Harpy claws are notoriously rotten with bacteria."

"Wonderful." I stomped away. Fear was making me irrational. I couldn't stand the thought of losing Mason, so I transformed all that worry into an emotion that I could more easily vent. Anger.

The harpies were gone for now, but I had no doubt the wounded one would send her harpy friends after us. We needed to get to the forest before then. But first, I had a bit of unfinished business.

I grabbed Grim by the scruff, like a mama cat with an unruly kitten.

He squawked as I pulled him around to meet my gaze. I gave him my best crazy-eyed look, the one that makes opponents falter in a fight. The one that said they faced someone who might not give a damn about dying but just wanted to get in a few good jabs before the end.

"That harpy was after you, wasn't she?"

Grim's front legs pedaled in the air. His back legs kicked up dirt as he scrambled to get away. But my fistful of fur held him fast.

"Tell me! Stop treating us like we're on a need-to-know basis and spill it!"

"Stop! Stop! I'll tell you!"

I let him go. He landed lightly and sprang away.

"That was uncalled for." He gave me a hard look as he smoothed down his fur with tongue and paw.

Mason stood up and leaned heavily on his good leg. "I think it was exactly called for."

"Oh, I see. A minute ago, you two couldn't agree on who should get the pleasure of flinging them self into danger first. But now you're ganging up on me."

"Answer the question, cat. Why are the harpies after you?" Mason's eyes were hard as flint. "Or let me guess. Those birdies are the Nether police, and you're a fugitive."

Princess snarled to show her support. Grim looked at the unifying anger on our faces and his little shoulders slumped.

"Fine. I will explain. But not here. Those birdies will return, and I don't want to be exposed out here when they do."

CHAPTER

23

The temperature dropped as soon as we ducked into the forest. Overhead, thick foliage blocked the sky. Trunks were tall and widely spaced, with the lowest branches fifty meters above us. Shaggy moss grew on the bark, or maybe that was bark. And long, willowy vines hung from the tallest branches. Ferns clustered between the trunks, masking leaf litter and hiding anything that crawled, hopped, or slithered through the underbrush.

As we walked in the quiet shadows, I was glad to have my sword back. When I fought the harpy, I hadn't even thought about it. The blade had been an extension of my arm for so long, it just felt natural to have it in a fight.

So maybe Grim was right. Maybe I could manifest wings if I really wanted them. But he'd also implied that finding Jacoby wasn't my top priority. And that was a load of ogre dung. There was nothing I wanted more than to bring Jacoby home.

I side-eyed Mason, who limped through the gloom with his lips pressed thin and his eyes shaded by furrowed brows. The fight with the harpy had been a disaster. We couldn't get out of each other's way. That didn't bode well for us living together. We were two independent souls who would be better off living alone. That didn't mean we couldn't date. But the thought of waking next to Mason, watching him enjoy that first cup of coffee in the morning, maybe standing at the fridge wearing only his shorts, making a funny face at the milk gone sour…that was living. Dating was just dating.

I sighed and caught up to him. I slipped my hand in his. He threw a glance over his shoulder and pulled his hand away.

Okay. I could be the bigger man here. "I'm sorry I stepped in front of you with the harpy."

He raised his eyebrows and shook his head.

"What? I apologized! What more do you want?"

"You don't get it, do you? You're so worried I'm going to get hurt, you'll jump in front of a bullet for me. Ever since…" He let the thought trail off, so I finished it for him.

"Ever since I ran you through with my sword, you mean? Or were you referring to me breaking the spell that kept you immortal? 'Cuz I did that too. So forgive me, if I'm trying to make up for it by keeping you alive!"

It was his turn to reach for me, but I yanked my arm away and sped up.

"Kyra, don't."

I ignored him and marched on, leaving him behind. It was a petty victory because his wounded leg slowed him down. I didn't care. I needed time alone to think.

"Don't get too far ahead," Grim called after me. But I ignored him too.

I pushed myself into a jog, needing the burn of exerted muscles to calm the fire inside me. Despite the alien flora, the forest was comforting and familiar. I half expected, half hoped to find a dryad stepping in our path or to spy a wood troll trundling home with a pack of kindling on his back. But except for a few small rodents, I keened no other life around us.

Princess darted off sideways. I could follow her trail by the rustling ferns and the occasional tip of ears or tail above the plant line.

Eventually, the path widened to a small clearing with the remains of a campfire and a pile of wood stacked beside it. On the other side of the clearing, the road continued into the forest. Around the camp, five statues stood like petrified sentinels. At the base of each statue, offerings had been left—small piles of stones, crowns of dried flowers and bones of small animals. Nothing inorganic. And nothing that would be of value to thieves.

The long Nether day was coming to an end, but I had enough light to study the carvings. The first one was a creature carved from one great log. It had two heads—hawk and lion. The feathers of the hawk and mane of the lion were carved in intricate detail. Only his flat, wooden eyes made him seem less than alive.

"I see you met Kodjinn," Grim said as he stepped into the clearing.

"Who is he?" I asked.

"He is anger and passion. And a Steward of the Nether. They say his feathers and fur burst into flame when emotion takes him."

Interesting. I moved on to the next statue. This carving seemed almost human, except for the multiple arms. The body was carved in a seated position. One pair of arms held an open book. Another pair met with flat palms overhead. A third rested in the lap. A sculpted gown draped over large breasts. The face was fine-boned and bearded with thick curling tresses.

"Sushanoo. Steward of forgiveness and reason. Master of the airy realms."

By now, Mason had joined us. His pale face told me his wound pained him, and I felt a pang of guilt for running away and making him rush to keep up. He said nothing about my childish pique, but joined Grim on the tour of the strange statues.

"And this is Nyami, Steward of love and ruler of the water realms."

The next figure had exaggerated eyes and a bouffant crown of hair. She posed with hands on her hips and one knee bent like a sassy teen. She wore a short skirt that seemed made of fish scales. It hugged her round hips. A cropped shirt of the same texture showed off her navel.

"Isn't that interesting?" I said.

"A little too 'look at me, I'm a goddess' for my taste." Mason turned away, dismissing her. I stopped him.

"No one ever said the gods were subtle. But look at her stomach."

"What about it?"

"She has a belly button."

I hadn't spent much time in college. My mother's cancer returned during my freshman year and my cousin Aaric came to escort us back to Asgard that spring. But for a few months, I'd stumbled through a bunch of classes, trying to figure out my major. One lecture that stuck out in my memory was an ethics of theology class. The professor liked to arouse vigorous discussions. Once he drew us into a debate over a provocative question. If man was made in God's image, then did God have a belly button? And if so, did that mean he had a mother? And if so, how could he be the All Mighty? It was a question that turned around itself like a Mobius strip with no beginning or end.

"I was thinking that Nyami and the other Stewards here might not be as all powerful as they want us to believe," I said.

Grim twitched his whiskers. "I suggest you don't tell her that to her face."

The next totem was a tall, handsome youth wearing a crown of leaves.

"Ganus, Steward of life and earth," Grim said. Ganus wore an ankh symbol on a chain around his neck. I had questions about how a symbol from Terran history ended up in the Nether, but Grim pushed us on to the last statue.

This one stood apart from the others. It was bigger, for one, and carved from alabaster stone, not wood.

"Dodona," Grim breathed, awe shining from his eyes. "The Oracle."

I studied this Oracle. She was a stately woman, square jawed and big-boned. Her hair was braided in a crown and she wore a great swath of material draped over her in many folds and tucks. Of all the Stewards, she seemed the least exotic, except for her size.

"So she's a bigwig, is she?"

Grim shot me a sneering look.

"She is Dodona, the giver of blessings."

"Right. And the others do her bidding?"

"The other are the guardians of the Nether. You might call them gods."

Having grown up with gods and sons and daughters of gods, I was less than impressed.

"As long as they stay out of our way, they can be as godly as they like."

Grim sat back in his disdainful cat pose, tail curled around toes, eyes half-lidded. He looked composed, but he had a tell. His ears never stopped twitching. Grim was nervous.

"What's the matter," I asked. "Are we stepping on some toes by camping here? Should we sacrifice a goat to the Stewards before we settle down for the night?"

"You jest, but the Stewards let us pass through their forest at their pleasure. At some point, we will have to pay their toll."

Mason stood in front of Ganus, staring at the medallion hanging around his neck.

"Don't you find that strange?" he said.

"Strange how?"

"The ankh is an Egyptian symbol. What's it doing on a god in the Nether?"

I'd been thinking the same thing. We both turned to look at Grim.

"What are you asking me for?" The cat gave us a wide-eyed look. Then he turned and headed over to the fire pit. "We'll stop here for the night. Be a good monkey with thumbs and light us a fire. It gets cold when the sun goes down."

I ignored the insult and peered at the bits of light poking through the canopy. "But it's still light out. Can't we keep moving?"

Grim tucked his tail around his toes. "No. We can't. The next campsite is too far. You don't want to be caught on the path at nightfall."

"Why not?"

The cat watched me with his unblinking gaze.

"Fine. Can we at least find something to eat?"

"You can do whatever you wish." He lay down and tucked his feet under his belly.

"I'll find some kindling," Mason said.

"Don't go far."

Without a word, he limped into the underbrush with Princess on his heels.

Oh, boy. I'd really pissed him off this time. I'd have to make it right, but first we needed fire, food and rest.

Blackened logs and ash filled a ring of stones, but the fire was long dead. I crouched and built it up with the few sticks available. While I worked, I felt eyes watching me, but when I turned, the statues' gazes were flat and wooden. I shivered. It would be a restless night under the watch of the Stewards.

My sword hadn't disappeared after the battle with the harpy. In the real world, I could easily light a fire with a spark of magic pushed through it. Time to test that trick here. I stuck the blade into the pile of sticks, closed my eyes and thought about *fire*.

I heard a snap of flames and opened my eyes to find a nice little blaze.

Grim watched me without lifting his head. The tip of his tail thumped and thumped and thumped.

"You know, you could have made a fire without the help of that noisy sword. If you want something. You need only think about it. But you must really want it."

"So you say. But here we are, stuck in a forest, when all I really want is to find Jacoby."

"Is it?"

I gritted my teeth and turned away. I wasn't going to get into that discussion again.

Mason returned and dumped a load of sticks beside the fire. "I hope that's enough to get us through the night." His face was pale and his lips white.

"Let me look at that leg," I said.

"It's fine."

"It's not." I didn't give him a chance to pull away. I pulled off the makeshift bandage. Still no blood. Gently, I prodded the cut and Mason winced.

"It's so strange. It's a fairly deep cut. It should bleed." I had no more bandages, so I re-wrapped the wound with the piece of pant leg.

Grim peered over my shoulder. "It's good he doesn't bleed."

"What do you mean?"

"If you bleed, you can die." Grim yawned and stretched. "As your ki turns to stone, you'll bleed much more easily. When that happens, it means your corporeal body back on your world is near death."

I looked at the scratch on my wrist from his claws. "If you bleed, you can die. Good to know."

"Hurts either way," Mason mumbled. The fact that he was complaining told me he was really out of sorts. Mason never complained. I'd seen him get shot in the leg and react only by gritting his teeth.

"You'll have to take it easy for a while."

I sat back and examined him. His pants were ripped and so was his shirt. Even his hair had finally relaxed and fell over his forehead in unruly curls.

"I have to say the whole ripped-shirt look is working for me, though. It's got a swashbuckling-slash-bodice-ripper feel to it."

Mason stared at me with flat eyes.

I sighed. He was still annoyed with me.

Princess hopped out of the ferns with a snake dangling from her jaws. She dropped it at my feet and gave me a big doggie grin, tongue lolling. Her muzzle was stained with blood. The snake wasn't her first catch of the evening.

"Thanks. I guess this is to share?"

She flopped to the ground, rolled and nearly squashed Grim. He hissed in her face. Princess favored him with a sloppy kiss up the side of his nose.

"Delightful." He scrubbed at his face with a paw and then moved to the other side of the fire.

Night fell like a wet blanket in the forest. One moment we were sitting in front of the fire enjoying a bit of roasting snake. The next moment, the trees and ferns disappeared into inky shadows. As the fire burned down, Mason and I huddled closer for warmth. It got cold fast.

Grim stayed in his fur-ball pose. His eyes were closing, but I wouldn't let him off that easily.

"You were going to tell us why that harpy was after you," I said. He slow-blinked at me, then stretched.

"We guides have our own rules." He stared into the fire as he spoke. The flames danced in his enlarged pupils.

"And you broke one."

"Yes. But she was worth it." His eyes took on a dreamy look. Of course, it was about a woman. Did that mean there were grimalkin females? Or had Grim fallen for some alien feline?

That was all the story I was going to get. Grim settled down again and curled his tail over his nose. Mason was exhausted from his wound and slept beside me with Princess at his back.

I had a hard time falling asleep. The idols of the Stewards were just visible at the edge of the firelight and in the dancing flames they seemed to leer at me. I lay down with my back to the fire and tucked my head under Mason's chin. His gentle breath blew across my forehead. I was cold, but eventually I sank into the shadow of sleep.

Kur nudged my hand. My ice-sprite tucked into the crook of my legs. My hand dropped to his soft, furry head, fingers sinking into the thick pelt...

That wasn't Kur.

I pulled myself from the dream to find Grim watching me with half-hooded eyes.

It seemed that warmth was worth being man-handled. A rumbling sound, like an avalanche bearing down on us, filled the night.

My fingers froze in his fur.

Grim's head jerked up. The sound stopped.

"Were you purring?"

He pointed his nose in the air and sniffed.

"Most assuredly not. I do not purr." He rose, his back arched to creep away.

"Stay." I reached for him and he flinched under my touch. I withdrew my hand. "Really. Stay. It's too cold to sleep alone."

With his head low, he slunk back to my side and curled into a ball, his back pressed against my thighs. He let out a puffed sigh. I resisted the urge to pet him again. I could leave him that bit of dignity.

With Mason at my back and Princess twitching in her sleep beside him, I finally let myself relax. My family was safe for the moment.

CHAPTER

24

e had a long slog through the forest the following day. Carved statues of the Stewards marked every crossroads in the path. These were totem style statues with the Steward heads piled one on top of the other and Dodona always placed as the crown. The four Stewards wore varying expressions of displeasure, rage and fear, as if the weight of the Oracle was too much to bear.

Grim seemed to know his way and didn't hesitate at any turning point, but I stopped at each statue for a moment, not in reverence, but in curiosity. They were so lifelike, I half expected them to jump down from their pedestals and follow us. Each totem was slightly different. In one version, Sushanoo carried scales, suggesting justice or reckoning. In another they were posed reading from a thick book, suggesting what? Pursuit of knowledge?

Only the Oracle looming over all of them was the same, with her braided crown and unerring gaze. She gave me the creeps.

Eventually, the dirt path changed to a gravel road. Grim picked up speed as if we neared our destination. The trees gave way to a swath of tall reeds with a river sweeping through it, and a boardwalk winding toward the water. It groaned underfoot and my first steps across the faded gray boards were hesitant.

A small lizard-like creature, winged and feathered in black with green badges on its shoulders, watched us from the top of a reed stalk. Grim bounded ahead and leapt. With his black-to-gray coloring, he became a flying shadow—darting, twisting, totally focused. The creature never saw him coming. Grim's jaws clamped onto its neck. He pivoted in the air and dropped gracefully to the boardwalk with his catch dangling from his mouth.

I sprinted forward. I don't know why. There was nothing I could do. The lizard-bird was dead before the cat's paws hit the ground.

"Grim!" I used my stern voice, the one that usually got results when Hunter or Kur were misbehaving.

Grim threw a disdainful glance my way. He padded to the end of the boardwalk, where it became a dock jutting into the river. A wooden boat was tied to the moorings. It resembled a Viking ship, with a square sail and a figurehead carved into the bow—the face I now recognized as Nyami, the beautiful Steward of water and love. Except on this carving, her mouth was open, lips pulled back in pain or anger.

I stomped after Grim, determined to have my say.

"Leave it," Mason held onto my arm. "Look."

Grim tossed his catch on the ground and turned to me. "I told you we'd have to pay the toll at some point."

Up close, Nyami's figurehead was more frightening than the idols we'd seen in the forest. Her teeth were stained black with bits of fur and feather stuck to them.

Lovely.

Grim nudged his offering with a paw, needing the monkey with thumbs to do his bidding. I glared at him, but in the end, I picked up the dead creature.

"I'm sorry, little one." I placed it in Nyami's wooden jaws. The boat seemed to shiver, and I keened a wave of power shuddering through it. That was some toll.

"All aboard." Grim hopped onto the deck. Mason unwound the ropes from the moorings.

I had a deep discussion with Princess about the necessity of traveling by boat. She had heartfelt, philosophical reasons why we shouldn't that went something like, "Aroo!" I told her she really needed to get her furry butt on the boat, and I got a whine, a grumble and a thorough head shake that sent spit flying. She crouched on the dock and covered her muzzle with both paws. Nothing I said would budge her. Finally, Mason picked her up. She whimpered and tried to climb over his back until he unceremoniously dumped her into the boat. It rocked wildly from side to side and my stomach lurched. Princess didn't like the motion either, and she flopped onto the deck with a grousing growl.

The faint wind was enough to fill the sail. We drifted with the current at a good clip. I hung off the side of the boat, hoping I wouldn't get to know what partially digested snake looked like. The water was clear and blue, but like the Nether's sky, it was the wrong blue. It was tinted purple like the bluebells that grew on the mountain near my grandfather's castle in Asgard. And it was full of spirits. They floated by our boat like spectral fish, sometimes staring up at me with wistful gazes, but mostly ignoring the boat's passage.

Our vessel was flat-bottomed and the water shallow. The riverbed glittered in the sunlight. Then I realized that the odd blue color of the water came from the stones lining the riverbed. Thousands—maybe millions of ki stones.

Oh, gods. How many lives had been snuffed out on this river? The thought did nothing to settle my stomach.

"You okay?" Mason's hand rubbed my back.

I nodded. Any words would come out with a load of stomach acid. But he didn't force conversation. He knew when I needed silent comfort. His hand was a warm and grounding reassurance between my shoulder blades. And I was just happy to have him talking to me again.

Ahead, a bridge arched gracefully over the river. From a distance, it didn't look high enough for the mast of our boat. We closed on it quickly. Two more Steward statues were carved into the abutments at each end of the bridge, like gargoyles peering down from the eaves. These statues—Ganus and Kodjinn had wings, and they looked ready to come to life and confront us. But we passed without waking them. I glanced up as we fell under the bridge's shadow. The tip of our mast cleared the space with inches to spare.

My nausea wore off, and I could sit back and enjoy the scenery. Not that there was much to see. Just the endless marshy riverbank. Every few minutes, another bridge appeared on the horizon. We sailed beneath them, one after another, with those silent Stewards watching from the abutments. We saw no other vessels on the water, though we passed several docks with boats tied off and figureheads bobbing in the current.

"Why so many bridges?" Mason asked. "Where do those roads go?"

Grim, who had found a patch of sunlight to bask in, opened one eye. I thought he wouldn't answer, but he yawned, stretched and sat up.

"The river is the only decent highway through the Nether."

"But the bridges…"

"They lead to doors."

Now I sat up, paying attention. "Doors like the one we came through?"

"Precisely."

That was a comforting thought.

"If we can't find our door again, can we use one of those?"

"Do I need to call your attention to the rules again?"

"Right, I know. Don't go through a door uninvited. But what if we have no other option?"

"Without the proper key, the doors are not an option. Just ask those unlucky souls."

Grim nodded his chin toward the next bridge, barely visible in the distance. The span writhed and twisted like it was a live thing trying to shuck off its skin. As we drew closer, it became clear that the bridge wasn't actually moving. Dozens of ghostly bodies clung to it, climbing along and over the struts.

"What is it?" Mason leaned against the rail beside me.

"Ghosts. Hundreds of them."

"Who are they?" I gripped the hilt of my sword.

"Pillagers. Conquerors. Idiots." Grim twitched his whiskers, which I was coming to recognize as the cat's version of a shrug. "Some shaman or sorcerer probably promised riches for invading another world. But once they got here, they couldn't leave. Happens all the time."

As our boat floated closer, the ghosts watched us in silence—a spectral line peering over the rail. They were vaguely humanoid with tall, willowy forms, long faces, and bald heads. And they all wore a look of hopelessness in their eyes.

"It's not right," I said.

"We can't do anything about it."

The hells we couldn't.

"Stop the boat, Grim, or by the One-eyed Father, I'll break one of your precious rules and bring those damned harpies down on our heads so fast you won't be able to say meow."

I held my sword up, feeling its power surge through me. I wasn't sure how

146

I could attract the harpies, but I'd think of something.

Grim bent and washed his toes for the thousandth time that day. I glared at him. He stared back with a calm, even gaze.

"I mean it, Grim."

He heaved a big kitty sigh. The shadow of the bridge fell on us, and the boat swerved for shore. The hull ground on rocks as we slid to a stop. I hopped out with Mason right behind me. He struggled with his lame leg to climb onto the dock. I opened my mouth to tell him to stay in the boat, then shut it. No babying here.

The steep bank was difficult to maneuver. I kept my pace slow, giving Mason time to catch up. A ghost flitted around us like a wasp looking for a sweet treat. The others seemed not to notice our intrusion, but continued their unrelenting vigil on the bridge. Loose rocks skidded under my foot, and I ignored the spirits to concentrate on the climb. A climb made harder because I had to carry my unsheathed sword. Why, oh why, had my subconscious mind not manifested a sheath and harness too? But try as I might, I couldn't will them into existence. Just like my wings.

A sapling made a good handhold, and I pulled myself up. I leaned over to help Mason over the ledge.

"Thanks." Sweat drenched his face and shirt. Like me wishing for a sword sheath, he was probably wondering why he couldn't wish himself healed.

I rested at the top for a moment. Below us, Princess paced beside the boat. She tried to scramble up the slope, but the scree slid her backwards.

"It's all right," I said in a soothing tone. "Wait there. We'll only be a minute."

The hound whined and sat on her haunches. Grim perched on the bow of the boat, next to the figurehead. He watched without comment.

Mason and I stood at one end of the bridge. I looked down the gravel road that lead away from it. A blue door stood about a hundred meters away. It was attached to no frame or wall. Just a blue door in the middle of nothing. Beyond it, the road disappeared into mist. I turned away. I wasn't ready to leave the Nether yet, and even if I were ready, I had no key to open that door. But I couldn't help thinking that there had to be some way to force it open, otherwise these people wouldn't have died trying.

I ran my hand along my thighs. In another world, my body sat in front of

Timberfoot's tree, with his fledgling roots twined around my legs. I couldn't feel those anchors here, and that made me worry that we would never find our way home. A strange door like this one might be our only way out.

"I wish I could see the ghosts," Mason said, interrupting my dismal thoughts.

"You really don't."

The ghosts had noticed us now. Some gathered in small groups. Others squatted on the bridge or stood on the rail. But all watched our approach with expressions ranging from lost to haunted to terrified.

"You're going to free them, aren't you?" Mason watched me with that steady, penetrating gaze he had, the one that always made me want to confess my sins. If he ever gave up alchemy, he'd make a great detective. Or a priest.

"Yes."

"You sure? Might get us in trouble."

"We're already in trouble, thanks to those two." I waved a hand at the cat and the hound waiting for us in the boat.

Mason worked a kink from his neck. "There are a lot of lost souls in this world. You can't save them all."

"No, but I can save these."

I didn't know why it was suddenly so important, but I couldn't move on with our quest until I freed these souls. Maybe I had a bit of the Valkyrie in me after all.

"All right, then." Mason winked and squeezed my hand.

As we crept toward the bridge, the only sound was the gravel crunching under our feet. Blue stones littered the wooden planks that stretched across the river. They flashed in the sunlight like beacons.

Come to me, come to me, they said.

My sword's magic is finicky. It works differently on humans and mortals than it does on fae or immortals. I had no idea what it would do to alien beings in an alien world. Usually, I pulled from the environment to prime my sword, but I couldn't easily access that power here. When I tried, I came up against the same block that prevented me from creating my wings. Instead, I drew on the well of power that lived inside me. Using my own magic could leave me weakened. Depleting my magic entirely could kill me.

I thought of Nori and hesitated. She'd been feeding Jacoby from her personal well for weeks. And now she waited for us to rescue him. She was counting on us. Could I endanger our mission and all she had sacrificed to be a Good Samaritan to these perfect strangers?

The spectral faces watching me were bleak. They had no expectations. No hope.

I nudged a blue stone at my foot. This could go very wrong.

"What's the matter?" Mason asked.

"Nothing. I'm just a little overwhelmed by how many of them there are." I filled my voice with concern for the spirits to mask the concern for my own well-being if this all went sour. Mason might accuse me of being overprotective, but it was a kettle-pot situation. Now that he could see the sunrise, he was determined to never let me fight another battle alone. But he couldn't help me here. If I was going to do this—if I was going to dip into my own magic—I couldn't let him know what it would cost me.

Valkyries have many skills. In the days of battle between the Aesir and the Titans, or the Aesir and the Giants, or the Aesir and any number of other enemies, we fought alongside the gods and their children. We were also cleaners. In the aftermath of great battles, we walked the killing fields and sent the dead and mortally wounded to the halls of Valhalla with a stroke of our blades.

I had never wanted that power. It seemed arrogant to me. Who was I to presume to judge a soul? But in the last few years, with the deaths of friends and family, and by facing enemies who channeled only hatred and evil…I had learned to accept my sword's soul-sucking ability for what it was. Not a judge, but a conduit. At home on Terra, I'd released spirits to the next plane of existence, regardless of who they were. Joran came to mind. The man who'd killed Alvin and Theo. The man who'd suffered from the slow death of a wound by my blade. I'd allowed him passage to the next realm because I was Valkyrie. That's what we did. Let the gods sort him out.

I had no idea who these ghosts on the bridge were, where they came from, or what their purpose in the Nether was. They could have been refugees or invaders. It didn't matter.

I scraped the tip of my sword across a blue stone. It sparked and turned gray.

A ghost sitting on the railing effervesced in a spray of blue light and winked out of existence.

Every spirit stopped. I felt the combined weight of their stares, like a wave of heat pressing down on me. But instead of feeling depleted, the freeing of that one soul bolstered me. I scratched another ki stone. Another ghost winked out. This one had been standing nearby, and as she went, her hand brushed my arm in a silent *thank you.* The contact jolted me like I'd been zapped with an electrical current. It tingled along my nerve endings, sending a rippling shiver down my spine.

I touched another stone. And another. By now, the ghosts understood what was happening. They swarmed me like eager children looking for sweets. I pushed through them to reach more stones. Faster now. Each release zinged through me, filling me with joy.

"Help me gather the stones." My voice was rough and breathless to my ears. Mason cocked an eyebrow at me but started collecting the stones. He piled them at my feet, and I drove my blade into the mound.

A mass of spirits blazed out at once. The sheer power of the release should have toppled me. In the Nether, I had no way to boost my wards. But instead of crumpling in a heap and convulsing with seizures, I felt strong and ready and full of joy.

Mason dumped another load of stones at my feet.

I could hear them now. The lost souls whispered their thanks, sang of their relief and joy to be reunited with loved ones. Oh, All-father! They'd been trapped here for so long. For eons! Their release sparked in me a feeling of utter gratitude—love condensed down to its basic form. The purest element in the universe.

And it filled me to bursting.

By the time I'd dispatched the last soul, I was laughing. Mason looked up at me with that pure element shining in his eyes.

"Now you look just as I remember you." His voice ground with emotion. "Now you look like my Kyra."

I stretched my arms wide and laughed again. I was strong! I was full of life. I was flying.

The golden wings spreading from my back felt so natural I couldn't imagine life without them. I flexed their powerful frames and rose higher.

A black figure shot into the air from below. Princess zipped by me. A long "Arooooo!" followed as the hound also discovered the freedom of flight.

CHAPTER

25

rim was furious about my side adventure. When I finally wore out the novelty of flying and dropped to the deck of the boat, he was pacing in agitation.

"You'd better hope you're back in your own world before the harpies learn about your little intervention back there."

"Why? I set a few souls free. They should thank me."

"The rules say—"

"I know. 'Don't disturb the ki stones.' Too bad. This place could use a bit of a shake up."

Grim's face looked like he was going to explode. Then he heaved a sigh, like the weight of the Nether was on his shoulders.

I itched to spread my wings again, but Grim wanted to continue along the river.

"We're almost at Port Dodona. We dock there and then we'll fly." He closed his eyes as if concentrating. I keened a little tug of magic from him, and the boat pulled away from shore, grinding against rocks until the current took us downstream.

I could barely contain the energy sizzling through my veins. Releasing those ghosts had fired me up, and I had trouble sitting still. The boat tipped side to side as I paced the short deck, fanning my wings like a butterfly just out of her cocoon.

Princess couldn't be convinced to sit still, not when she had the whole sky to explore, and she circled above the boat. A stray wind buffeted her, and she tumbled through the air until she caught the current again. Her wings were black with bone-white ridges and feathered in downy soft fluff. She took to flying like she'd been born to it. Terrific. Now, along with the squirrels, no bird would be safe.

With a sigh, I tucked my wings in. As soon as they snugged against my back, they disappeared. I spun around.

"They're still there. Look." Mason shrugged and his wings popped out. "They only appear when you want them."

I concentrated and keened the growth of my wings before I felt them. I couldn't help the grin that spread across my face. "Pretty snazzy, huh?"

"Pretty and snazzy." Mason reached over my shoulder to stroke my wing. I shuddered down to my toes, as if he'd plunged his fingers into that deep well of magic inside me.

"Do you feel that too?" I ran a finger across his silky feathers. His eyes popped, then smoldered with a darker intent. He pulled me to him, our wings enveloping us like a shield against the world. Little lightning bolts of desire tingled along the edges of our feathers where they touched.

"I can see some very practical applications for these wings." His voice rumbled next to my ear, and he trailed kisses along my neck.

"Get a room!" Grim hollered from the foredeck.

I jerked my wings closed as heat rushed up my cheeks.

Mason was having none of that. "If you've got a room for us, I'd oblige. Until then, shut it, cat." He planted one more deliberate kiss on my lips, slipping me his tongue for good measure.

Over his shoulder, I could see Grim's tail thumping the deck. His eyes slitted. Mason grinned and retracted his wings too. I rubbed my hands down my filthy jeans as if smoothing down a ruffled ball gown.

I leaned against the rail. Mason joined me and we watched the riverbank slide by. Fog whispered through the reeds, though the day was clear and dry.

"That was pretty incredible back there." Mason's hand covered mine. "I couldn't see the ghosts, but I felt it when you released them. Hard not to. It was amazing. You were amazing."

Unreasonably, I felt tears prickling my eyes.

"I wish you could have seen them."

"It was enough to see you. I haven't seen you that happy...ever."

"That's because you make love with your eyes closed." I grinned and bumped him with my hip.

He turned one of his dark looks on me, the kind that mothers warn their daughters away from. Then he lifted my fingers and kissed them. Overhead, Princess howled.

"Are we okay?" I said.

"I should be asking you that. I was pretty grumpy yesterday."

"You were."

"I'm not used to being in pain." He flexed his knee. His leg was better today, though the odd, bloodless wound hadn't closed. "I never thought much about pain before. The sunrise always took it away." He smiled, but it didn't reach his eyes. "I guess I was a little spoiled."

I lifted his arm and wrapped it around my waist. He pulled me tighter against him.

"That's my point," I said. "You need to be more careful."

"And you need to stop jumping in front of every danger that comes my way."

I ground my teeth against the answer I really wanted to give him, and said, "I'll try. But it's not in my nature to let those I love get hurt."

"And it's not in my nature to let others take care of me."

I laid my head against his shoulder. "We make a great pair. Are you sure you want me to move in with you?"

He kissed the top of my head. "Never been more sure of anything."

"Arooo!" Princess dive-bombed, snapping her wings open at the last second and spraying us with dog drool. Her antics reminded me of Ollie when he was learning to fly, and the thought tugged at my heart.

"Why do you think she got her wings the same time I did?" The question had been nagging at me since we left the bridge.

Mason squeezed my fingers. "You're pack. She's just following your lead." He gazed at the river bank sliding by as if his mind's eye saw something more interesting. "I think that's how she followed you into the Nether. You're her alpha."

I nudged him with my elbow. "Is that why you followed me, too? Am I your alpha."

A slow grin spread across his face. "I'd follow you anywhere."

Grim jumped onto the deck beside us. "If you lovebirds are done, we're coming into port. Now be a good monkey and grab the rope," he said to me. "Tie us off to the mooring when I say. And for the love of the Stewards, get that hound down here before she gets lost in the mist!"

"For someone without opposable thumbs, he sure is bossy," I grumbled as I readied the rope. Mason whistled for Princess, and she crash landed on the deck in a tumble of feet, fur and feathers.

The mist was thickening, and within minutes it smothered our boat. The deck became slick under foot. A rumbling sound turned both our heads. Grim was poised on the bow of the boat, looking past the figurehead. I expected to see another bridge looming in the distance. Instead, the forward horizon disappeared in the fog.

The rumbling noise grew thunderous.

"It's a waterfall!" I shouted over the crash of rushing water.

And we were heading right into it.

"What the hells, Grim? Turn the boat!"

The cat sat alert but unwavering. Mason gripped the railing. His face was drawn and pale as he stared into the looming mist. Droplets of moisture hit my face and clung to my hair. Princess let out a howl that got lost in the deafening roar of the waterfall. We were almost upon it. And then the boat swerved.

"Prepare to disembark!" Grim jumped to the deck.

The boat cut across the current as if pulled by a line. A dock ghosted from the mist and we bumped against it. I jumped onto the dock and tied off the line.

Grim hopped out on nimble feet. Mason, hindered by his bad leg, climbed out awkwardly. He wasn't helped by the slobbering hound who pushed past all of us and took off down the dock. Grim followed her and they were already disappearing into the mist by the time I helped Mason onto the dock. He waved me forward.

"Go after them. I'll catch up."

I glanced from his pain-filled expression to the dense mist, undecided.

"Go!"

I had promised not to coddle him, so I turned and jogged into the mist.

I caught up to Princess first. She snuffled at something in the grass, and I called her to me.

"Stay close." The hound whined, but walked at my heel. I sunk my fingers into her collar of fur, glad for that anchor. The mist swirled around us, oppressive and disorienting. I had to trust that Grim was guiding us in the right direction. I could just see the flash of his silver tail ahead.

The roar of the waterfall lessened, and the mist parted like a curtain, spitting us out onto a barren desert. Underfoot, hard-packed sand was cracked and desiccated under the glaring sun, making the ground a field of tiny obstacles to trip us.

I shielded my eyes, but could see no landmarks in any direction. Mason limped through the wall of fog to join us.

"Now we fly." Grim arched his back and sprang into the air. His silver wings sprouted and flapped, taking him higher.

"Aroo?" Princess stuck her nose up, scenting this new air.

"Go ahead." Her bone-white wings burst open, and she took off after the cat.

"Shall we?" Mason's wings quivered behind him.

I tensed my own wings and jumped.

155

26

veryone dreams of flying at some point in their lives. Dream flying is amazing—soaring, banking, diving. The wind across your face is never too harsh. Currents tingle over your skin. I remember waking from such dreams disappointed with the limitations of my earthbound body.

Flying for real wasn't like that.

At first I marveled at the freedom, the power in my wings, and the joy of being one with the sky. That got old fast. The sun was relentless. Sweat poured off my face to be whisked away in the wind. Then we flew higher, not as high as the planes that used to grace Terran skies, but high enough that the air was chill. My shoulders ached almost immediately, from using muscles I didn't even know I had. My sword was a millstone in my hand. As my fingers went numb, I could no longer grip it.

The blade tumbled away.

"No!" I dove after it. The wind tore tears from my eyes and when I blinked, my sword was gone. I fluttered to a halt and hovered in the air. Hovering was harder than flying, and I couldn't do it for long. Grim swooped around me.

"Leave it!" he shouted.

"I can't!" My gaze scoured the rocky ground, looking for the telltale glint of the blade.

Grim lashed out with his feet. His claws caught my shoulder, but it was more of a shove than a scratch.

"The blade wasn't really here in the first place," he said. "When you need it again, it will appear."

He turned and flew away. I watched him go until he was a silver dot against the sun. Mason had waited for me and I didn't want to stall him any longer. I sucked in a deep breath of the cool air and followed our guide.

Below us, the desert wasn't completely empty. We passed over ruins of ancient cities and crashed vessels, suggesting that once, this world had been inhabited by an advanced civilization. Not anymore. The only evidence I saw of people was the odd caravan of seekers plodding over the rocky desert. Their faces turned upward as we passed.

"I guess they haven't mastered flight yet," I yelled, pointing at the caravan below. Mason smiled but didn't respond. Conversation was difficult at this height.

A few minutes later, a stone fortress came into view. Grim wheeled around as we flew over the structure.

"Dodona's Labyrinth," he said with that gleam of awe in his eyes that showed up every time he spoke of the Oracle.

Now I saw that the structure wasn't a fortress. It was open to the sky, a square stone-walled space about the size of a city block with a maze of more walls inside. I spotted only two entrances on opposite ends of the outer walls. Twin statues of Dodona guarded the gates on either side. Beings milled around the gates. I squinted. They weren't ghosts, but live people. I was too far away to see what had them clustered by the walls.

While I examined the strange labyrinth, wondering at its purpose, I wasn't paying attention to the changing wind currents. A strong gust tumbled me ass over tea kettle and I plummeted, free-falling until I had the presence of mind to stretch my wings again. Mason dove to catch me, but I'd already righted myself. He seemed to take to flying like a natural. Princess spiraled by us, mimicking my near-death plunge.

"You okay?" Mason asked.

"Fine." That was all the response I could muster. In truth, the fall had shaken me. Mason nodded, and we flew on, leaving the mystery of Dodona's Labyrinth behind us.

Minutes or hours later—time had lost all meaning—Mason faltered. His right wing dipped, and he lost altitude. I banked and flew closer to investigate. The bandage around his shin was stained dark red.

"You're bleeding!"

His jaw was clenched tight against the pain.

Blood wasn't good. What had Grim said? If you bled in the Nether, you could die in the Nether. Did that mean we were running out of time? Was Nori frantically trying to keep our mortal bodies alive in the dryad grove?

Whatever it meant, Mason couldn't go on much longer. I patted the pocket of my shirt, reassured by the weight of my ki stone.

I pushed myself to catch up to Grim.

"We have to stop!" I yelled. The cat didn't spare me a look.

"We keep going." His fluffy cat butt shimmied as he flew, and his tail streamed behind him like a silk scarf.

"Mason is—" I didn't get to finish that thought.

A shadow blanketed us, and a screeching caw pierced my ears. Yellow talons grabbed the grimalkin around his hips. Grim yowled, and I lost sight of him in the flapping mass of harpy wings.

"Hey!" I shot forward with no plan, only an instinct to help. The harpy turned her owlish face to me and grinned, baring broken and blackened teeth.

Then she dove with Grim clasped in her claws.

CHAPTER

27

Princess plunged after them. I banked and turned to find Mason already descending. He landed badly and crumpled to the cracked desert floor. Princess landed beside him. She barked furiously at the harpy who had Grim pinned with one massive clawed foot. I circled the scene to get a better idea of the harpy's intent.

Her wings were mottled gray, brown, and black and spread behind her like an angel of death. Frizzy black hair sprouted from her head, leaving her scalp bare in patches. Naked from the waist up, her ponderous breasts hung to her stomach where wrinkled gray skin faded to plumage and powerful raptor haunches. She had short arms with stubby, childish hands and these held open a scroll as she read out a proclamation.

"The guide known as Grim Grimalkin is to be detained on suspicion of obstructing the natural flow of spirits in the Nether. Grim Grimalkin will immediately surrender his badge of office. He will remain in custody until the Tribunal of Stewards decides his fate." The harpy rolled up the scroll and it disappeared. "Do you accept these terms?"

Grim was panting hard. The harpy increased the pressure on his chest and he squeaked.

I landed on the dirt, ignoring the jarring pain through my knees.

"Hey, Angry Bird! Let him go!" I had my sword out and ready. Mason moved to stand beside me, one stone arm raised and shaking. Princess growled. I sank my free hand into fur and felt rage tremble through her.

The harpy turned a dark glare on us. "This is none of your concern, *human.*" She sneered on that last word like it was an insult. This wasn't the time to correct her about my true parentage.

"You could at least let him speak. Or does your justice system rely on gagging your victims?"

The harpy curled her lip, and it quivered as she considered me. Gold irises with slitted pupils accented her apple-sized eyes. To her, I was less than a bug, a nuisance to be ignored or treated with harsh indifference.

After a moment, she leaned back, loosening her hold. Grim squirmed from under the talons. His fur stuck up in all directions and he rolled his shoulders, settling his pelt. His tail twitched across the hard-packed sand.

"Do you accept the terms?" the harpy repeated.

Without taking his eyes from her, Grim raised a paw, licked it and tidied his whiskers. He was smooth, I had to give him that. The harpy terrified me, and I wasn't the focus of her wrath.

"Do I have a choice?" Grim said.

The harpy cocked her head.

Grim heaved out a sigh. "Fine. I will meet the Tribunal of Stewards, but the Guide Handbook, section fourteen, paragraph three, clearly states: A Guide may not be detained for any reason if that detention should endanger the life of a Seeker. In such cases, detention must be deferred until the Guide has successfully escorted the Seeker through the Nether and accomplished the spiritual goals of said Seeker." He smiled, looking at me, not the harpy. "It is our raison d'être, you might say. Even the Stewards cannot interfere with the quest of a lawful seeker."

I was impressed that he could recite the rules from memory. Maybe that came from years of study. Or maybe he'd boned up on the relevant points for just such an occurrence. Either way, I didn't like the implications. As long as we stayed in the Nether, Grim wouldn't have to face that tribunal. I glanced at Mason, whose face was tight with pain. We didn't have much time here, anyway.

The harpy wasn't impressed. She flexed her jet-sized wings as if to overshadow us with her might. I covered my eyes as the flapping stirred up dust. She stomped around, her claws tearing up chunks of ground.

The birdie was having a temper tantrum.

Finally, she came to a decision and settled down. Her tiny hand reached into her feathered under-wing and produced a gold collar, which she snapped around Grim's neck. He spit out a hiss in protest and scrambled backwards, but it was too late. The collar was in place. I keened strange magic coming off it, like it circled him in an invisible cage.

She turned to me. "Finish your quest, seeker. We will find the grimalkin again."

She cranked her wings and leaped into the air.

I rounded on Grim. He was grooming his ruffled fur back into place.

"You're way too complacent about this." I stood over him, hands on hips. "She sounded serious." The cat continued to pull at his silky fur, nuzzling at the spot where the harpy had gripped him in her talons. "Hey! I'm talking to you! They're going to kill you. Don't you care?"

He twitched his whiskers and turned to look over the barren landscape.

"Do you know how many souls, I've ferried through here?" He didn't wait for my answer. "Six hundred and forty-two thousand, two hundred and eleven. Including you three. The Nether never changes."

The number stung me like a heated branding iron. So many! How long had he been here?

"I don't remember my life before the Nether. I had a family once, but their faces are blurred in my mind. I can't even remember the name my mother gave me. Death is my only way out of here. So sure. I'll give it a try."

"You're trapped?" Mason asked.

Grim nodded. "Cursed to guide seekers on their quests for all of eternity. For my sins." He grinned that Cheshire grin again.

"I hope the sins were worth it," I said.

"Can't remember most of them." Grim's tail gave a gentle swish.

Mason ran a hand through his hair and turned to walk away into the desert. I could hear him mumbling in French. He'd only recently broken his own immortality curse—or rather, I'd broken it for him. Seeing another being weighed down with such a burden hit him hard.

Princess bounded after him, leaving me alone with Grim. I sat in the dirt and reached out a tentative hand. As my fingers combed down his back, he half closed his eyes. When I reached for his head again, he ever so slightly leaned into my touch.

"I'm sorry that happened to you. Whatever your crime, I'm sure it didn't deserve an eternity of service to those harpies."

"The harpies are just enforcers. The Stewards will decide my fate."

CHAPTER

28

Flying over the endless desert, I couldn't fathom how we'd ever find First City. The dry, cracked sand flats stretched as far as I could see in every direction. We were all exhausted. Even Princess had quit the loop-de-loops and settled in for a determined but steady flight. Grim harried us any time one of us fell behind. We flew into an ever-darkening sky. Behind us, the sun edged toward the horizon.

"We must get there before sundown!" Grim shouted into the wind.

Finally, a dark spot appeared on the desert floor. As we flew closer, the spot grew into a circular city of dark structures rising from the sand, surrounded by a wall of stone. Unlike the other cities we'd passed over, this one wasn't in ruins. Buildings of white stone shone in the last light. The wall surrounding them was tall, solid and imposing. A black cloud hovered like a billowing hat over the city. Lightning crackled and rain fell within the walls, but left the surrounding desert dry. It looked like a fun place.

Grim glided around the city to land on the other side, outside the only gates in the wall. The rest of us followed, landing with a crunch of hard-packed dirt under our shoes. Our shadows stretched long and thin behind us. Shadows cast by the walls inched along the sand to our feet. The gate loomed in front of us, a black hole in the white stone wall.

Grim trotted forward, then stopped.

"We're too late!"

A grinding noise announced the closing of the gates. A set of wooden doors three stories high and belted in steel slowly shut, sealing off the city with a final clang.

"We'll wait for morning." Grim sat in the dirt and began worrying at that spot on his back again.

"Wait for morning? No way." I gazed up at the gates. Two columns flanked the doors. Once again, each was carved with the heads of the four Stewards, mounted one on top of the other and crowned with Dodona's striking face.

I was tired, but we were so close. We couldn't stop now.

"We can fly over the walls." I looked at Mason. He stood on one foot, favoring the other. Blood caked his pant leg. He looked even more like white marble than usual. It wasn't fair to make him go on without a rest, but he just nodded.

A long, low wail rose from inside the closed city, followed by a soul-breaking scream.

"That's why we wait," Grim said. "The cleaners are more active at night. We rest and, in the morning, we'll have a better chance of finding your friend."

I didn't know what the cleaners were, and I didn't care.

"And what kind of chance does Jacoby have?" I balled my fists, trying to keep my voice even and rational. "One more night might be the end of him."

"How long has he been lost?"

I made a quick calculation in my head, but I couldn't even guess how long we'd been in the Nether.

"It's been over a month already."

Grim's whiskery eyebrows shot up. "And his corporeal form was alive before you came here? That is most unusual."

I thought of Nori feeding him sips of magic for weeks.

"We had help from a healer."

Grim nodded. "Then he has learned to survive First City so far. He can do it one more night. We make camp here." He trotted off, his silvery pantaloons swishing in the fading light.

"We'd better find shelter," Mason said. "It looks like rain."

I wrapped my arm around his waist, partly to feel him near me, and partly so he could lean on me as we walked toward the gates.

The shadow of the city wall fell on us like a shade being pulled down on a window. I blinked as my eyes adjusted. The temperature dropped and goosebumps rose on my arms. Dust swirled around my feet as the wind picked up, and my eyes felt gritty with sand. Lightning crackled over the city again, followed by another of those eerie wails. It would be a long, unpleasant night stuck out in this desert.

Trash from abandoned campsites lined the wall on either side of the gates. A canvas sheet was stretched over broken tent poles, and it snapped in a sudden gust of wind. Black scars and chunks of charcoal marked old fire pits. A cart with only one wheel was dumped on its side and abandoned. And mingled among all this debris were those awful blue stones, along with ghosts that floated apathetically along the wall.

My sword appeared in my hand, anticipating my visceral need to release those spirits from an eternity of mindless wandering. Tension I hadn't even realized I was holding released from my shoulders. I swung the blade in a figure eight, loosening my wrist.

"Don't." Grim appeared from the shadows and butted against my shins. His tail wrapped around my leg.

"Why not?"

"Not here. We don't want to call attention to ourselves."

I stared him down for a moment, but he was unrelenting. My hand itched on the hilt of my sword.

"For once, would you listen to me? It is my job, after all, to steer you through this quest."

I lowered my sword, but it didn't disappear into its spectral sheath. I hadn't found the knack of calling it up and dismissing it with my thoughts. Instead, it reacted to my baser wants, and I had no way to school those.

"Fine. But so far, I have to say, you're a terrible guide."

Grim bowed his head, and his whiskers twitched. "That's because I was meant for loftier things."

We made camp beside the gates. They were solid wood, grayed by time and sanded smooth by whirlwinds off the desert. The faces of the Stewards on the flanking totems were stern and their eyes seemed to follow me as I moved around camp. I plucked a flapping canvas tent off a broken frame. Mason pulled a damaged cart to lean against the wall, and we rigged a shelter. Then we scavenged for anything we could burn. There wasn't much—a few splintered wooden shields, some arrow shafts and tent poles. Mason pulled the last wheel off the cart and added it to the pile of kindling.

The sun had gone down, and the temperature was dropping fast. The odd storm that circled above the city continued to lash us with sand-scouring wind, but so far, no rain.

Princess disappeared among the piles of rocks at the base of the wall and returned with a fat lizard in her mouth and dropped it at my feet. Flecks of blood on her muzzle told me she'd already eaten. This was my share.

"Thanks." I wasn't hungry, but I knew we'd need to keep our energy up if we were going to make it through the cold night.

I built a fire while Mason dressed the lizard, and we roasted it on a spit. A small fountain next to the gates provided water. It seeped from the mouth of a Nyami carving and puddled in a basin. I dipped my fingers in it and touched them to my lips. The water was warm and stale, but I drank my fill anyway. What choice did I have? I reminded myself that I could only die if my corporeal body died back on Terra.

Maybe. Hopefully.

Princess stretched out on the ground and was soon fast asleep. I envied the hound's ability to shut out the rest of the world and sleep whenever she was tired. After hours of flying, my body ached for rest, but my mind churned on.

The fire lit Mason's face. He was brooding. And tired too. I could see it in the dipping line of his shoulders and the creases at the edge of his eyes. Probably wondering how he got mixed up in such a disaster.

On the desert plains, insect messengers flashed like fireflies. We were never far from the harpies' watch.

The lizard crackled in the flames. Mason removed it from the spit and partitioned it three ways. Grim plucked at his piece with dainty bites. I gobbled mine down even though it burned my tongue. After a few bites, I slowed.

"You know what's been bothering me," I asked. Grim glanced up, but continued to gnaw on his dinner. "Why do we need to eat here? Why do we sweat in the heat and shiver in the cold? Our bodies are still on Terra, presumably, in some kind of stasis, but very much alive. We're simply astral projections of ourselves here. So why do our astral bodies act so much like... bodies?"

Grim chewed and watched me silently.

"I have a theory," Mason said quietly. "I've been thinking about how Princess and I followed you through the door. The answer to that question is right here." He raised his hand and made a slashing mark above his head. "Like I can almost see it but not quite reach it."

I nodded. That's how I felt about everything new we encountered in the Nether.

Mason continued, "I need to build blocks of understanding to get there. One of those blocks came to me as we flew today." He straightened his back and cracked his neck from side to side. "We're spectral beings here, but we're interacting with a spectral plane. So our bodies feel real."

I chewed a tough bit of lizard and considered his words.

"So you mean in our world, ghosts can't interact with anything because they aren't on the same spectral plane."

"Exactly."

"And the ghosts here? I've seen them float right through solid rock."

"They're out of phase with this world, too. They should have moved on to another plane, maybe one that vibrates at a different spectral frequency."

"Critter wrangler rule number eleven," I said. "If it bleeds, it can die." I glanced at his wounded leg stretched out before him.

"Maybe." He rubbed a hand over his face. "It's a working theory."

"It's not a bad theory," Grim said. "Except that the Nether isn't a world in the sense that you understand it. No one is born here. No peoples claim it as their home. The Nether is the space between worlds."

After dropping that little bomb, he set about licking his back again.

"What exactly does that mean?" I asked. Grim's nose scrunched up as he chewed on a matted clump of fur. Then he sat up and sighed.

"It means that the people who built the few cities you see in this world, did something very bad. Magic on an apocalyptic scale. It knocked their planet out of its dimension, killing every living thing on it instantly. Because of its unique status, it became a nexus for other worlds. It's much easier to open a door to the Nether than directly to another world. The Stewards understood this and claimed the world for their own."

"And what do they get from a dead planet?"

"Power," Mason said quietly. "Every seeker who comes through here pays tribute to them in some way or another. That kind of belief is the currency of a god's magic."

I thought about that for a while as I forced down the last of the stringy lizard meat.

"And her?" I pointed to Dodona's head topping the nearest totem. "How does she fit into this neat little scheme?"

Grim bristled at my offense. "The Oracle does not scheme."

"Yeah, but is she a new god like the Stewards or is she one of those who blew this world out of sync in the first place?"

"The Oracle just is. She will be here long after the Stewards are gone."

He went back to cleaning his back. He was being a bit obsessive about the hygiene tonight, even for him. I leaned forward to get a better look.

"Is that blood? Let me look." I pushed his nose away. His lip curled and he let out a hiss. It was adorable. "Forget it," I said. "I've been hissed at by scarier things than you. Now let me look."

The fur on his back rose and his eyes squinted to slits, but I ignored him and parted his fur.

The harpy's talon had punctured his side. Dark blood oozed from the wound. I was still confused about my relation to life and death in the Nether. But Grim was pretty clear. He had no corporeal body elsewhere.

"Mason, could you find something to hold water and bring it to me?"

Mason rose, and the shadows swallowed him as he searched the ruined campsites for a pot.

"This is going to hurt, but I need you to sit still." I stroked Grim's silky fur, and he didn't flinch from my touch. I took that as tacit permission to continue. He sucked in a breath as I pulled at fur that had stuck to the wound. The puncture was deep, and blood was already clotting over it. That was the problem with puncture wounds. They healed too quickly, often leaving debris and bacteria inside to fester. There was nothing I could do about it now.

"Here." Mason returned and handed me a metal helmet filled with brackish water. He also brought a relatively clean piece of cloth and a small knife.

"Thanks." I smiled at him. It was like he could read my mind.

I cut away the clotted fur and then washed the wound, hoping I wasn't making it worse with the less-than-clean water. The skin on his back twitched like a horse shucking off a fly. But other than that, he sat through my ministrations without fussing. I cleaned out as much blood and dirt as I could, wishing I had antiseptic cream. Wishing for my sword had called it to my hand. Why not antiseptic? But no pot of ointment magically appeared. The convoluted workings of the Nether made my head hurt.

I sighed. "That's the best I can do." I threw the bloody cloth on the fire and rinsed my hands in the remaining water.

Grim inspected his wound, then settled in a loaf pose by the fire. "Thank you."

"You're welcome. I hope it doesn't get infected."

Grim half-closed his eyes. I leaned against Mason, stealing some of his warmth, and he put an arm around me. Princess pedaled her feet in her sleep, chasing a dream. The rest of us fell into the thrall of the fire. Our little shelter wasn't much protection from the wind that whipped the sand up in erratic dances. The fire had burned low, and we had no more wood. I tucked my head into the hollow between Mason's chin and collarbone, so thankful that he was here with me.

"So how did you end up here?" Mason asked.

I thought Grim wouldn't answer, but after a long pause, he began to speak.

"I was a foolish kit, looking for adventure. My father wanted me to be a *dukun*, a shaman of my people. Like he was and my grandfather before him. I had other ideas. I used his teachings to travel to the Nether, and I tried to break through a door. The Stewards sentenced me to be a guide in payment for my crimes. And so here I am."

"How long ago was that?" I asked.

Grim's whiskers twitched. "Long enough that I no longer remember my father's face."

"That seems harsh."

"It is their way."

"So what did you do to upset the Stewards this time? You said it had to do with a woman."

Grim looked away. "She needed my help. I couldn't leave her to wander until her body died in some other world. Not again. Not another one."

"You helped her break out of the Nether." I said. He nodded again.

He'd helped someone in need, so she wouldn't end up as a blue chip of stone and a disembodied spirit. And the Stewards were going to punish him for it.

"And you can't leave? You have to face this tribunal?"

"Maybe once I could have left. But not now. Not with this." He hooked one claw on the gold collar embedded in the fur at his neck.

That night, we all slept badly under our makeshift tent. The wind blew in gusts that snapped the canvas. Inside the city, the wailing came and went. Princess stretched herself along Mason's back and I huddled against his chest. His arm was a heavy but warm weight over my shoulder.

And a silky, silver-black cat slept in a ball against my stomach.

29

hen I woke the next morning—stiff and cold from sleeping on hard ground—the gates to the city stood open. I rose, stretched out the kinks, and drank from the fetid fountain. We had nothing to eat, and I didn't want to waste time hunting. Jacoby was in that city. I wouldn't make him wait for me any longer.

Inside the gates, the storm cloud churned overhead. The bizarre rain that only fell over the city had fizzled out, but our feet slipped on slick cobblestones. A wide boulevard led away from the gate through the ruins of stone buildings. Windows were bare of glass. Doors hung open on crooked hinges. The streets were swept clean, but when I peered inside a building, I found broken furniture and crockery with a heavy covering of dust.

And ki stones. They were everywhere. Piles of them clustered in the abandoned buildings. More were scattered along the oddly tidy boulevard.

I stood in place, turned in a circle, and realized what was really bothering me about this city.

"Where are all the ghosts?"

Mason was right behind me. His body heat lay like a shadow against my back. His voice rumbled in my ear. "I've got a bad feeling about this."

My sword appeared in my hand, drawn by the fear gurgling in my gut.

"Put that away!" Grim dashed around our ankles.

"What?"

"Your sword!" He arched his back and hissed at my blade. "It's bleeding magic! You'll call the cleaners down on us!"

I'd never seen him so agitated. I shook my hand, as if that would dispel the sword to whatever ether it had come from. Nothing happened.

"What are cleaners?" Mason asked.

"Just get rid of it." Grim danced around. The hair on his back stuck straight up.

"I can't!" Panic now made me grip the hilt tighter.

Mason held my elbows and turned me to face him. "Look at me. Look right here." He pointed two fingers at his eyes. Gods, I loved those eyes. Silver-gray and deep enough to get lost in.

"Take a deep breath. Now close your eyes."

I did, and he pulled me closer so that my head rested against his chest.

"Listen to my heartbeat."

The thum-thump-thum-thump filled my senses and when his fingers closed over mine, I let him take the sword. The flat of his other hand rubbed the small of my back. It was comforting and empowering all at the same time.

When I opened my eyes, he greeted me with a smile.

My sword was gone.

"As soon as you let go of it, it disappeared," he said.

"You're so good at that." I snuggled against him again, not wanting to relinquish the feeling of safety I found in his arms.

"At what?"

"At talking me off the ledge. Will you always do that for me?"

"Always." He kissed the top of my head.

"Are you two going to mate right here in the street? Or are we going to find your friend?" Grim's tail slashed back and forth, and his gaze roamed up and down the deserted road.

"Calm your whiskers, furball." Mason showed him his teeth. "Before we go anywhere, why don't you tell us about these cleaners?"

A shiver ran along Grim's fur. He leaned in and whispered, "First City is a holy site for pilgrims from many worlds, but there's a reason this place is so bare. The Stewards like to dissuade devotees from sticking around too long."

That didn't sound ominous at all.

"I thought you said the cleaners only came out at night."

"Mostly. But magic calls to them, so let's try not to catch their attention."

I shuddered. My sword was called a soul-sucker, but in truth, it offered release. From the sounds I'd heard last night, the cleaners weren't so benevolent. We had to find Jacoby, and fast.

"Where to?" I asked.

"I can't say. First City has its own rules. You're the one who's supposed to have a connection to your friend. You must find him. But I suggest you do it before nightfall."

"And when will that be?" I didn't have a good grasp on the Nether's clock. Hours passed like days.

Grim's whiskers twitched. "When the light goes out."

"Helpful. Thanks."

We saw no one else as we moved down the road. The vacant windows felt like eyes watching us. The only sound was the grinding of sand against cobblestones under our feet and it seemed unnaturally loud. Princess's normal exuberance was dampened, and she walked quietly at my side.

Mason limped along in a dark mood. "This place makes my skin itch."

I peered through the window of a nearby structure. Inside, dust covered a long counter. Sand had piled against it. A few broken pots were visible on shelves lining one wall. They were also covered in dust. Shadows lurked in every corner. There were dozens of places for a small dervish to hide. And this was just one of hundreds of buildings. The enormity of our task hit me like a battering ram.

Overhead, the storm cloud spit out a jagged flash of lightning.

"Do you think we should split up?" I asked Mason.

"No. We really shouldn't." His eyes had gone dark and his right arm was stone. He expected an attack at any moment. But from what?

I really wanted my sword. I shook out my hands to keep myself from calling it back. I could feel it in my bones. Something was already watching us.

We move quickly up the cobbled road. I peeked into each house on the right. Mason checked those on the left. We covered two blocks like that until we came to a town square.

I glanced up the boulevard that wound around a small hill with a fortress at the center of the city. There was no way we could check all these buildings in a day.

"We need a better plan."

During our search, Princess had been jumping through open windows, chasing down the few rodents scurrying through the ruins and generally being a nuisance. She'd gotten over her initial hesitance and now thought we were out for a fun afternoon adventure.

"Princess, come!" The hound bounded from under a toppled cart where she'd cornered a rat-like thing. She was panting and dripping drool onto the cobblestones.

"Sit."

She collapsed onto her haunches and watched me, expecting a game. I could give her a game.

"Let's play hide and seek. You want to do that?"

She pranced and whined.

"Good girl. Now listen. Jacoby is hiding. Can you find him?"

Princess whined.

"Go on! Find Jacoby!"

Mason leaned against a stone wall, his arms crossed over his chest.

"You really think that will work?"

Princess watched me with her head cocked, waiting for instructions.

"Probably not."

Hell hounds didn't understand words. They understood magic. And she knew Jacoby. She'd lived with his comatose body in my apartment for days and traveled with him for miles in the Inbetween. So I filled my mind with images of Jacoby, his smell, the softness of his fur, and the feel of his magic. I wrapped all that up in a package and sent a pulse of command, "Princess, *finn!*" *Search!* She let out a woof and turned in a circle.

"Stop that!" Grim pounced on my foot. His teeth clamped on my boot.

"Hey!" I shook my leg to dislodge him.

Princess snuffled around as if looking for a scent. Then she raised her nose to the sky and let out a howl that would make a werewolf proud. It worked! With her nose to the ground, she followed Jacoby's magic signature.

Mason and I trailed after her. Grim darted back and forth, paws bouncing him off the sides of stone buildings.

A long, low wail came down the road with a rush of wind that pulled at my hair and whipped the sand up from the cobblestones.

"Oh, no, no, no!" Grim froze, fur standing on end. His tail pointed straight for the sky.

A strong gust of wind knocked me into a wall. A wail followed—a chasmic reverberation, stretching, stretching, *stretching*…and rising to tear away all reason.

"Run!" Grim shot forward and turned at the next intersection. Princess took off after him, barking like mad. My head rung from colliding with the wall. Mason grabbed my hand and pulled me after the others. My feet seemed to belong to someone else, and I tripped over the cobblestones. Only Mason's firm grip kept me from sprawling on my face. As we turned the corner, I glanced backward.

Something black hovered on the road. Taller than the first story windows, the cleaner wore shadows like a ragged cloak. They flapped about a face that was hidden under the dark hood and marked only by yellow glowing eyes. It raised a skeletal hand and pointed at us. The rest of its arm was lost in a black sleeve that morphed and misted like smoke.

I skidded around the corner. The creature let out another of those lacerating wails.

My sword appeared, reacting to my fear. I dropped it like it was made of burning embers and it disappeared.

I ran.

"In here." Mason ducked into an alley that led between two buildings. Grim pranced impatiently in front of a wooden door. It was closed, but several of the boards had been torn away, leaving a hole big enough to crawl through. Grim went first. Mason followed and then me. Princess stood in the alley, four legs braced to spring. Her lip curled and she let out a deep growl.

"Princess, no!" I whisper-shouted. She wasn't listening. Hell hound attack mode had taken over. I reached through the door and grabbed a fistful of her ruff. "Come!" The hound whined as I pulled her away, but she tucked her tail and scooted through the door to crouch at my heel.

We were in some kind of storeroom. Shelves lined the walls. A few held old empty crates and amphora-like pottery. The air was stale and dusty. I held back a sneeze. With my hand on Princess's back, I could feel her bristling with the need to attack.

"Now what?" I asked.

Grim bonked his head against my leg. "Make yourself small," he whispered.

I keened a sudden absence beside me, like Grim had disappeared.

The cleaner's wail filled the surrounding darkness. It grew as the creature advanced down the boulevard. Just like Princess tracked Jacoby by his magic signature, the cleaner was tracking us.

Beside me, Mason sat with his eyes closed. He felt light years distant instead of only a few inches away. I sucked in my magic and tried to mimic the earthy magic around me. I'd been learning to reel in my magic in this way, mostly to blend into the environment when I was on the job hunting pests. Before now, I'd only managed to harmonize with natural environments and the green magic of plants, grasses and trees. I had none of that in this bare cellar. Still, I wrapped my protection around myself and extended it to cover Princess, hoping against all rational hope that it would fool the cleaner.

Seconds passed. Minutes.

We huddled in the dark as the cleaner's wail crescendoed. It paused at the head of the alley. Wind blew bits of debris in through the broken door. Then the wail dimmed as the creature moved off.

Still, we waited. My legs cramped under me.

Mason rose, grabbed Grim, and pinned him to the wall.

"Is there anything else you want to tell us about this place, cat? Are there bugs that will eat our eyeballs? Quicksand to swallow us whole?" He shook the grimalkin. Grim hissed and chomped down on his wrist, not hard enough to break the skin, but hard enough to show he meant business. Mason let him drop to the ground. Grim shook out his fur.

"Just the cleaners. And I told you not to use your magic. It attracts them."

"He's right." I rubbed a hand over my eyes and dug fingers into the pulse at my temples. "I should have listened. What are those things, anyway?"

"The Stewards keep them around to clear out the…ah, spiritual debris. There's usually only a few of them because they're very territorial."

"I get that. But what are they exactly?"

"Lost souls. Really old and powerful souls."

My stomach churned. That's what would become of Jacoby if we didn't find him. He'd either be eaten by one of those demented cleaners or he'd turn into one.

"Is it safe to keep moving?" I asked.

Grim's big green eyes shone in the dim light. "It's never safe in First City."

While we crouched in the dark, the storm intensified. Rain spattered the ground in the alley. Water leaked through the broken door into the storeroom. But in minutes the downpour eased up, leaving puddles and mist behind.

"Wait here." Mason squeezed through the door. I poked my head out and watched him splash up the alley. He paused at the main thoroughfare with his back pressed against the wall. Slowly he peered around the corner, waited a breath, and ran back to us.

"Coast is clear. But I suggest we move fast. Can that hound really find Jacoby?"

Princess's ears perked up. She darted through the door and pressed her nose to the ground. She was tracking magic, not scent, so I hoped the rain hadn't washed the trail away. With a soft woof, she picked it up and dashed down the alley.

I clamped down on the shout that almost burst from my throat when she disappeared around the corner. Grim ambled after her, unconcerned that the hound might get lost or run into another one of those cleaners. I ran. The cobbled road was slippery, and I skidded onto the main boulevard, twisting one knee painfully.

Far ahead, Princess ran in circles, whining.

"I'm coming, I'm coming." I worked out my injured knee on the run. With his limp, Mason couldn't run full tilt. He caught up as I stood at the entrance of a marketplace.

"What is it?" His breath came shallow heaves.

"I don't know."

Princess danced around whining. Grim leaped onto a barrel, then to a stack of crates.

Under the weight of the storm cloud, the square was shrouded in shadow. Lighting crackled, illuminating the scene in stark relief before plunging it back into gloom.

I took a few hesitant steps forward. Three-story buildings bracketed every side of the quad. Their crumbling facades were impressive, and the architecture hinted at a government, religious or business sector, definitely a main hub of the city. The square itself was laid out with walkways leading from the center like spokes on a wheel. Each walkway was littered with old carts, crates, barrels, broken tables and smashed pottery—remnants of a once busy market.

Princess danced with impatience at the far end of the square. We wove through the debris to find her standing over an unbroken amphora—an urn with a spike on the bottom to drive it into the ground. Like the Greek amphorae I'd seen in history books, this one had faces carved on it too, but none I recognized.

I looked back at the facade of the largest building that dominated the square. Something was etched into the gray stone above the massive double doors. Time and the relentless sand sheering off the desert had scrubbed much of the carving away, but yes, I could see them now. The gods watching from on high. Except they weren't the same faces I'd seen in the forest and on the boat figureheads. These were other gods, lost to time and memory.

And now the cleaners made sense. Prayer is a powerful form of magic. Only gods had the skills to harness it properly. The Stewards didn't want pilgrims coming to First City and wasting their prayers on dead gods. They needed those tributes for themselves.

Looking at the stern faces on the carvings, I wondered what they had done—what unbelievable and destructive magics they had unleashed—to shift their entire world out of phase. And how close had the humans of Terra come to making the same disastrous mistake during our Flood Wars?

I shivered. Maybe the Stewards were right. These old gods didn't deserve the honor of prayers.

Princess pawed at the ground beside the amphora. She nudged it with her nose.

"What is it?" Mason asked.

"I don't know." The urn was half hidden under a more broken pottery. I rolled it into the open, surprised that it was intact. Standing up, it would have been as tall as my knee, but it lay on its side, the spike at its foot only a broken stub. One of the handles was also missing, leaving a jagged shard of pottery in its place.

Princess sat beside the urn. Her face was full of expectant energy. If she were a bomb-sniffing dog, I'd have said she found her target.

"That's too small for Jacoby to hide in," I said.

She let out one sharp bark that sent some critter scurrying from under the rubble. The hound didn't even give chase. Her whole being was focused on the urn.

"Fine." I grabbed the remaining handle and propped the jar upright. The opening was about as wide as my palm, but the neck narrowed before it flared out again. I peered inside, hoping that a snake or a scorpion didn't jump out to bite me on the nose. It felt like looking down the barrel of a rifle.

"Can you see anything?" Mason asked.

"I don't know. The neck is too narrow. Hard to see the bottom. Hold it for me."

Mason took the amphora in two hands.

So far nothing had burst from it, so I risked a closer look. Something *was* in there.

"Tilt it a bit that way, toward the light."

I pressed my face to the opening.

Eyes peered at me from the bottom of the urn. Two big eyes framed in a ruff of curly gray fur.

"By the One-eyed Father!" I reached into the urn, but my hand stuck in the narrow neck. I yanked it back. "Break it! Break it now!"

Mason stared at me, confused by my outburst, so I grabbed a stone and smashed the head off the urn, not caring that I was destroying an artifact of immeasurable age.

There, inside the belly of the urn, sat Jacoby, no bigger than my fist and curled into a ball.

He jerked upright, blinking in the sudden light.

"Kyra-lady?" A small, tinny voice cracked like it hadn't been used it in a long time.

"Yes, Jacoby. It's me. We found you!" I scooped him up. He was so small! Jacoby, who had once stood nearly three-feet tall, now fit in my palm.

I tried to raise him to my eye, but his legs were unsteady and the motion knocked him down. I set him on a crate and crouched at his level.

He was too thin, dirt matted his fur, and he quivered like a newborn foal. I petted him with my thumb, making soft comforting noises. He clutched my finger in both hands. Huge eyes peered up at me.

"I told you we would find you," I cooed.

His little lip quivered. "I was so lost. Nobody cames. I thoughts I be's alone forever."

"I would have come sooner, but I didn't know how to find you. I'm here now. We're going to take you home." My heart felt too big for my chest.

"Home?" His eyes glistened and the fringe of fur around them perked up. He threw both arms around my finger, hugging it to him.

And he grew. One minute, he was two inches tall. The next, he was expanding, stretching, and growing, until a full-sized dervish sat before me.

He jumped off the crate and whooped. Princess got in on the act and bounded to his side, barking and wagging her tail.

I turned to Grim. "What in the hells?"

"In the Nether, you are as you see yourself." He sniffed with his nose in the air. "I believe I explained this already."

Before I could answer him, a blue slug slunk from the remains of the amphora and floundered toward Jacoby. The dervish windmilled his arms and jumped backward with a yelp.

"No! Don't lets it touch me!" He teleported a few feet away. The ki ported with him. Jacoby scrambled backward, but the little blue stone homed in on him no matter where he turned. Princess barked and chased him. Jacoby finally plunked down on the ground. He kicked his legs out in front of him and the slug rubbed up against the bottom of his foot, content to have contact.

Jacoby glared at it.

"Disgustings! I runs and hides, but it finds me. Always."

179

"It's okay." I sat beside him. "It's your ki. It likes you."

Jacoby squinted at the slug. Then his eyes opened wide. "My ki?"

"Like your soul," Mason said. "It needs to be close to you. You should eat it. That way it will be safe."

Jacoby wrinkled his nose. "Gargoyle makes fun."

"No, he's telling the truth. Look. I have one too." I pulled my little jeweled worm from the pocket of my shirt. It was a little bigger than Jacoby's and sat like a ball of warm gelatin in my hand.

"And you eats it?" His eyes were baseball wide.

"Well, yes. Mason ate his. And so did Princess. Grim here says it's the best way to keep it safe."

Jacoby scrunched his nose and squinted at me. "But Kyra-lady not eats it."

"Not yet. But I'm keeping it close."

"I keeps mine close too." Jacoby grabbed his ki in his fist, putting aside his disgust in that whimsical way he had. Princess egged him into a game of chase and they ran through the market.

I stared at the wriggling thing in my hand. I couldn't do it. I couldn't swallow my own soul. Mason watched me with an expression somewhere between amusement and patience.

"You're going to have to get over that soon," he said. "I don't think it would be a good idea to go home with your soul riding sidecar."

"I know." I would do it. Just not right now. I tucked the ki back into my pocket.

The trilling moan of a cleaner echoed from somewhere outside the market.

"We need to go," Grim said. "Before the sun sets." He jumped down from the crate and turned in circles.

"Wait! We found Jacoby. You said our door would appear as soon as we accomplished our task."

The cleaner trilled louder.

"We need to go now!" Grim dashed off, jumping lightly over the market debris.

"When I catch that cat, I'm going to wring his neck," I said. Then I followed him back into the maze of streets.

The cleaners were active in the fading light. And we weren't the only souls lost in the city. As we slunk along the shadows, a scream echoed through the cobbled alleys. No telling which direction it came from, but someone had fallen to the Stewards' custodian monsters.

We huddled against a rock wall. Grim's tail lashed the ground as he peered into the gloom ahead of us. Behind him, Jacoby crouched in a ball, trying to make himself small again. Princess pressed to my side, and I could feel her trembling against my leg. And Mason had my back, like always.

We moved like some many-legged beast, dashing to one corner, stopping until Grim checked it out, then creeping to the next until we made it back to the courtyard in front of the city gates. It was a fifty meter dash across open ground.

"We don't have much time," Grim said. "The gates will close soon." His ears were twitching in all directions.

We scrambled forward, but the gates had already started their lumbering path to closing. Halfway across the courtyard, Mason's bad leg gave out on. I caught him as he crumpled.

"Go without me!" he shouted.

As if I would.

I propped my shoulder under his arm and dragged him forward. He grumbled about my stubbornness. We were a dozen paces away when the gates closed with a bang. The echo was like the lid slamming shut on our tomb.

I leaned Mason against the gate, and he slid to the ground. Jacoby hopped from foot to foot and Princess stared into the darkness, a low growl rumbling from her chest.

"Now what?" I whispered to Grim.

"We fly."

I glanced up. The wall around the city was easily three-stories high. Lightning shot from the petulant cloud and seized a nearby tower. It wouldn't be an easy flight, but we had no other choice.

"Jacoby, do you have wings?" I asked.

The little dervish cocked his head. "Wings?"

"Like these." I willed my wings to appear and they stretched behind me, strong and supple.

Jacoby twisted his neck to peer at his back and fell over trying.

"No wings." He pouted.

"Then you port outside the gates. Can you do that?"

He stuck a finger in his ear and scratched. "Yes."

"Good. Do it now. Wait for us out there. We'll be coming over the wall."

He disappeared.

As soon as she'd seen my wings, Princess manifested her own, and she now hovered above us. Grim also stood ready with his silvery wings spread wide.

"Take Princess and go," I said to him. "We'll be right behind you."

Grim gave a big, put-upon sigh. "Come on, you stupid hound. Let's go."

I reached out to help Mason stand. "Can you make it?"

He snarled at me, but grabbed my hand and pulled himself up. I let him have his mood because his breathing was ragged and sweat dripped down his face. He balanced on his good leg, lips pressed into a thin line.

"What's the matter?" I asked.

"Can't…my wings. I can't retrieve them…too much pain." He panted through those last words, then tried again. Pearly white wings burst from his back. His smile was a little wobbly, but I could see he was relieved.

"Good. Let's go."

A trilling, clicking sound made me turn.

The cleaner raced across the courtyard, black cloak flapping.

"Kyra, Move!"

I couldn't. It was too big. Too fast.

I registered Mason's words on some level, and my prey-brain, the one that also shouted for me to get the hells out of there, agreed. But my sword appeared in my hand and I raised it.

The cleaner moved insanely fast. His feet barely skimmed the cobblestones. Was it alive? Human? Ghost?

Ten paces away. Clawed arm raised. Eight paces. The black hood fell back, revealing a ghoulish face, large eyes, flat nose. Six paces. Desiccated lips drew back from a full mouth of razor teeth with incisors as long as my little finger. Two paces.

Duck!

A clawed hand ripped through the air where my head had been. I rolled, hit bony legs and slashed wildly with my blade. The cleaner fell over me and landed on Mason, who screamed in pain or rage. I scrambled from under the creature's feet and lanced my sword downward into his leg. He hissed and twisted, trying to claw my face.

I pounded the pommel of my sword, driving it deeper into his leg, pinning it like a bug to a specimen board. Blood leaked from the wound and I grinned.

Critter wrangler rule number eleven. If it could bleed, it could die.

Mason hammered the cleaner with his stone arm, catching it on the shoulder. The beast turned his attention to this new threat. I wrenched my blade free and swung it like I was batting for home. His head flew off his shoulders in a spray of blood and landed with a sick splat. It rolled to a stop against a rock.

The body toppled, crushing Mason against the cobblestones.

"*Osti de tabarnak de sacrament, de câlice de criss de merde...*" Curses poured out of Mason. I pulled the cleaner off him and he rose on unsteady legs, shaking dust from his hair and eyes.

"Thanks." He didn't look thankful. His arm was still stone, as if he waited for the next attack. He'd already made it clear he didn't like me putting myself in danger to save him. We'd have words about the fact that I protected him from the cleaner instead of flying away.

Later, I thought.

I took a deep, steadying breath. "Ready?"

His eyes scanned the shadows, but he nodded.

We flew over the gates and fell onto the sand. Princess barked, and Jacoby hopped around us. I rose and hugged them. We needed a moment to catch our breath. What I really wanted was shelter and a few hours of sleep, but those would have to wait. We were too close to ending this madness.

"What now?" I asked the grimalkin. He sat on a broken cart bed, in that perfect cat pose, upright with ears perked and tail curling around his toes.

"What do you mean?"

"You said my door would appear when I needed it."

"No." He licked his paw and washed behind one ear. "I said your door would appear when you'd done what you came to do."

"Right. Job completed, remember?" I pointed at Jacoby. "Do I need to fill out a customer survey or something?" I was tired, bruised, hungry and generally pissed. I'd had enough of the Nether and its fun and games.

"Come on, Grim. Why can't I go home? I did what I came here to do."

"Did you?"

Tiny muscles in my fingers went rigid as I imagined choking him. The cat watched me with his calm gaze.

"Fine. What's next on the agenda?"

"I suggest we return to your anchor. You may find your answers there."

"My anchor? You mean my father's tree?"

"Precisely."

That was days away! Even if we flew directly there, we'd still have to face the harpies, the unbearable heat and whatever charms this world-that-wasn't-a-world had to offer along the way.

Grim had moved on to washing his feet now, completely oblivious to the rage building in me.

Mason pulled me aside.

"Hey, have some water and cool down." He dipped a cup into the fountain and handed it to me. My hand shook as I took it.

"I can't."

"You can't what?"

"I can't do this anymore. I can't fly, float or run. I can't make that journey back again. We came so far. We did it. Now I want to go home. It's not fair."

I threw the cup on the ground. Water splashed over my feet. I knew I sounded like a child and I couldn't help it.

Mason put two hands on my shoulders. "It's going to be okay. We got this far together. We'll get home together."

I nodded but wouldn't look him in the eye, not until he tipped my chin up, forcing me to meet his gaze. And what did I see there? Confidence. Not in himself. Confidence in me. His gaze polished away my rough edges and left only the best parts of me.

I smiled a shaky smile, and he leaned in to kiss me.

"Mmm, salty," he said with a grin.

I kissed him back, letting my lips brush over his stubbled cheek.

"Mmm, bristly."

He leaned his forehead against mine.

"As soon as we get home, I'm taking a long hot shower."

"I'll scrub your back if you'll scrub mine."

"Deal."

I took a deep breath and turned back to Grim.

"Okay, I'm ready. Let's go find our tree. We're flying?"

"Not exactly." Grim's whiskers twitched. He jumped down from his perch and trotted around all four of us. His tail whispered against my shins, across Jacoby's chest, around Princess and Mason. With each touch, I keened magic building, encircling us like a wand doused in fairy dust.

And then he teleported us away.

CHAPTER

32

f I never had to be teleported again, it would be too soon. I landed with a thump on grass and staggered to all fours to heave out my insides. With the entire contents of my stomach—which thankfully wasn't much—laid out on the grass, I rolled onto my back and stared at the blue-green sky. My eyeballs were sweating.

"You okay?" Mason's shadow fell over me. He reached out a hand, and I pulled myself up.

"Yeah, you?" My stomach settled into a low grumble.

"Not my favorite mode of transport." He rubbed the back of his neck and flexed his shoulders like he'd just woken from a long sleep. "But it's better than flying for hours."

"Well, that was bracing." Grim's fur was standing on end. He twitched his back and tail to settle it.

"I thought you said that teleporting was against the rules?" I said.

"It is. But since I'm already going to hang for breaking the rules, I decided we should take the direct route. It's not an exact science, but look."

I glanced into the sun. Princess and Jacoby were chasing each other on the grassy plain. They seemed unaffected by teleportation. My father's tree loomed behind them in the distance. As far as the eye could see in every direction, the landscape was flat and bare, carpeted with that scrubby grass.

We started walking.

The tree was farther than it looked. I worried that Mason wouldn't make it, but he limped along, his eyes fixed doggedly ahead.

There was no door waiting for us in the tree trunk.

"Now what?" I stood with hands on my hips, staring into the oak's branches.

"You know what you need to do." Grim found a patch of fading sunlight and curled into a ball. He watched me with sleepy eyes. His tail tapped the ground lightly.

"I don't."

Mason took my hand. "I think Grim is suggesting you have some unfinished business with your father."

I snatched my hand from his grip.

"Unfinished business? Like asking him why he left me and my mother? I don't care. I haven't cared about that in years. Or do you think I need to forgive him? That's so cliché." I crossed my arms over my chest and hugged myself. "And besides. There's nothing to forgive. Because I don't care. Remember?"

Mason listened to my epic ramble with one cocked eyebrow.

"Okay. No forgiving. Maybe you just need to talk to him."

I gave him a black look. He held out his hands, like trying to tame a feral animal.

"It's worth a try. Unless you want to find another door out of here."

I glanced at Grim, who was pretending to sleep in the sun. Finding another door meant going back down that river. And even then, we had no guarantee that the door would lead back to Terra.

I paced a few steps away from them all. I needed to think.

Something bumped against my knee. I looked down at Grim's fluffy face.

"You really think this is necessary?" I asked.

"I do."

"How do I know you aren't stalling so you don't have to face the Tribunal?"

Grim sat on his haunches and sighed. "You don't. But I promise I'm not afraid of the Tribunal. I've been a guide for so long, I don't even remember my life before. And you might have noticed that the Nether is rather dull." He turned to look out at the endless gray-green plains. "I'm ready for something new."

"The Tribunal will kill you. You said it yourself."

He looked back at me over one shoulder. He was grinning. "Dying would be something."

By the One-eyed Father, I didn't want his death on my conscience. I didn't want to speak to my DNA donor either, but it seemed I wouldn't get my way with either of those things.

Grim bumped his head against my leg again.

"I'll come with you. It will be my last task as guide, to record your meeting with the dryad Life Tree."

My resistance crumpled. I could do this. I could face the father who abandoned me like day-old leftovers and talk to him about my feelings. Then I could go home and leave Grim to his fate. Easy peasy.

"You'll really come with me?" My voice sounded as meek as a small child left out in the rain.

Grim lifted his chin. "Speaking to a Life Tree is a great honor. I will bear witness and record the events for posterity."

"I'm going too." Mason limped between me and the grimalkin.

"You won't." Grim thudded his tail. His eyes were sleepy, but I wasn't fooled. This was Grim's try-me-and-you'll-feel-my-teeth look.

I took Mason's hand and pulled him aside. "It's okay. I can do this on my own."

He crossed his arms and stared me down. "We've had this conversation before. Just because you can, doesn't mean you should."

"I know. But this time, I really should. I need to face my father alone. Please understand. I…." Words failed me. It wasn't that I didn't want to share my innermost feelings with Mason. I just didn't know what those feelings were yet. Was I angry at my father? Scared to disappoint him? Worried that he'd turn away from me? Until I knew, I wanted to face him without other emotions muddying the playing field. And Mason definitely came with his own kit of emotions.

He searched my face and somehow saw what I couldn't put into words. He nodded and lifted my hand to his lips.

"Be safe."

I SAT ON the grass in front of the tree. The sun had set, leaving only a faint glow on the horizon. I laid my palms flat on the ground. The prickly grass did nothing to calm my jitters.

Grim marched around me, muttering in a language I didn't understand. I keened magic building in him like a charge of static. Jacoby and Princess had worn themselves out and sat beside Mason a few feet away.

Finally, Grim stopped pacing and stood before me. Since I was sitting, his eyes were level with mine. The hair on his back stuck up like quills.

"You may touch me," he said, like he was offering a benediction.

I reached out and paused. "You sure?"

He sighed and settled his fur down.

"Of course. It is necessary."

I placed my hand on his back, just above his lashing tail. A shudder rippled up his spine. He turned and snapped at my fingers.

"Not there. Here." He ducked his head under my hand. "Now don't move."

I resisted the urge to dig my fingers into his fur and rested them lightly behind his ears.

Grim closed his eyes. I felt his muscles tighten. No, that was wrong. It was more like a side-to-side shake, impossibly fast, like a video screen that flicks out of phase for an instant.

It passed, and I was again sitting under my father's tree.

But everything was different again.

I stood up and examined the tree. It was bigger, the leaves more vibrantly green. A bright sun dappled through the branches. A light wind tossed the leaves, and they glinted with gold highlights. The effect was dazzling, like the stars shining bright enough to be seen in daylight.

Mason and the others were there, but they seemed far away, and nearly lost in a ball of darkness. It was night in the Nether. I saw myself sitting next to Grim, my hand resting on his head. We were as still as stone carvings. Mason paced around us. His hands were fisted, and he looked like he was hanging onto his composure by a thread. Princess matched him pace for pace, and Jacoby bounced along beside them. They were all eerily silent and flickering, like an old movie from a rundown projector.

I ran to Mason and grabbed for his hand. My fingers went right through it like he was a ghost.

Or maybe I was the ghost.

I turned in a circle.

Not too far away, another version of myself sat cross-legged on the ground with Jacoby cradled in my lap. Princess and Mason crouched beside me. We looked like hollow-eyed revenants who had lost their way. That was me, back in my own time and space.

And here I was, a third version of myself. I looked down at my feet. They were wrapped in thin white roots.

So I was in my father's world.

I tried a hesitant step. The roots didn't keep me in place, but moved with me.

A small sound like the clearing of a throat made me turn. Grim stood in the dappled sunlight filtering through the oak's canopy. He was bigger here, and his silver coat gleamed like it was made of crushed diamonds.

"Where are we?" I asked.

Grim scratched his ear with his hind leg.

"We're still in the Nether. And on Terra. And in your father's world. The Life Tree acts as a kind of nexus. You're seeing the three worlds where you exist right now. We're in the place they overlap."

Three worlds. Three Kyras. How many times could a soul be split before it crumbled into nothing?

I suddenly felt like an over-stretched balloon ready to pop. I gulped in air and let it out in a panicky exhale.

"Take it easy," Grim said.

"That's easy for you to say. Your soul hasn't been bisected like some organ under a microscope. And, hey! Why aren't you on two planes as well?"

It was true. The cat didn't exist on the other plane with Mason and the others.

Grim lowered his eyes and whispered, "Because I have no soul. No ties to any world. The Stewards took those away when I became a guide."

"At least you're not in manacles." I lifted my foot to show him the roots wrapping around my ankle. No matter how I moved, they clung to me but never hindered me.

"You asked the Life Tree to be your anchor. And just as your father anchored you, you have anchored the others."

I followed where he pointed. He was right. More hair-thin threads intertwined with the roots around my ankle. These were golden and more like vines than roots. I bent down to hold one in my hand. Immediately, I felt Princess's wet tongue slide up the side of my face and heard her distant, "Aroo?"

I dropped her vine and picked up the second. It buzzed like an over-active bumblebee, and it was hot enough to burn my fingers. Definitely Jacoby. I dropped it and reached for the last vine.

A ripple of love-worry-yearning stroked me. That one was Mason. I held onto it a little longer. I could smell his distinct scent—male heat and hot stone—as if his hands had left it on my skin and hair. Reluctantly, I put down his vine.

Those ties weren't chains. They were bonds that stretched into another world. They would never snap. And they were with me all the time. In my world, they would be invisible, but that didn't make them any less strong. In the Nether and on Terra, my family might not feel them, but I would always know they were there.

"I understand." My father's anchor was the same bond of family, even if I had never acknowledged it.

I turned back to his tree. The sun glinted through the branches, making it difficult to see it clearly. I squinted up at the leaves that shifted and whispered against each other in the constant breeze. My hair had come loose from my braid and blew into my eyes. To keep my fingers busy, I re-braided it while I considered my options. Was my father here, hiding somewhere in the tree? Was *he* the tree? Or was he some vague and alien presence that I would never be able to relate to?

"You should say something," Grim said. "Let him know you're here. Life Trees can be hard of hearing, but that's only because they spend so much time listening to the universe, it can be difficult to focus on one voice."

I looked up at the tree.

"Hello, Timberfoot." I felt stupid talking to a tree.

Grim head-butted me again. "Keep going." He stepped a few paces away to give me some privacy.

I tried again.

"I thought maybe we could talk before I go home. Grim seems to think… well, he's my guide here, and he says that in this space between worlds we might be able to meet. That is, if you want to."

I held my breath.

The leaves rustled, and I looked up into the branches, expecting…what? A great looming godlike face? But this wasn't The Wizard of Oz. And I certainly wasn't Dorothy.

A man sat on the first solid branch of the great oak. His legs dangled in the air. He jumped lightly to the earth, lighter than a man of his size should. He was much taller than me, and I had to look up to meet his gaze. Way up. The sun shone through the leaves behind him, forcing me to squint. I couldn't see him in the glare, and I got only an impression of solidness. And redness. He wore a red tunic over brown pants. His hair was red gold and curled in crazy waves. A darker, russet beard covered ruddy cheeks and chin.

His voice rumbled like thunder. "Hello, Daughter."

CHAPTER

33

I didn't know what to say. Should I call him Dad? Father? Sir? I had given up the childish need for a father long ago. When I moved to Asgard, Baldyr filled that role, and I stopped looking back at those early years when I'd felt abandoned by this stranger. A stranger who now stood before me with a half grin plastered on his face, expecting some response from me.

And all I could think was—why was he so tall?

I clasped my hands together, feeling the soft bones and dimpled knuckles of a child. Those hands ran up my stomach, across my flat chest and then to the pigtails bobbing beside my cheeks.

He wasn't tall. I was small.

Grim's words came back to me. In the Nether, you appeared as you wanted to be. And for some unknowable, inner-soul reason, I wanted to be a little girl.

"I am glad you came." His voice boomed. I clapped my hands over my ears.

"Can you not do that?"

He smiled and held out both giant hands. "I usually only speak to the spirits and the stars. They are very far away."

"I can hear you just fine."

He arched one russet eyebrow at my tone.

"I'm sorry." I softened my tone. "I just don't understand why I needed to come here."

"You did not want to come?"

"Not really. Right about now, I should be heading home with them." I pointed to the ghostly figures of Mason, Princess, and Jacoby, who waited for me beyond whatever barrier separated my father's world from theirs.

"And yet, you are here. There must be a reason." He stood watching me with an enigmatic look on his face. I couldn't decide if he was smirking or smiling. Every time I tried to look him in the eye, the sun poked through the tree branches behind him and blinded me.

In the unsettling, unquestionable way that dreamscapes change, we suddenly shifted to a clearing in an oak grove. Timberfoot stood by a table in the center of the clearing. He was lit from above, though I saw no light source, and he was trimming a bonsai tree. The *snick-snick* of his clippers was too loud in the quiet.

I was barely tall enough to see over the surface of the table.

"Do you live here?" I turned in a circle to inspect the grove. The trees made a barrier as dense as a wall and their leaves met overhead in a high ceiling. It had the homey feel of a den.

Snick-snick. A tiny leaf fell on the table. Timberfoot looked at me and smiled. "It is where I am."

Right. This was going to be one of those conversations.

"Do you know why I'm here?"

Snick-snick. Another leaf fell.

"Yes." He studied the bonsai. The trunk bent like it had been blown over in a strong wind and held there. It was some sort of fruit tree with tiny red berries clustered in the glossy leaves. He turned its pot in a circle, examining it from all angles.

"I want to go home," I said.

"So go." He didn't look at me, but continued to turn his bonsai. Turn and snip. Turn and snip.

"I can't. Not until…"

Not until what? What did I want from this man? So many things. And nothing. As a child, I had wanted him to come to my school plays. Wanted him to drive a sedan like other dads and come home for dinner, grumpy and tired from a day at the office. Later, I wanted him to show up in the emergency room the first time Mom collapsed, to take the responsibility of making her better from my shoulders.

No. That wasn't entirely true. I liked the responsibility. The nurses and doctors always told Mom how lucky she was to have such a mature, caring daughter. At home, I'd hear their praises in my head as I swept the kitchen, did the laundry. Let Mom sleep. Made sure she didn't work too hard. Never abandoned her.

Abandon.

How many lost, hurt and sick creatures had I taken in over the years? How many of those were salves for my own feelings of abandonment?

I understood all of this in the moment it took Timberfoot to snip another leaf from his tiny tree.

Snick-snick.

The sound scraped away the last scab over those old wounds.

"All right, I admit it!" The words burst from me. "I hated you for leaving me. And Mom. She refused to talk about you. At night, I would hear her crying sometimes. And then she got sick, and I was alone to take care of her. I was ten." My voice cracked and my chest tightened. "I was alone because you weren't there! How could you leave us? What was it? You found a better offer? I know about you and Queen Leighna. Were we not royal enough for you?"

My tiny hands pummeled his thigh until he caught them both in one of his. Tears and snot ran down my face as the dam of my pent-up feelings finally broke.

"My child." He sat on the ground and pulled me into his lap, wrapping his arms around me, rocking until my sobbing storm blew itself out.

"I did not leave you willingly. Look." He waved his hand and a dark spot shimmered in the air before us. It turned mirror-like, first reflecting the red-bearded dryad holding a tiny girl on his lap. That image faded, replaced by a dim room with walls of stone. A man slumped against the wall, legs splayed across the floor and hands covering his face.

"What is this?" I asked, hiccuping as I caught my breath. He held me tighter. Tension rippled through his arms.

"Watch."

Seconds went by. The clang of a metal latch rang out. The man rubbed his eyes and looked up. It was Timberfoot's face, younger and less imposing. His hair and beard were longer, tangled and dirty from neglect. His clothes were filthy, bloody rags. He rose and moved across the room. It was a cell.

Another figure opened the door. I recognized him and jerked backward, coming up against my father's hard shoulder. It was Esot, the oread who'd kidnapped me and brought me to Underhill as a prize for the upstart fae prince.

"It's all right," Timberfoot said. "But you must watch." His big hand covered my tiny ones to still their trembling.

"Time to play," the oread in the vision grinned. Light from a sconce on the wall outside the cell caught his face, and I realized it wasn't my kidnapper. This oread had a broader forehead and a flatter nose. The woody protrusions that crowned his head were more pronounced, but they were from the same tribe.

He grabbed Timberfoot by the arm and dragged him down a long, dimly lit and smoky hallway.

"They tortured me for years, not because they had to. Because they wanted to." Timberfoot narrated the scene. I wanted to look away, but the images consumed me.

Timberfoot tied to a rack, arms and legs splayed, head dangling like a dead man. Timberfoot being whipped. Timberfoot kneeling before a throne, his hands bound behind him. A line of oreads took turns kicking him until he toppled lifeless to the floor. Timberfoot lying on a stone alter while a blazing brand was pressed against his thigh.

Timberfoot screaming.

"Stop it!" I turned away from the sight and buried my tear-stained face against his chest.

"I do not wish to scare you, little one. But you must know that I did not stay away willingly."

I looked up at him through watery eyes. "Why? Why would they do that?"

His lips set in a grim line. "Because oreads are a bloodthirsty tribe. They invaded our lands, killed our people. But we dryads don't believe in war, so my mother sent me to treat with them, to make a deal that would bring peace. Instead, they took me hostage, hoping to force my people to give in to their demands."

"Lisobet would never do that." I knew Grandmother well enough. She wouldn't give in to terrorists, not even for the sake of her son.

"No. She would not. And so I was their prisoner for years. You were only a day old, when I got the urgent call. I would not have left you. But my people…they were being slaughtered by the hundreds. I could not abandon them."

He waved his hand again, and the horrible images of torture melted away.

"How did you endure that?" My voice was so small, like I was asking Dad to scare away the monsters under my bed. Only these monsters hadn't come for me. They'd come for him. They'd taken him from me before I was old enough to see his face.

"I endured so you would not grow up without a father. I knew that if I could stay alive, I would get back to you."

"How long?"

"I don't know. Years."

"But you got away. You must have. The stories…about you and Leighna and Underhill."

"She told you."

"Yes." I craned my neck to see his eyes—to read the emotion the fae queen's name invoked—but the sun still blinded me.

He was quiet for a long moment, perhaps deciding how much he wanted to tell his daughter.

"I woke one morning, expecting to find my usual bowl of gruel for breakfast. Instead, I found the door to my cell open. The fort was abandoned, and all the oreads were gone. At the time, I thought my mother had finally beaten them back and I would find dryads waiting for me in the forest." He shook his head. "I found only destruction. A war I hadn't even known was coming had consumed the world."

"The Flood Wars."

"Yes. The world was on fire. Even so, I tried to find you and your mother, but you were gone without a trace."

"Mother was sick. We were in Asgard by then."

I felt a hot splash on my cheek. He was crying.

"Natalia was my first love, and I never forgot her. Nor you." He gripped my hands in his. My fully grown hands. Sometime, during his telling, I had grown to my adult size. Suddenly, I felt foolish sitting in his lap, but I didn't want to move. Circled by his arms, I was safe and surrounded by love.

"I am also sorry that you were alone for so long while your mother was ill. I should have been there. I should have taken care of you both."

"Thank you for telling me." I felt wrung out, like my lungs had been stomped on until I couldn't take another breath.

My father rocked me and we each remembered times that were better forgotten.

"Why did I never know any of this? Why didn't Lisobet get word to my mother?"

"I do not know. That is a question for Lisobet to answer."

Oh, she would. When I got back, I'd have some choice words for my grandmother.

I wiped my eyes on my sleeve and stood up. My father followed me. It was easier to think of him like that now. My father. Maybe he'd never be Dad or Daddy, but at least the cavity that had been festering in my spirit all these years was now filled.

"Thank you for agreeing to be my anchor while I looked for my friend."

"I am honored that you asked." He bowed his head. "And thank you for this." His finger lifted the chain around his neck. Leighna's pendant dangled from it.

"She was a good friend. And she loved you very much."

His lips dipped into a frown. "She is gone, then?"

"Yes. She died trying to protect the city she loved."

He nodded. Then his far-away gaze turned back to me.

"I have a gift for you too." Like a magician plucking a coin from behind my ear, he produced a golden acorn and dropped it into my hand. It was smooth and buzzing with potential energy like a wind-up toy ready to be released. "For your daughter."

"My what?"

But he only smiled and put his two great hands on my cheeks. His gaze peered right inside me. This time, the sunlight didn't blind me, and I stared into the same blue speckled eyes that I saw in the mirror every morning.

"Stay safe." He kissed my forehead.

Then the sun sparkled behind him again. I shut my eyes against the brightness and when I opened them, he was gone.

I turned to Grim, who was sitting in the great tree's shadow.

"I'm ready to go back now," I said.

Grim nodded. He stood and trotted over to tuck his head under my hand. I keened the magic building in him as he built the bridge to bring us back to the Nether.

His fur was soft under my fingers. I would miss the little pain-in-the-ass when all this was done. I wondered if he would miss me. No, of course not. After the Stewards were done with him, there would be nothing left of my guide.

I braced for that uncomfortable shift between worlds.

"Wait!" I stepped aside, breaking the connection between us. "What if…" A crazy, foolish, and possibly deadly idea was growing in me.

"What?" Grim's fur was sticking up again as the pent up magic primed him. "We must get back now."

"Just give me a minute." I patted my shirt pocket and found my ki. I pulled it out, and it sat in my palm, strangely warm and heavy for its size.

Here's hoping this thing regenerates like a liver.

I pulled off one of the tiny pearls along its spine. There was no blood. It was like pulling apart a gummy worm. I buried the pearl beside the roots that tethered me to the Life Tree.

Laying my hand on the dirt, I pushed magic into it, willing the bit of ki to grow. A tiny gold vine sprouted.

"Come here." I waved Grim closer. His eyes were wide, his back rigid.

I fanned the little vine, like I was feeding oxygen to a fire. It grew and twined around my father's thick chains, wrapped around my ankle, and twisted itself up with the other ties that bound me. Then it lashed itself around Grim's hind paw.

"What did you do?" He turned in circles like his feet padded on a hot plate.

I felt the new connection blaze into being. It squeezed my heart painfully, then it settled along with the others—Mason, Princess, Jacoby, Gita, Errol, Clarence, those who'd found their way into my life over the years.

"You feel it too, don't you?"

Grim stood with his back arched and all his fur standing on end like a Halloween cat.

"It's okay. You're family now."

He snort-sneezed and shook his head. "It won't be for long. The Stewards will see to that."

"For however long it is." I smoothed down his fur. He didn't shy away but laid his head against my leg, panting as he reclaimed the soul taken from him so long ago.

Finally, he looked up at me with huge, sad eyes. "We should go back to the others now."

Grim put his paw on my foot and the scenery did that odd shifting thing again, like I'd been looking through off-kilter binoculars that suddenly came into focus.

We stood by the oak surrounded by the endless grassy plains.

A blue door was set in the tree trunk.

"Kyra!"

I turned to greet Mason. We were finally going home!

34

Cautiously, I approached the door. Would it open? Had I finally fulfilled the mission of my heart so the Nether would let me out of its grasp? I didn't think I could handle another disappointment. My emotions were scrubbed raw. I wanted time to curl up under a warm blanket and process them—a process that would probably involve large quantities of ice cream.

I laid my palm against it the wood, feeling the rough grain and the new connection to my father. The door opened under my touch. Mist filled the doorway, but I keened the others waiting for us—Nori and the dryads.

Grim sat in the shade of the oak tree. The sun dappled his silver coat. His tail curled around his toes, and flicked like a steady heartbeat.

My heart tripped in my chest.

Mason leaned against the door frame.

"You're not going to leave him here, are you?" A tired smile hid in the corners of his mouth. It hit me then, how long he'd been following me on this mad quest. How long he'd been uncomplaining and supportive as I tilted at broken windmills. How long it had been since his smile lit his eyes.

I shook my head. "I can't. Give me a minute."

I turned back and crouched to put myself at Grim's eye level.

"I guess this is goodbye," I said.

He watched me with half-lidded eyes.

"I wanted to say thank you for everything you've done for us."

Still no response, but he lifted his nose as if catching a stray scent on the breeze.

"You know, you could come with us." I snuck out my hand and stroked the silky fur on his shoulder. He didn't shy away.

"There's no reason for you to stay here. Mason has a big barn that our goblin friends are renovating. You'll love it. There's a forest for you to hunt in, and—"

"I cannot go with you." He sidestepped out of my reach, and I let my hand drop.

"Why not?"

"I must face the Stewards and pay for my crimes."

"But you'll pay with your life."

"Perhaps. But at least someone will remember me."

He butted me gently with his head and rubbed himself along my shin from his crown to the tip of his tail. So like a cat. Just when you're completely frustrated with them, they go and do something unbearably cute.

"Without the sanction of the Stewards, I wouldn't survive to take a breath if I stepped into your world" Grim said.

"So, let's get their sanction."

The cat flattened his ears. "One does not simply negotiate with the gods."

"Maybe one doesn't. But I do. I'm coming with you."

I rose before he could argue and faced Mason, ready to fend off his objections. But when I laid out my arguments, he nodded.

"Fine. Let's go see these Stewards."

"Nuh-uh. You have to go back and take care of Nori and Jacoby." And the One-eyed Father only knew what kind of mischief Princess would get up to without supervision.

"Not going to happen." Mason crossed his arms. "You go, I go."

I sighed. I really didn't want to have this conversation now, but it was a long time coming. I picked through my thoughts carefully, trying to parse together a coherent argument that wouldn't put him on the defensive.

"You're being ridiculous."

Okay, parsing wasn't my strength.

"Ever since I broke your curse, you seem to think you need to keep me under surveillance twenty-four-seven." He opened his mouth to speak, but I held up my hand. "I'm not finished. I survived seventy-nine years on various worlds without you. I don't need you to babysit me."

His eyebrows lowered, and he studied me with quiet intensity, eyes filled with a storm of pique and pain. I pinched the bridge of my nose, closed my eyes, and ground down the last ridges of my molars.

"Let me try that again. I understand how hard it was for you to be forced onto the sidelines when I fought Gerard and Polina. But you don't have a debt to pay because of that."

He rubbed the back of his neck and looked away. "That's how you would see it. And I know you well enough that nothing I will say will change your mind. Kyra Greene is on a mission."

He grinned that little flirty half-grin that made me want to kiss him and smack him. Not necessarily in that order.

"Go take on the Nether gods. But be safe and come home to me. That's all I ask. I love you."

Oh, damn. Now I felt like a tool. My eyes betrayed me by leaking all over my face and he gathered me into his arms.

"I love you too," I said, muffled against his chest, so it came out more like "I lmf mootoo."

He held my face in his strong hands and wiped away my tears with his thumbs. His eyes raked over me, like he was scraping away one last memory.

Then he stepped toward the door.

A raucous cawing filled the air and a flock of harpies landed on the grass before the Life Tree. One harpy held a glowing scroll in her stumpy human hands.

"Kyra Greene of Terra?" Her voice was brittle as burned glass.

"That's me." I stepped forward, putting Mason and the others behind me.

"You have broken the rule of life and will answer to the Tribunal of Stewards." Behind her, the other harpies cackled like a murder of crows on a bloodstained battlefield.

CHAPTER

35

A harpy grabbed my arms and pulled them roughly behind me. The excitement of the capture had her riled up, and the breeze from her wings tossed my hair as she fanned them.

Mason swore in French as he lashed out, but in moments, he was seized too. His captor loomed over him, a full head taller, wings outstretched as if she might fly away with him in her grasp. She yanked him backward, and his head clashed with her pendulous breasts.

Three more harpies held down a squirming Princess with their taloned feet. Jacoby seemed to have disappeared. Then I spotted him lurking near the open door in the Life Tree.

"Jacoby, go! Get home!" I urged.

The dervish stuck one finger in his mouth, considering. By the gods, I hoped he listened to me for once. The harpies marched us into the grassy clearing and I lost sight of him.

"Where are you taking us?" I craned my neck to look my captor in the face and nearly got a mouthful of sweaty boob. Yuck. She pushed me down to sit on the grass. Mason's captor did the same to him. Princess continued to fight. She growled and a harpy hissed. Good girl. I hoped she ripped a chunk out of her.

"Settle your hound or we'll skewer it," said the harpy holding Mason. The one behind me yanked upward on my wrists and my shoulders screamed.

"Let her go! She won't leave without me."

The harpy holding Mason glared at me. I glared back. Princess half-snarled, half-howled and another harpy yelped.

"If you don't let her go, I can't be responsible for what she does to you."

The harpy held my gaze for one moment longer, to prove she was a bad-ass bitch, then snapped. "Release it." The harpies holding Princess jumped back and the hound burst forward, snarling and spitting. Her hackles were raised and her eyes burned with fury.

"Princess, to me!"

She backed up a step.

"Princess, *hael*!" I laced my words with a jolt of magic, and the hound slunk to my side, growling up at my captor.

Jacoby slipped up to lean against her outer flank.

Damn. He should have gone home, but I couldn't worry about that now. The harpies didn't seem in a hurry to take us anywhere.

"Why are you holding us?" Mason asked. "We've done nothing wrong."

"That has yet to be decided," said the harpy holding him. She seemed younger than the others, though her face was a maze of wrinkles. She grinned like a hawk spotting prey and licked the side of his face. Mason's lip curled in disgust, but he didn't lash out in any other way. Good man. There was no reason to give them an excuse to abuse us. Not yet, anyway.

I strained in my harpy manacles to look behind me. A half dozen of the bird-crones waited with wings folded. "So what are we waiting for?"

"The Stewards," Grim said. He hadn't been detained. The collar around his neck was the only surety the harpies needed.

Suddenly, the air shimmered and a monumental stone slab appeared on the grassy plain. It was a table with four large chairs along one side. And on these sat the Stewards.

The Tribunal had come to us.

At one end of the stone table sat a giant stone statue of Dodona, partially nude and wrapped around an obelisk. That wasn't suggestive at all. A fire burned in a small hearth at her feet. She loomed over the Stewards, her face stern and watchful like a school matron waiting for her charges to misbehave.

On their thrones, the Stewards watched me with impassive expressions. I recognized the faces from the statues in the forest. Kodjinn with his two heads and predatory gaze. Sushanoo, the intersexed Steward that Grim called the Fair One. Nyami lounging in her chair like a belly-dancer at rest. And Ganus on his throne, a step higher than the others. He seemed somehow both youthful and stern.

The harpy let go of my wrists and shoved me forward. I stumbled and rammed into the sharp edge of the table. I rubbed my forearms and looked up at the boyish face of Ganus.

"Kyra Greene, you have been charged with creating life. How do you plead?"

I opened my mouth to answer, but Mason beat me to it.

"This is ridiculous! We came here as seekers in good faith. You have no right—"

A harpy swept his legs out from under him with one swipe of her great wing. He fell hard. I heard air whoosh from his lungs. The harpy pressed her great taloned foot on his chest. His face turned red as he tried to suck in air.

Ganus ignored the altercation. His eyes never left my face.

"How do you plead?" His voice boomed with authority, and I keened a touch of compulsion magic in it. I took a moment to ramp up my wards.

"I beg the Tribunal's pardon. You took us by surprise. We expected the guide to be the one facing your judgment."

Ganus's eyes flicked to the grimalkin. "The guide's transgressions will be addressed later. How do you plead?"

This guy was unswerving in his methods.

I glanced at Mason. He was standing but still held fast by the harpy. His arm had gone to stone. He nodded at me, ready to take my cue. If I wanted to fight, he'd fight. My sword was only a thought away. I could feel Princess trembling with unspent fury beside me. And Jacoby could turn this place into a dust bowl of a tornado if he wanted to. Only Grim's loyalties were unknown to me. But even without him, my little band of misfits packed some decent fire-power. Would it be enough to overpower a few harpies and some self-righteous gods?

My father's tree, with the door home, was only a stone's throw away. Instinct screamed at me to run for it. The harpies were lined up in front of the door and would make us pay for such insolence, but they weren't my real worry. My real worry was the Stewards. Gods could boast any sort of magic, and historically, they were ruthless in its execution.

Critter wrangler rule number twelve: don't ever try to appeal to a god's good nature.

With that in mind, I studied the other Stewards. If Grim was to be believed, each had a secondary gift, emotions they ruled. My best bet would be to speak to Sushanoo, Steward of reason and forgiveness. Not because they would treat me fairly—a god's idea of fair rarely made any sense to an underling—but because I wanted to understand their accusations before I made the decision to fight.

I turned and bowed.

"Great Sushanoo, I humbly beg for your notice." I could play the dutiful supplicant. I'd seen hundreds of supplicants come to beg favors from my grandfather, Baldyr.

Sushanoo inclined their head, just enough to let me know I could go on breathing for another minute. Their six arms were folded across their chest.

"Please, great Steward, can you clarify the accusations? How exactly have I created life?" I held open my empty hands as if to show I wasn't hiding some strange life form on my person.

Sushanoo leaned forward. They were thin and pretty, with curly black hair, full breasts and a beard that would make a Viking proud. "You gave life where life had been denied. Only the Stewards may revoke such a punishment." Their voice was melodic and smooth.

I gave life? What in all the hells?

I glanced from face to face. The other Stewards watched me with indifference. Kodjinn's hawk head cocked to one side, as if I might be a fat, tasty rabbit. Ganus picked fluff off his tunic and Nyami leaned back in her chair, one leg hanging over the armrest while she ate from a bowl of purple berries. Had Dodona's statue moved? It seemed like she watched me now, but before her eyes had been fixed on the Stewards.

Silky fur touched my hand. Grim head-butted my fingers to get my attention.

"They mean me. Your little trick with the vine. In effect, by giving me a part of your ki, you tethered me to you. But long ago, the Stewards cut all my ties to other worlds, trapping me here to do their bidding."

"Punishing you for your transgressions," Ganus corrected. Kodjinn's lion head let out a roar to punctuate that idea.

The Stewards didn't like that I had freed one of their slaves. I chewed on that for a moment, then bowed to Sushanoo, trying to appear humble, when really I was holding in my rage behind gritted teeth.

"Great Sushanoo who is master of the air, surely you understand that the wind blows in many directions at once."

Sushanoo leaned over the stone table. A stray wind tossed their hair, making them look fierce and wild.

"Go on."

I didn't really know where this argument was taking me, but I pushed on.

"Grim has served you faithfully and has earned this new chance at life outside the Nether. When I gave him the vine, I did not understand that he was bound to you in such a way. But I would do it again. All creatures deserve to live free."

Sushanoo's lips thinned until they disappeared in the thick beard. A ripple went through the other Stewards.

Ganus leaned forward. "So your argument is that even if you weren't ignorant of our laws, you would still have broken them?"

I heard Grim groan.

"That's not what I meant!" I looked from Steward to Steward and found no hint of forgiveness.

"Kyra Greene," Ganus said, "you have been found guilty. By the Oracle's will, I sentence you to death." Ganus pounded his gavel on the table. The sound reverberated like a cell door slamming shut.

"No!" Mason shouted and jumped forward, breaking away from the harpy. His fist turned to stone. He was ready to take on these supposed gods. "Grim, tell them it's a mistake!"

The cat wound around my ankles, then jumped onto the table.

"I demand trial by Dodona's Labyrinth!" he shouted. "If the accused is blessed by the Oracle, she must be set free!"

The Stewards turned toward Ganus. He frowned, wrinkling his youthful brow, then declared, "We must consult the Oracle." Ganus raised his hand and pointed. "Leave us!"

Grim jumped down from the table and trotted toward the oak grove.

I was too stunned to move.

Mason dragged me away, and said, "Maybe your father can intervene."

"I don't think so. He has no influence in the Nether." I took his hand and pulled him after Grim.

"What have you gotten me into?" I asked the cat.

Grim sat with one back leg sticking in the air as he washed his thigh. It was a nervous gesture, I now realized, and had nothing to do with being calm and collected.

"It's your only chance. You must walk Dodona's Labyrinth to gain her blessing. Then the Stewards can't touch you."

I thought of the pilgrims I'd seen lined up outside Dodona's maze and the ki stones littering the field outside it. My only chance of survival was painfully slim at best.

"Can it be done?"

"It has been done four times in the history of the Nether, if you believe the Stewards."

"Four times? You mean the Oracle blessed them?" I looked back at the Stewards, who were feeding something into the fire on the hearth at Dodona's feet. From this angle, it looked like the statue's head was bowed in acceptance to the offering.

Grim twitched his whiskers. "If you believe their stories, then yes, the Stewards were the first to be blessed."

"And you believe them?"

Grim lowered his leg and began to work on his toes. "I believe the Stewards won the Oracle's favor," he said between licks. "I don't believe they were the only ones."

"So if I win, they won't be asking me to join their little clique. I'm okay with that."

A whistle came from the Tribunal.

"They're waiting for us." Mason took my hand, and we walked back to the stone table.

Ganus stood. His crown of gold laurel leaves shone like a halo. I glanced at the stone Oracle. She seemed as impassive as ever, but was now staring straight at me.

"The Oracle has accepted your right to run the labyrinth. Should you survive it, you will win her favor."

Mason stepped forward.

"I offer myself as Kyra's champion."

"No!" I shouted at the same instant that Ganus banged his gavel and said, "Done."

CHAPTER

36

nce the Oracle was involved, it seemed that the rules of the Nether no longer applied. Five harpies grabbed our arms in their talons and teleported us in a blink. My guard dropped me to hard-packed ground on a bluff overlooking Dodona's Labyrinth. Below us stretched the unforgiving and seemingly endless desert. Pilgrims massed before the labyrinth's wall, dozens of alien races mingling uneasily to pay their respects to the Oracle.

Grim, Princess, and Jacoby were also dumped onto the sandy bluff. I jumped to my feet and looked around.

The Tribunal was already there. The Stewards sat on their thrones, looking bored. Dodona's statue had shifted positions. She was no longer wrapped around the obelisk, but sat with her elbow resting on a knee and her head cradled in her palm. She stared out over the desert.

"Where's Mason?"

Except for the harpies that brought us, the bluff was empty.

"Don't panic," Grim said. "At least not yet. The birdies have taken him to get ready for the trial. They will bring him when he is presentable."

I didn't like that. He could be anywhere, and the harpies could be doing anything to him. I realized that I'd been gripping my sword in my fist since we arrived. I dropped the blade, and it disappeared into the mists of the Nether. That was a trick I'd miss once we were home.

Home. Gods, I wanted to be done with this business. I shook out my hands and shaded my eyes to look down at the labyrinth. We faced one of the two gates into the maze. It was guarded by the biggest statue of Dodona we'd seen so far. Her head topped the labyrinth wall. I could see the crown of a second Dodona statue poking over the walls on the far end of the labyrinth where I'd seen the other entrance during our brief flyover on the way to First City.

The pilgrims had spotted us. Some began to shout and point. A few pressed their faces to the ground in reverence.

Grim sat beside me. "They will go home with an amazing story to tell. If they go home."

"What are we doing here?" I wasn't into small talk at that moment.

Grim sighed. "This is Dodona's trial. Your champion will have to run the labyrinth. If he makes it through, the Oracle will bless him. If not...."

He didn't need to finish that thought.

I turned my attention to the field in front of the gates. Wagons, tents, weapons and other debris were partially covered in glittering sand. Ghosts flitted among the pilgrims and the ruined camps too. Now that I was looking for them, I spotted more lost spirits, pale in the bright sunlight. They stood before the wall beside the gates, arm raised in supplication. Or they poked through the remains hidden in the sand.

"What's with all the ghosts?" I said.

"Petitioners for Dodona's blessing. Failed petitioners."

The sparkle in the sand was from ki stones. Thousands upon thousands of ki stones. The squandering of all those lost souls nearly choked me.

"How exactly does one earn Dodona's blessing?"

Grim stared at the field, his ears perked forward. "Some come through the doors just to touch the wall of her labyrinth. It's said to bring good luck and heal the sick. Others want a more...substantial reward. They will run the labyrinth. If they make it through, they win Dodona's favor."

I studied the maze. It didn't look too complicated. Wasn't there a trick to getting out of a labyrinth? Were you supposed to take only left turns? Only right turns? I couldn't remember, but it had to be more complicated than it appeared.

Dear gods. What had I gotten us into?

I glanced at the Stewards who sat on their thrones waiting for the spectacle to begin. Only Nyami seemed impatient. The Dodona statue had turned her back. When had she moved?

I walked over to the great stone table and placed my hands on the flat surface to keep them from trembling. I stood in front of Nyami who slumped with one leg flung over the arm rest, her foot tapping the air with unspent energy.

"Blessed by the Oracle," I said. "What exactly does that mean?"

The pretty Steward lifted her nose and sniffed. Kodjinn answered instead.

"It is different for everyone. I, for example, found the power of fire. My friend Nyami here, is mistress of the watery depths." He leaned in as if to impart a secret. "You can see why she's bored. Too much desert and not enough water on this planet." He sat back. His leonine muzzle grinned.

"But you all went through the trial?" The Stewards nodded in unison.

I shot a look at Dodona, who'd changed position again. She leaned forward to watch over the Tribunal with a beatific smile. "So gods do have a belly-buttons. Interesting."

Nyami frowned and looked down at her stomach. She wasn't the brightest bead on the rosary.

I left the Stewards and went back to the edge of the bluff to study Dodona's maze.

So the Oracle's favor was godhood. Why would anyone in their right mind want to be a god? That way lay megalomania. The old saying about absolute power corrupting was absolutely true. Even my great-grandfather, the one-eyed Odin, had his moments of unbridled cruelty. And he was one of the more benevolent gods.

I had more questions, a lot more, but the harpies had returned with Mason. He was barefoot and dressed in a simple white tunic. His damp hair stuck to his forehead, and his skin shone with a ruddiness from scrubbing. I didn't want to think of what that bath had been like under the tender ministrations of the harpies.

I stepped forward to go to him, but Grim cut me off by swirling his tail around my ankles.

"Let me speak to him first. I'm still a guide. I will help him as much as I can."

I bit my lip, hoping the pain would stop me from crying, and nodded.

Grim took Mason aside. They conferred in low voices that I couldn't make out.

The wind tossed up dust from the desert, and it scoured any exposed skin. This was a dismal, unwelcoming place. Even Princess and Jacoby felt it. They didn't run around or tease each other. They just sat, looking up at me with big, worried eyes.

"Everything will be fine. We'll be going home soon." I hoped I wasn't lying.

I rubbed my arm where the harpy's talons had pinched me. She'd given me a good scratch, and I frowned at the red line etched across my skin. It oozed blood. That wasn't good. It meant my body was starting to fade back home.

If I could bleed, I could die.

Mason too.

He stood looking over the plains with Grim at his side. The grimalkin was no doubt explaining what Mason would face inside the Oracle's maze. His tail swished across the sand, as if to emphasize his point. Mason cut him off with a sharp word. Grim sighed and turned away. He saw me watching and shook his head.

Mason's gaze caught mine, and we met halfway across the windy bluff.

"You okay?" I slipped my hand in his.

"Peachy." He squeezed my fingers.

"You don't have to do this."

"Do you think those fine ladies will release my from my pledge?" He pointed to the harpies standing guard. "Or the Stewards?"

I thought of Ganus and his gavel. When it had fallen, sealing the deal, I'd keened a rush of magic. A pact that had been established and could not be broken.

"I guess not."

I didn't want him to take my punishment. I wanted to fight my own battles. I wanted him to go home and live out his long but mortal life.

But my anger had faded, and I wouldn't argue with him again. Not now. Not when we might only have a few minutes left.

He laced my fingers with his and wrapped my hand around his back.

"I wanted more time." He pressed his forehead gently against mine. "But somehow we've gone from having eternity, to having a lifetime, to having only minutes."

"It's my fault." The tears started in my gut, burned up my throat and were unstoppable as they carved hot lines down my cheeks.

"Not your fault." He wiped the tears with his thumb, then kissed the trail they'd left on my skin.

"It is." I couldn't explain how. Despair took away all my words. But it was my fault. Kester was right. I was a magnet for mayhem.

"I should be there with you." If the tables were turned, nothing would stop Mason from facing the Oracle with me.

I glanced at the harpies, and a dangerous idea came to me. Dangerous and perfect. I reached into my pocket and pulled out my ki stone. It felt more solid. Weightier. It was less slug-like and more stone-like than before. Another sign that we'd worn out our welcome in the Nether.

I broke off one of the pearly protrusions and handed it to Mason. At the last moment, my fingers closed around the pearl and I turned to Grim.

"Will this bring down the wrath of the Stewards again?"

Grim shook his head. "He already has a soul. Gifting him a piece of yours isn't a crime."

I held out my hand to Mason. "Will you?"

"I will." His eyes bore into mine. He opened his mouth, and I popped in the piece of ki. He swallowed.

"You too." He cupped my hand that held the rest of the ki stone. "It will ease me to know you're safe, in one way at least."

I could give him that. I swallowed the stone. It lodged in my throat and I gagged. Mason pounded me on the back and I choked it down.

Jacoby squirmed in between us and held up his own ki with a tiny pearl broken from it.

"Mister Mason? I thanks you for finding me." Mason crouched and took the pearl from Jacoby.

"And I thank you." He swallowed it. Princess, not to be outdone, licked him from chin to ear.

Mason made a rough sound that approached a laugh and tousled the hell hound's ears. Then he turned to me, and the many worlds we inhabited fell into a hazy background. It was just me and Mason. He held my head in both his hands. His fingers tangled in my hair. I turned into one palm, to feel it against my cheek—skin to skin as we were meant to be.

His eyes were lit with a hint of dark humor. He leaned in and kissed me. His lips caught the corner of my mouth, then drew me in deeper. I opened to him. This wasn't about passion or romance. It was a hard kiss, a claiming, and when he finally pulled away, he left my lips tingling.

My fingers gripped his arms, digging into the bare skin.

"I don't know how to let you go."

"You do."

"I can't."

"You can."

"She won't let you off easy."

"I know."

"And you won't heal with the sun anymore." Spikes of guilt and fear and rage stuck in my throat. I could neither bring them up nor swallow them down.

Mason gently unclenched my fingers and wrapped my arms around his waist. I ducked my head and leaned it against his chest, keening the toll of his heart.

"Remember when you faced Gerard Golovin without me?" He whispered into my ear, words for me alone. "I let you go. It nearly killed me, but I had no choice. And now you will let me go. You'll find the strength because you have to." His lips found the sensitive hollow behind my ear and blazed a path to my chin. I turned into his kiss and his mouth closed over mine. The taste of him was intoxicating. His magic enveloped me. It buzzed over my skin, pulsed through my veins and matched my heartbeat thump for thump.

Finally, he took my shoulders and pushed me away, far enough to look me in the eye. "And there is no blame to lay for breaking my curse. You gave me a gift. I'd say it was the best gift, but we both know that one happens between the sheets. Ooh la la, baby." He twisted his hips, grinding himself against me.

I didn't want to laugh, didn't want to give into his attempt to lighten the mood, but a sound—rough edged and nearing hysteria—burbled from my throat followed by a hiccup.

Mason showed me his bad-boy grin.

"You can't do this. I won't let you." My voice cracked. I felt a thousand years old.

"It's already done."

I pounded my fists on his chest. But I had no fight left in me.

"It's not fair. It should be me. I'm the one who broke their stupid rules."

"It is exactly fair." He dipped his head to meet my eye. "You take care of everyone. Jacoby, Princess, Ollie. Me. You never stop to consider the repercussions to yourself."

"That's not true."

"It is. Ever since you broke my curse, you've been jumping in front of every stone thrown my way, treating me like I'm made of glass."

"But you are! Next to the power of a god, you'll shatter. And there will be no more sunrises to put you back together."

He shrugged. "Nor for you. So it's time you let someone take care of you for a change."

I squirmed in his arms.

"I don't know how to do that."

"We'll figure it out together. I promise."

He was so sure of himself. So sure that he'd beat the Oracle at her little game and come back to me. I wished I had his confidence.

"It is time," Ganus said, his voice booming like he spoke through a megaphone. "The postulant must take the field."

Mason turned to Grim. "Any last words of advice?"

"Remember, you are as you want to be," Grim said. "So want to win."

Mason's gaze met mine and held it. "I want it."

Two harpies came for him. I clung to his hands even as they wrenched him from my grip.

"Love you."

"I know." He held his hand against his heart where a little piece of me now lived. "I love you." His words whipped away in the wind as the harpies grabbed him under each shoulder and jerked him into the sky. They flew him to the far side of the labyrinth. Pilgrims shrieked and scattered as the giant birdies bore down on them. The harpies dropped Mason in front of the gate. From our angle, I couldn't see him land, but that had to hurt.

"Hey!" I shouted and darted toward the Stewards. A harpy stepped in front of me, blocking the way. Grim circled my ankles, swishing his tail around me.

"Leave it," he said. "Come with me."

I glared at the harpy. She hissed and showed me her serrated teeth in a parody of a grin. I followed Grim to the far end of the bluff where it curved around the labyrinth.

"Until he's inside, we can watch from here," Grim said.

Down on the plains, Mason lay crumpled on the sand. He stood up, shook the dust off his tunic, and faced the doorway into the labyrinth.

My crew ranged themselves around me like a shield, but I knew they couldn't protect me from what was about to happen. I put one arm around Princess and laid the other hand on Jacoby's shoulder, taking comfort where I could.

"If he succeeds...." The words grated like sand. I cleared my throat and tried again. "If the Oracle blesses him, will he be forced to stay here as a Steward?"

Grim side-eyed me, but didn't answer.

I nudged him with my toe.

"Now's not the time, Grim. I'm not one of your seekers and you aren't my guide anymore. I need to know. Now."

For once, the cat actually looked scared. "I would tell you if I knew. I swear it. But I don't know the answer. I've never met anyone who survived the blessing. Except for them." He nodded toward the Stewards.

I thought of all those ghosts on the field, probably just a fraction of the souls who came seeking the Oracle's blessing. All those postulants had tried and failed.

My heart turned to ice.

Grim butted me with his head. "I can tell you what will happen next."

I nodded, numb now as the shard of ice in my chest spread to my limbs, my stomach, and my thoughts.

"He must find the path through the labyrinth. Dodona won't make it easy. She'll test him at every turn."

"What kind of tests?"

"It could be anything. She's particularly fond of elemental trials."

"So fire or water?"

"Air, earth, light, dark, sound, silence. Any of those are fair game."

"That doesn't sound so bad."

"It's bad. She can make those elements take any form. I once saw a postulant driven mad by a simple smell. But that's rare. I think Dodona was bored that day."

Terrific. Mason wasn't just facing the whims of an Oracle. Dodona was probably a bit mad. After eons of being top dog, most gods started to believe their own hype. And that's when the megalomania kicked in.

I glanced at the Oracle's statue. It had moved again when no one was looking. She now sat upright with her nose stuck in the air. An eager smile lit her alabaster face as she gazed over her monstrous labyrinth—her own personal torture chamber.

Mason strode toward the door, and suddenly there was no more time for questions or second-guessing. The gates opened, releasing a flood of ghosts. They flew at Mason and he ducked, covering his head with his hands. After a moment, he stood up and gawked at the mob of ghosts as they dispersed.

Oh, gods. I bit down on my lip to keep from crying out. My tiny piece of soul was already affecting him. I'd given it to him to help, to be a part of his trial, to stay by his side in the only way I could. Instead, I'd infected him with my attributes and now he could see ghosts.

I'd just made an already impossible task harder.

CHAPTER

37

ason pushed through the ghosts loitering by the gate. To his credit, he got over them much quicker than I did when I first started seeing spooks. Inside the labyrinth, he turned right and jogged along the outer passage. At the first intersection, he turned left, then left again. He slowed as the turns became sharper, with less space between them, and he made his way toward the center of the maze. I was impressed by his unerring sense of direction.

He encountered no obstacles other than being surprised by more ghosts and a tumble of rockfall that blocked the passage. He put a hesitant foot on the rocks, testing them before adding his weight. His hands crept upward, looking for handholds, testing each before committing.

My fingers squeezed Princess's ruff as the seconds passed. I kept expecting something to pop out of the pile and attack. Mason placed another foot. The rocks shifted. He adjusted and moved on. Another step. Another handhold.

He crested the top and climbed down the other side.

I let out a ragged breath.

Part of me wanted this to be over one way or another because another tiny flame inside me had started to hope that he would make it through unscathed. And that hope was more terrifying than the numbness of despair I'd wrapped myself in.

Then I spotted something running along the top of the walls. From this distance, it was too small for me to make out, but it moved more like a crab than a rodent, skittering for a few feet, stopping, then jerking forward again. Long black legs flexed, and it leaped from one wall to another.

Beside me, Grim groaned.

"What is it?"

"Gremlin." The creature stopped at a bend in the maze. Rocks were piled on the wall. The gremlin stood upright, displaying a long skinny body and stick-like arms and legs. It mounted the rocks and thumped its foot. The sound echoed like a drum.

Inside the maze, Mason paused. The gremlin was ahead of him and around the bend. Mason hadn't seen it. He'd only heard the noise, and he turned in circles, trying to pinpoint the source. The creature thumped again. Mason took a hesitant step forward. The gremlin's thumping sped up to a rapid staccato, and as Mason turned the corner, rocks began to slide.

"No!" My sword reacted to my need and appeared in my hand. But I could do nothing with it. I could only watch as the rockslide crashed in a cloud of dust. Princess paced along the bluff, but my feet seemed as heavy as cement blocks.

The gremlin beat his chest and let out a shrill ululation before scampering away.

I waited, trying to swallow, feeling my heart had lodged in my throat. The wind picked up, blowing away the dust. The rockfall was still as a tomb. We waited in a silence that amplified all my fears. Mason was dead.

Then the pile shivered. A rock flew off the top. Another fell down the side as a hand punched through. Mason's stone hand. Then his head. He dragged himself out like a zombie rising from his grave.

I sucked in a deep breath and exhaled a small bit of gratitude. If Dodona thought to beat him with stone, she didn't know much about gargoyles.

His face was gray with dust except where blood leaked from a gash on his forehead.

"He's bleeding!" I rubbed the small wound on my arm. The blood wasn't just a sign of Mason's vulnerability. It was a reminder that we were desperately short on time.

"Is that it? Is she done?" I clutched Grim's fur a little too hard.

"No. Watch!" He squirmed from my grip.

Mason raised his face toward us, either looking for encouragement or to comfort me. Then he limped onward. One more turn and he reached the nucleus of the labyrinth—a square with a lone tree growing from the center.

A bare tree, little more than a black trunk with a few odd branches spiking toward the sky.

From our angle, I could see all of this center square except one corner. Mason entered from the opposite side and stopped. He was scouting the space, wondering where the next ambush would come from.

A shadow blocked the sun. I looked up, shielding my eyes. A black shadow slipped across the sky. It moved quickly, like it had its own propulsion, and settled over the center square of the labyrinth.

"Oh, no!" Grim settled into a sphinx pose and hid his face under his paws.

"What?" I ignored his dislike of being touched and shook him. "What is it?"

He looked up with wide eyes. "A deceptor."

"What does it do?"

Grim hesitated.

"Tell me now!"

"It's darkness."

I paced to the very edge of the bluff. The Stewards hadn't moved from their perches. Below us, Mason stumbled around the center square as if he couldn't see, even though he was plainly visible to us.

"Darkness?" I said. "That doesn't seem too bad. He'll figure it out."

Grim also stood and twined around my shins.

"You don't understand. It's not simply the absence of light. It's a darkness of the mind. A deceptor distorts reality. A minute lost in its shadow will feel like an hour to Mason. He won't be able to find his way out, and to him it will feel like he's been wandering in darkness for days, until he eventually gives up."

"He won't!"

Grim leaned against me. He seemed to need the anchoring touch as much as I did. Princess pressed herself against my other side and whined.

"Mr. Mason wills be okay?" Jacoby gazed up at me. The fringe of fur around his eyes quivered. I tucked him against me too, as if I could insulate myself from the horror below with fur, fangs, and claws.

Mason tripped over a loose cobblestone and fell against the dead tree in the center of the labyrinth. He pulled himself upright, groping the trunk like a blind man. With hands held out in a shield, he crept to the outer wall.

221

Then he trailed one hand along it, looking for the break that would mark the doorway out of the labyrinth's nucleus. He stumbled twice over rocks or sticks on the ground, inching ever closer.

I held my breath. Mason tripped and I jerked my hands forward as if I could catch him. I couldn't. And it broke my heart to see him looking so lost.

Go on…just a bit further.

Mason's hand trailed off the wall into the passageway.

And he kept going. To him, the gap didn't exist. In another minute he was on the other side of the opening, hand still trailing along the wall.

"What? How…?" I didn't even know what question to ask.

"It's the deceptor," Grim said. "It deceives."

Mason circled the square again. When he came to the wall closest to us, I lost sight of him for grueling minutes. I stretched my neck until it ached from the tension, as if those extra inches would make the difference. Finally he emerged on the other side, still seeking the exit.

He made another laborious circuit, tripping, stumbling, seeking, sometimes crawling. How long had he been under the deceptor's influence? Thirty minutes? An hour? How long had that seemed for him? Hours? Days?

He was tired now, hanging onto the wall instead of searching it. Eventually, he turned toward the center, hands stretched out before him. When he hit the dead tree, he slumped to the ground, braced his arms on his knees, and hung his head in defeat.

No! He couldn't give up. He wouldn't.

"Come on. Get up!"

Was he asleep?

He raised his head. From this distance, I couldn't see his eyes under the shadow of his brow, but I felt them. He was asking for help.

I raised my blade to the sky and sunk all my will into it. The sword blazed with light.

"He won't see it," Grim said.

"He doesn't have to," I said through gritted teeth. He just needed to to feel it.

The shining sword attracted the attention of the deceptor shadow. Lightning crackled from it—jagged fingers that reached for the blade.

The Stewards turned as one to gape at my audacity. I could almost hear their exclamations. *How dare she interfere with the Oracle?* I bet their belly buttons were quivering with outrage. They huddled in a circle to confer.

"Kyra! You must stop!" Grim danced around my feet. "If they find you are interfering, they will punish you!"

"You said it yourself. Mason can't see me."

I had nothing left to lose.

I fed magic to my blade, sinking all the love I had for him into it. I added my hopes for our future. I thought of how we'd bring my menagerie to settle in his barn. How he'd clear some drawers in his bedroom for my panties and bras. We'd learn each other's morning habits. He'd scold me for drinking too much coffee, and I'd ply him with a proper breakfast of bacon and pancakes. He'd give in just to please me.

And I thought of the acorn in my pocket, a promise from my father that one day I'd have a daughter. If Mason died, if he gave into the deceptor's madness now, that wouldn't happen because there would never be anyone else for me.

Come on, Mason. Look through the darkness.

Lightning hit my sword. The blade absorbed the energy and glowed brighter. The next crack of lightning split the dead tree at the center of the maze, knocking Mason from his lethargy.

He stood and rubbed his face as if wiping off years of dust.

He smiled grimly and staggered away from the tree. This time, when he hit the wall, he moved with assurance to the doorway. His hands ran over the empty space as if it were a solid wall. Then he pushed. His arms sank into the shadows. He pushed again and his body followed. In another instant, he was through to the passageway, blinking in the bright sunlight. He lifted a fist and shook it, then turned and half-ran, half-limped down the passage.

Thunder cracked, loud enough to deafen, and the deceptor shadow exploded.

The Stewards favored me with savage glares.

"What? I didn't do anything. It's not like he could see me through your little trick, right?"

The Stewards turned away and settled back into their roles as vigilant witnesses. I resisted the urge to stick out my tongue and na-na-na-boo-boo them.

Jacoby hugged himself into a ball at my feet. I collapsed beside him and he crawled into my lap. He was shaking. So was I.

"It's okay," I soothed. "He made it. It's over now."

Mason jogged along the stone corridor, making turns when he came to intersections, sometimes turning back when he hit a dead end. The maze wasn't particularly complicated, and he soon found the last turn. The final corridor was a long one, running nearly the full length of the maze to the exit that would spit him out in the desert right in front of us. He hitched into a limping jog as he realized that freedom was within reach.

He was going to do it. The Oracle had done her best to stop him, but he'd won through! I stood up, gripping Jacoby in my arms so tightly, he squeaked.

Something crawled from a crack in the walls and chased him. It skipped along, opened wings, and hopped into a short flight. Its long tail whipped back and forth as its lizard-like body undulated, picking up speed and gaining on Mason.

Grim hissed, and puffed himself up into a silver fur ball. "Salamander!"

The creature hopped along the top of the wall, flexing leathery wings wide.

It burst into flame. The fire engulfed it but didn't consume it. Monstrous wings flexed, opening wide. Flames licked off the wingtips like feathers. Then, when Mason was three strides from the exit, the creature dove and wrapped him in a fiery embrace.

Mason screamed.

CHAPTER

38

is spine tensed into a rigid arc. His head shot back. Flames choked off his screams. The fiery creature hugged Mason's arms to his side, engulfing him in the inferno.

He was burning up!

Dear Odin, great-grandfather of my heart, if you have any purview on this world, please help him!

The salamander turned blue, like flame at the heart of a candle wick. It no longer resembled lizard or bird. It was pure fire.

Mason fell to his knees, then to his side.

The salamander winked out of existence like it had been snuffed.

Princess raised her snout and howled.

I was frozen to my spot. Mason was dead. Burned to a crisp by the selfish Oracle.

Except he wasn't a blackened lump. He lay naked and unmoving. His clothes had burned away, but other than that, he seemed unharmed.

Jacoby slipped his hand in mine. I looked down at his sweet face. He smiled, popped the last of his ki stone into his mouth, and swallowed.

"Kyra-lady, don't cry. Fire can't hurts us."

Was I crying? I wiped my cheeks, surprised when my hand came away wet.

I turned toward the Stewards, fully intending to kill them. My sword agreed, and it pulsed in my grip.

I took two steps and fell over Grim, landing hard on one knee.

"Don't," Grim said. "Look."

I raised my head.

Mason rolled to his hands and knees.

My heart crashed to a stop, then hammered against my ribs like it was trying to break free from its cage.

Slowly, Mason reached one hand forward. Then the other. His right leg followed. He wobbled and collapsed inches from the exit.

"Come on, come on. Don't let her win." My hand ached on the hilt of my sword. The blade vibrated, feeding on my tension.

For the longest minute of my life, Mason didn't move.

Then he reached again, pulling himself across the gravel, one painful inch at a time, until he collapsed on the sand outside the labyrinth.

Grim trotted over to the Stewards and Ganus bent down to confer with him. I couldn't hear what they said, and I didn't really try. All my focus was on the still form lying in the sand below.

After a moment, Ganus rose and said, "The human is blessed by Dodona."

"What does that mean?" I called out, but the Stewards turned away.

The Oracle's face didn't seem so benevolent now. The statue stood straight as an arrow pointing to the heavens. Her brows hunched over wide eyes and her mouth was pursed as if frozen in the act of forming a curse. To hells with her. Mason had beaten her at her game, and she could go suck rocks for all I cared.

None of them mattered now. Only Mason mattered. The cliff at my feet sheared off at an angle too steep to descend. I ran for the far end, where the slope was less severe, then descended, running, sliding, skidding, not caring that the scree tore at my hands.

On the desert floor, my feet sunk into sand and every step took the effort of ten. Pilgrims cried, prayed and screamed. Some were singing. I ignored them all.

Mason lay motionless before the gates. A pack of curious ghosts hovering over him. I fought the distance between us, the sand that slid under each of my steps, and my lying heart that kept whispering, *he's dead he's dead he's dead.*

I dipped into a gully and momentarily lost sight of him. When I topped the dune again, Dodona stood on the rise. Her fists were clenched and her mouth warped in an ugly sneer.

"Get out of my way, bitch." I snarled right back at her. "He beat you fair and square."

I blinked and the next thing I knew, I was lying flat on my back. Dodona was poised above me, her arm frozen in the backswing of a slap.

An unnatural wind tossed eddies of sand around us. I shut my eyes against the grit as I scrambled away. When I opened them, the statue had jumped again. She blocked my path, grinning with evil intent, her arm raised for another slap.

"BY YOUR INTERFERENCE, YOU FORFEIT YOUR RIGHT TO A TRIAL!"

I slammed my hands over my ears. Her voice boomed across the valley. It was the voice of a god, a voice that should never be heard by mortals.

"YOU WILL DIE!" Dodona's face was no longer the face of a serene oracle. Rage bulged her eyes and creased her forehead.

My sword popped into my hand. I slashed upward, catching her on what would have been the soft underarm on a human. Sparks flashed as the blade bounced off stone.

Her face flicked into a new expression—this one determined and haughty. A flash of motion and her hand grabbed the point of my sword. I jabbed forward, expecting to slice through her hand and skewer her eye.

Instead my arm froze. A shot of pure energy pulsed up the blade. My jaw locked as the Oracle's magic seized me.

I'd tasted a lot of magic in my time, from the sweet kiss of a clover to the acid burn of a pissed-off chimera. Dodona's magic was familiar. It scorched my nostrils with the stink of sulfur. It crowded my ears with the screams of the eternally damned.

Dodona was no god. She was pure demon.

Secure in her mastery over me, she dropped the glamor of an alabaster statue. Her skin was as pale as the dead, but she was alive.

By the One-eyed Father, she was a full-blooded demon, alive and ready to fight.

She hissed. I gagged on the rotting stench of breath that seemed to erupt from the bowels of whatever hell had spawned her.

"You. Will. Die." Her face twisted into an evil parody of her former beauty. Eyes turned yellow and bulging. Mouth drew back in a vicious smile to reveal teeth sharpened to blackened points—teeth designed to tear flesh from bones. Her grip on my sword tightened. Blood leaked from her fingers and coursed down her arm. She didn't care. She had all the power, and I had none.

I could only watch, frozen, as she pressed forward. The pommel of my sword hit my breast bone, a deeper thud against the booming of my heart. Sweat stung my eyes. I couldn't move to shake it away. I could barely breathe with the demonic magic hurtling through my veins, taking over every one of my bodily functions.

She was right. I would die here. After everything we'd endured, after coming this far into an alien world. After Mason sacrificed himself for me. I would die anyway at the whims of a demon.

The hissing shriek of a pissed off cat came a moment before he landed on Dodona. Grizzly-sized paws tore the flesh across her chest and shoulders. The creature could only be Grim, but it was as big as a bull. He opened jaws spiked with wolfish teeth, sunk them into her neck, and ripped out a chunk of alabaster flesh.

Dodona screamed.

The grimalkin tore into her throat again and again until the demon's screams faded to a gurgle of blood and viscera.

Dodona teetered for another moment, eyes wide, fingers twitching. Her magic let go of its grip on my heart. I wrenched my blade away. The false god fell with a boom that reverberated like the breaking of a world.

Grim jumped away, but I wasn't done. My sword screamed for justice. It had been violated by that foul magic and now it wanted blood. With hands shaking on the slick grip, I raised the blade and let it drop. Dodona's head rolled away with a hiss. Sour smelling smoke poured from the edges of her lacerated flesh. I fell backward, not wanting to breathe it in and landed at the feet of the grimalkin.

For days we'd been hiking through the Nether. Our guide had been a handsome, sometimes even cute cat, larger than most, but still passable as a house cat. Not so for the beast that stood panting before me now. On all fours, he could easily look a grown man in the eye. His silver fur had blackened with rosettes like burning embers along its back.

"Grim?"

He turned to me and snarled. His mane had grown and framed a face that only hinted at feline. The jaws were too wide, the nose flat with flaring nostrils. And the eyes had shifted from emerald green to raging red. He reached out with one great paw, claws extended, and touched the demon's body, laying claim to the kill.

"It's okay. You did good. You stopped her." I raised both hands, one still gripping my sword. The grimalkin hissed at the blade. I let go, and it disappeared.

"No one's going to hurt you. Or me." I held my hands out to show him I was unarmed. Princess appeared at my side. A growl rumbled from her chest. "Stop it. We're done fighting. Jacoby, take Princess to Mason. Let's give, uh… Grim some time to calm down."

Princess followed Jacoby, but I didn't lose eye contact with Grim. Finally, he settled down. With one claw, he dragged the body closer and sunk his teeth into her flesh.

I turned my back, betting that he was too busy with his prize to chase me, and sprinted across the sand.

Mason lay flat on his stomach, naked and bald, his skin raw and red. Unmoving.

I crouched by his side, afraid to touch him, afraid to feel his skin already cooling, afraid to find an absence in the universe where his magic should be. Princess and Jacoby peered at him too. None of us moved.

A couple of pilgrims gave into curiosity and approached. Princess lashed out, barking and showing her impressive teeth. After that we were left alone.

Sand blew across Mason's already scoured skin. He groaned and turned his head. More sand caked his cheek and stuck to his cracked lips. His eyes fluttered open. Even his eyelashes were burned away.

"Mason?" My voice was small in the big desert. He didn't respond. His eyes were fixed on me, but they had no animation. Was he even in there?

"Mason?" I laid a hand on his shoulder. He flinched and I quickly withdrew it. My fingers left white welts on his flame-red skin.

I sent Jacoby for water. Mason rolled onto his side. He sucked in a breath and it came out in a whistling wheeze. I helped him sit up.

He was completely hairless—no brows, no stubble. With his red skin, he looked like a baby bird fallen from the nest. I didn't care. He was beautiful. And alive.

"Kyra?" His eyes finally focused on me.

"I'm here. You made it." I squeezed my hands to keep from touching him. Jacoby returned from the fountain with a stone bowl full of water. Mason took it with shaking hands, drank some and hissed when it sloshed onto his bare legs.

"Can you stand?" He nodded. But when I reached for his elbow, he waved me off.

"Don't." His lip curled and I could see him fight for control over the pain.

I backed up. "I'll go find you some clothes."

A deliberate throat clearing sound made me turn. The Stewards had descended from the bluff. They watched us with expressions ranging from amused (Nyami) to aghast (Sushanoo). Ganus's gavel hung from his fingers as if he'd forgotten he was holding it.

He cleared his throat again. "Kyra Greene of Terra…"

"Don't start with me and your rules!" I marched up to him and invaded his space. For a god, he wasn't very tall and my nose nearly bumped his. "You can take your rules and your harpies and your dead oracle and shove them up your divine ass."

Ganus smiled and stepped back.

"Well, yes. We could do that. Or we could escort you to your door and bid you farewell."

I tensed, ready to recall my blade and continue the fight.

"Wait. What?" Had I heard him right? "You'll let us go home? Why?"

Ganus glanced at the other Stewards, who found something really interesting to look at in the dirt.

He sighed. "For longer than your race has existed, we've been under the yoke of that…oracle." He frowned on that last word. "In her stone form, she was invulnerable. That's why she chose to move and speak only when necessary. In her arrogance and eagerness to punish you, she forgot how fragile flesh can be."

"If you can bleed, you can die," I murmured.

"Exactly so." Ganus's smile was that of a headmaster to a brilliant if unruly pupil. "You have freed us. And to show our appreciation, we will provide you safe passage."

I squinted at him. There had to be some trick. A god's favor always came with a price.

"Passage for me and my friends?"

He nodded once.

"*All* my friends. The grimalkin too."

We turned to glance at Grim, who looked up with mad, red eyes as he gnawed on the fat meat of Dodona's upper arm. A growl erupted from him, and he lifted his bloody muzzle to hiss at us.

Yuck. That would put me off sushi for months.

"Will that hurt him? I mean…she's a demon, right?"

"Yes. Do not be alarmed. The hell cat was raised on demon meat, no doubt. It will not harm him."

Hell cat? Wasn't that interesting.

"And the oracle? Is she really dead?" There were few creatures that could survive decapitation, but I'd never fought a demon before.

"Dead?" Ganus closed his eyes as if he were reaching out with his keening sense. "Not exactly. But close enough that we can banish her from our world."

"What will you do after that, with the Nether?"

"That is none of your concern. Go take care of your lover now. I will make the arrangements to dispose of the demon." He snapped his fingers and a dozen harpies surrounded Dodona's body.

Grim must have decided his lust for blood was sated enough not to take on the harpies. He slunk away to begin the long process of washing gore from his fur.

It took me longer than I liked to find clothes. Most of the camps around the labyrinth's gate were long abandoned. Anything useful had been looted, scattered, or rotted away. I finally found a robe that was so threadbare it was almost see-through. It might have once been white, and I wondered if it was a postulant's robe.

When I returned to the gates, the Stewards had taken Dodona's body away—including all the bloodstained sand—to proceed with whatever ritual would keep the demon from returning. The grimalkin had shrunk down to his normal size again. He licked a paw and rubbed it behind his ear to clean the last bits of blood from his fur.

"That was an impressive transformation," I said. "Scary as hell, but impressive."

The cat scrubbed behind his ears and licked his whiskers, his gaze never leaving mine.

"So what are you, exactly? Shape-shifter? Hell cat?"

"Jaguar would be closer than cat. And not *hell* so much as *night sun*."

"Night sun?" I was too tired in body and mind to understand what he was saying.

"Yes, the night sun. You might call it hell or the underworld. My people were not so afraid of death as yours. They revered their dead and kept their ancestors around long after they were gone."

"I see." I really didn't.

"Like I said, you can call me grimalkin. Makes things neater, don't you think?"

"Sure." I sighed and hauled my body over the last sand dune to find Mason standing upright. Swaying, but standing. I offered him the robe.

"Not yet." His voice grated like charcoal. "Too sensitive."

I tucked the robe around my arm.

"How do we get back to Timberfoot?" I asked Grim. Mason wouldn't be able to fly even if he could manifest his wings.

Grim twitched his whiskers in a cat smirk. "The Stewards gave me special dispensation to teleport. Just this once. It seems they don't really want a new Steward joining their ranks." He inclined his head toward Mason.

Was Mason a Steward now? What did that even mean?

I had little time to contemplate it. Grim did his thing, twining around us and dripping magic off his tail until all five of us were wrapped up in his spell. I had a moment of that black, sinking feeling, then I fell to the grass in front of Timberfoot's tree.

Mason screamed as he landed. I ran to his side, but he was already sitting up. His jaw cut a rigid line as he hung onto his pain.

"Let's go home." I held out my hand. This time he took it.

I turned to Grim, who sat as though planted in the grass.

"You're coming, right?"

He looked across the plains at the world that had been his home for centuries. But was it really a home? He had no ties to it anymore. He looked through the misty door. His tail swished.

"I know it's scary," I said, "but we'll be right there with you. You'll always have a place with us."

He sighed and came to stand beside Princess. She stuck her tongue in his ear and gave it a good lick.

"Back off, mutt." Grim shuddered but didn't move away. I thought both my little hell beasts would get along just fine.

"Are you ready?" I asked Mason. He nodded.

About to step through the door between worlds, I had one irrational moment of panic. Would Terra still be there? Maybe we'd been gone for an eon and my world had already been decimated by some cosmic catastrophe. There was only one way to find out.

I stepped through the door.

From the archives:

GRIMALKINS: NOT YOUR AVERAGE HOUSE CAT?

May 11, 2077

Definition of Grimalkin from the dictionary:

a cat (archaic)
a spiteful old woman

Hmmm. Not much to go on there. But why am I asking about grimalkins? Just for kicks and giggles. In my line of work, I never know what kind of creature I'm going to come up against next. It's best to be prepared for anything.

So grimalkins, do they exist? I believe so, considering we could probably slap the name "grimalkin" on any cat-being. I imagine they would be rather wise, noble and patient creatures.

I'm not sure where the spiteful old woman reference comes from, but hit me with your grimalkin stories.

COMMENTS (7)

I had a cat familiar once who was smarter than most toddlers. His name was The Gentleman, and he used to bring me presents every morning. Not dead birds and mice like you might think. The Gentleman brought me pretty leaves, flowers, pine cones, and even a gemstone once. He would drop them at my feet while I drank my tea, and wait for me to notice so I could tell him what a considerate gentleman he was. If ever a cat deserved to be called Grimalkin, it was he.
cchedgewitch (May 11, 2077)

> Definitely a gentleman and a grimalkin. Thanks for sharing.
> *Valkyrie367 (May 11, 2077)*

———•———

We have a tradition of animal spirit guides in my clan. I was chosen by a cat. Even though he is long gone, his spirit still guides me every day. Maybe this is a form of grimalkin?
Ahanu (May 12, 2077)

> That's a lovely tradition. And yes, I think grimalkins would make excellent spirit guides.
> *Valkyrie367 (May 12, 2077)*

———•———

The spiteful old woman reference stems from the "malkin" portion of the term. Grimalkin may be a blending of gray and malkin, which was and archaic term with several meanings, one being a low class woman. Or it might also have been a diminutive of the girl's name, Maude.
ThatWordGuy (May 14, 2077)

> Thank you! I find etymology fascinating.
> *Valkyrie367 (May 14, 2077)*

>> I wish my students did too. It would make grading their final papers a lot easier :(
>> *ThatWordGuy (May 14, 2077)*

EPILOGUE

opened my eyes. I sat in the dryad forest. The standing stones of Iona Park were barely visible. I blinked and rubbed my eyes, but they didn't become any clearer. Night. It was nighttime.

My joints creaked as I stretched. When I tried to stand, a wave of dizziness came over me.

"Hold there, cousin." Thorn grabbed my elbow and helped me up.

"How long…" My tongue was thick and dry in my mouth and I couldn't form the words.

"You were gone nearly a day. We were getting worried."

Another dryad hurried forward with a cup of water. I grabbed for it greedily.

"Slowly." Thorn held onto my hand, forcing me to take small sips.

Nearby, Nori sat with Jacoby in her lap.

She smiled. "He's awake. Or he will be soon. I can feel him now." Her hand on his chest rubbed the grizzled fur. Jacoby opened his eyes.

"Kyra-lady?"

"It's me. You're safe now."

"You founds me?"

"I did, but you should really thank Nori here. She kept you alive until I could get to you."

Jacoby turned his huge eyes on Nori. Her own were raw with lack of sleep and now they began to shed the tears she had been holding in for so long.

"Thanks you, Nora-lady." Jacoby buried his face in her stomach and hugged her.

I found Princess standing guard over Mason. Another pair of dryad healers were trying to get a look at him, but the hound wouldn't let them.

"Princess, stand down! Let them do their work."

The hound shifted her haunches and sat. I bent to kiss her head and whispered, "Thank you for looking after him." She whined and her tongue darted over my chin.

Mason lay half in and half out of the circle of leaves and sticks. His glossy black hair fell over his forehead. A week of stubble covered his cheeks and chin. And his clothes, while rumpled and stained, were intact. Other than the fact that he wouldn't wake up, there were no traces of Dodona's trial on him.

After a brief examination, the healer turned to me with a frown.

"I find nothing wrong. No wounds or bruises. I detect no illness. He is alive, but unresponsive."

"He's tired," I said. We were all tired. "And his body may not show it, but his spirit was badly wounded. Please make him comfortable. And give him time." The healer nodded and signaled for his assistants to pick Mason up and carry him to a room in the canopy.

I needed rest too, but first I went over to my father's tree. The door in the trunk was gone. I laid a hand on the tree, then leaned in to press my cheek against the rough bark.

"Thanks, Dad."

I looked around at my tribe. Dryads, critters, a former gargoyle and even a demon. This was Terra's strength.

But someone was missing.

Grim.

He'd come through the door. I was sure of it. Now that I was aware of the bonds tying me to my family, I could feel him. Maybe he'd taken off by himself to explore his new world. I'd miss the little pest, but I'd have to be happy knowing that he was alive and free. It was the way of rescuers.

We spent two days with the dryads while their healers worked on Mason.

My grandmother had not waited for our return. Apparently, ranger business took her away soon after I'd fallen into the trance that took me across two worlds. I tried not to resent her for that. But it was easy to see how she'd let her only son lounge in an oread prison for years.

She left me a note.

I had to leave before you woke. I hope you found what you were looking for. I will see you in Montreal next spring, as per our deal.

Lisabet

P.S. Watch out for Kester Owens. He is not what he seems to be.

Kester appeared to be a demon in love with a dryad. I'd had enough with demons, and I hoped that soon I wouldn't have to watch him at all.

I sighed. And put down the letter. It was so like my grandmother. Succinct and cold. I wasn't happy about entertaining her in Montreal. But a deal was a deal.

I slept for thirty-six hours straight and woke with Princess snoring softly at my feet. Jacoby was sprawled across the bed, gangly arms and legs taking up most of the space.

I crawled out from under the heavy sheet and stood, taking a moment to let a bout of dizziness pass, then left my little treetop pod. Outside, the sky had darkened to match the shadows under the dryad canopy. Everything was one color—twilight. Not a hint of wind stirred the leaves. I breathed in the moment. I was alive. Jacoby was alive. Mason was alive.

Mason!

I'd left him in the care of dryads, fully intending to stay awake long enough to see him recovered, but one of the healers had offered me tea—dosed no doubt with a sedative—and that was the last thing I remembered.

We were in the small village near Iona Park. The Life Tree was renowned for its healing powers, so a decent sized medical facility had been established nearby. I headed there now. My feet felt heavy and clumsy on the rope bridge between trees. I could see small fire pots dotting the canopy. I was all turned around and I stopped to get my bearings.

An elderly dryad couple (I could tell they was elderly only from the deep resonance of their magic) looked up from a fire pot set on a platform outside their small pod.

"Can you show me where the infirmary is?" I asked.

"Let me take you there." The old dryad rose and wiped his hands on a cloth before handing it to his wife.

"I don't want to disturb your dinner," I said.

"It is no trouble. I am Bensayer. Please call me Ben." He held his hand out to indicate that I should precede him down the next bridge. When I hesitated, he added, "It is a great honor to offer aid to the World Jumpers."

"Is that what they're calling us?" I'd been called worse, but I didn't feel like we'd earned a nickname.

"I would like to hear about your time spent in the Nether. I am archivist for the Lekythoi Clan. Your words will educate generations of my people."

I turned to him, making the rope-bridge swing. Ben smiled patiently and braced his legs wide while I hung onto the flimsy rope rail like a life line. When the bridge calmed, I cleared my throat and said, "I would like that, but we will be leaving for Montreal soon. Tomorrow, I hope."

"Perhaps we can correspond, then?"

His open expression seemed so eager and honest, I couldn't refuse him.

"Uh, sure. Lisobet knows how to get in touch with me."

Four immense oak trees anchored a platform for the healing clinic. Alcoves were built into the surrounding trees, used as treatment and convalescent rooms. Several fire pots hung from a large tripod in the center of the square. A dozen dryads sat before them on woven reed chairs, enjoying a quiet meal. I breathed easier when I saw Mason sitting before the fire, chatting with Kester.

Ben left me with a curt nod and a promise that he would write soon.

Mason sipped from a mug of tea or broth. He looked better. His skin had lost that unhealthy pallor. He saw me studying him and smiled. A young dryad offered me a cup of broth, and I sat in the empty seat beside Mason. After a moment of awkward silence when I arrived, the dryads went back to murmuring their private conversations.

"The canopy is quiet," Mason said. "I like it."

"This is a raging kegger by dryad standards."

We listened to the gentle night sounds of the forest and sipped our drinks.

"Are you ready to go home?" he asked.

"So ready."

KESTER SAW US to Manhattan's north gate and got our car out of impound. He shook my hand and then Mason's.

"It would be nice if we could finish our railroad project," he said.

"I promise, one way or another, I'll get your road built." Mason frowned. "Oscar has been hounding me to take over for him. So maybe I'll even run for Senate."

Kester laughed and clapped him on the shoulder. "Welcome to the club, brother."

The train ride home was a special kind of hell. Jacoby was recovered and full of unexpended energy. He thought it was great fun to taunt Princess into chasing him around the tiny car. Nori regained some of her energy, which she used to complain about the smell of dog, the lack of personal space and hygiene, the dry food rations and about a million other inconveniences.

But we made it home in record time. And when the car door opened for the last time, we were greeted by a pack of goblin children, all eager to play with the hound and the dervish.

That gave the Mason and me a much needed break.

Twelve hours later, I stood in his kitchen—now my kitchen—trying to convince my tired body to wake up. I should get home and check on Gita and the crew. I should walk Princess and look in on the barn renovations. I did none of those things. I stood frozen by the window, a glass of juice forgotten in one hand, watching dawn tint the sky.

A loud rumbling noise, like a jackhammer heard from afar, broke into my thoughts. I put down the juice and went into the living room to investigate.

On the hearth by the dying fire, two cats were yin-and-yanged. One was charcoal gray, the other pure white.

Grim opened his eyes, cutting off the rumble.

"Was that you? You're going to wake the dead with that purr."

He yawned and stretched out his arms, pulling the female against him. She opened one eye and bit him on the nose.

"Oh, she's feisty. I like her."

Grim settled his face into the pile of fur. His tail thumped on the stone hearth.

I snuck back upstairs and out of my clothes. Then I slipped under the covers and snuggled my chilly back against Mason's steamy chest.

Morning chores could wait.

Dear Reader,

I hope you've been enjoying Kyra's journey so far. It seems like Kyra and Mason are all snug in their new home. I didn't want to leave you on a cliff-hanger, but I also didn't want you to think that there are no more adventures to come. So please enjoy the sneak peek at Book 5 of the Valkyrie Bestiary Series (as yet, untitled) below.

And you probably know that authors love reviews, but do you know why? Reviews are important because they help other readers know what to expect from the book, they let me know how my books are received by readers, and they help booksellers decide which books to show to new readers.

If you enjoyed this book I would be grateful for your honest review. It can be as short as you like. Even a few positive words will go a long way. And I'll try to make it as painless as possible. Use the links below to find the review site of your choice.

Want to find out more about Kyra's world?

Learn more about the Valkyrie Bestiary series at KimMcDougall.com including deleted scenes and more series fun.

Or join Kim McDougall's reader group to get the latest release updates and a free eBook at sendfox.com/wrongtreepress.

Poke around at Kyra's blog at ValkyrieBestiary.com.

Other places you can follow Kim McDougall: Amazon, BookBub, Goodreads, Facebook, Twitter, or Instagram.

Sneak Peek

Valkyrie Bestiary Book 5 (untitled)

MASON FOUND ME gazing out the kitchen window at the goblins who were busy renovating the barn. He was flipping through screens on his widget, catching up on everything he'd missed while we were gone.

He lifted his gaze long enough to smile and drop a kiss on my nose. "What are you doing?"

"Plotting out how I'll fill the barn with cages, terrariums and aquariums. I can't believe all that space will be mine."

"All that space and more. You just ask and I'll build you another barn." He grinned. "Two barns." His arms circled me, his widget now forgotten in his hand. I leaned back feeling the tolling of his heart against my back.

"I want to start every morning just like this." His voice was soft in my ear and full of power like a prophecy. A shiver ran through me. The feel of him wrapped around me could still weaken my knees. His lips blazed a trail down my jaw, and I turned to meet them with a full kiss.

A gentle cough told us that Dutch had entered the kitchen.

"Excuse me."

We both turned. Dutch was the impeccable serving man. He would never make a situation more uncomfortable by addressing the fact that we were both in our sleepwear—long t-shirt for me and shorts only for Mason—or that we'd been about to baptize the kitchen counter.

"Oscar asked to speak with you as soon as you returned. He indicated that it was of the utmost importance."

A sigh rumbled through Mason. He stepped back and ran his hand through his already sleep-mussed hair. "Fine. I'll call him now. Is there more coffee?"

"I'll make some," I said. Mason headed for the den to make his call, and I turned to the sink to rinse and refill the coffee pot.

Dutch gently but firmly took the pot from my hands. "Please, miss. Let me."

I stood back feeling suddenly like an intruder as he prepared coffee.

"I didn't mean to get in your way."

"Not in my way." Dutch smiled. It turned his usually rigid face kinder. "It's my job."

I'd taken care of myself since I was a child, when my mother first got sick. Being fussed over by a servant would take getting used to.

I smiled back and tried to put some assurance into it.

Since Dutch was taking care of breakfast, I decided to check my widget too and see what I'd missed while we'd been away.

I had full confidence in Emil, especially since Gabe was mentoring him. There were several messages, all about upcoming job bookings and one marked urgent. I clicked on that one first.

Emil wrote:

> Kyra,
>
> This message came through your business mail, but I thought you'd want to see it asap. I hope everything is OK. Call me as soon as you're back on the grid.
>
> Emil

Another message was attached.

> Hey cuz,
>
> It's been a few years, hasn't it? Hub locked me up on bogus charges. I'll tell you all about it when I see you. But I need about 1500 credits for bail. Can you help a girl out? I figure you sort of owe me anyway.
>
> Gunora

Minutes passed while I stared at the screen. The words were all there in the proper order. Verbs, adjectives, nouns. Everything standard sentences needed to make sense. And yet they made no sense.

Mason returned to refill his coffee.

"Everything all right?" He poured his cup and then one for me.

"Yes. No." My mind churned with possibilities and implications. "I got a message from my cousin Gunora."

"A dryad cousin?"

"An Aesir cousin. Aaric's sister."

"How is that possible? I thought you were the only Aesir on Terra."

"So did I."

I put down my widget and gulped my coffee like it was whisky. It shouldn't be possible that Gunora was in Montreal. When I left Asgard, fleeing from my guilt and pain over Aaric's death, I burned down Bifrost, the rainbow bridge that joined Asgard with Terra. No other Aesir could follow.

"Kyra?" Mason took my cup from my hand. "What does she want?"

"What? Oh." I turned to him and realized that he'd asked the question three times already. "She's in jail. She wants my help."

"We'd better get to Hub Station then. I'll get dressed."

I stopped him with one hand on his arm. "You don't have to get involved."

He plucked my hand off his arm and kissed my fingers. "She's your family. You're my family. Ergo, I'm involved."

Make sure to join the reader group at KimMcDougall.com *to get news about upcoming books.*

ABOUT THE AUTHOR

If Kim McDougall could have one magical superpower, it would be to talk to animals. Or maybe to shift into animal form. Definitely, fantastical critters and magic often feature in her stories. So until she can change into a griffin and fly away, she writes dark paranormal action and romance tales, from her home in Central Ontario. Visit Kim Online at www.KimMcDougall.com.

Made in the USA
Columbia, SC
25 September 2021

46203257R00148